THE **ORANGE CURTAIN**

THE
ORANGE
CURTAIN
JOHN SHANNON

An Otto Penzler Book

ORION

First published in Great Britain in 2002 by Orion,
an imprint of the Orion Publishing Group Ltd.

Copyright © John Shannon 2000

The moral right of John Shannon to be identified as the author of
this work has been asserted in accordance with the Copyright,
Designs and Patents Act of 1988.

A CIP catalogue record for this book is available
from the British Library.

ISBN 0752846981

Printed in Great Britain by Clays Ltd, St Ives plc

The Orion Publishing Group Ltd
Orion House
5 Upper Saint Martin's Lane
London, WC2H 9EA

For Ken Meier

Thanks to Spencer Olin, Martin Schiesl and Vu Pham
for sharing their expertise about Orange County with me.
Any mistakes or exaggerations are my own.

Vulnerability may have its own private causes,
but it often reveals concisely what is wounding
and damaging on a much larger scale.

—John Berger

one

The Gods Hate the Obvious

When Billy Gudger got home from work, he knew they'd done something to his front door.

It wasn't the scratch on the little Sanskrit plaque there that clued him in, because he'd made that scratch himself when he'd screwed it up directly under the peephole: *The gods love the obscure and hate the obvious.* He'd had it made up in devanagari writing, that strange alphabet from northern India that looks like Chinese ideograms doing chin-ups under a bar. He was probably the only person within miles who could read it, and even if some scholarly immigrant mailman from India happened upon it, some mailman who'd taught himself not modern Hindi but ancient Sanskrit, even then the reader would not know that the plaque concerned, not just a rather banal Eastern homage to idiosyncrasy, but a thing, eccentric and quite physical, that Billy carried within his head.

Billy couldn't quite put his finger on what the problem was with the door, but he could always tell. He peered closely at the brass knob and the dead bolt, then leaned very close and studied the brown-painted surface in small sections, stopping for a moment only at the scratches where he tended to rest his plastic laundry tub when he unlocked the door coming back in from the big house in front where his mom lived. He never left for even a minute without locking up.

I will pay anything to find her, *anything*, the voice on the phone had said. Come to my shop please.

I'll be right there, he'd replied, and he headed straight down the 405 toward Orange County. The last time he remembered being there had been his daughter's ninth birthday command visit to Disneyland—three, no four, years back. Even then Maeve had seen it as something of a sociological experiment—testing what girls her age were supposed to enjoy.

Jack Liffey wasn't really a detective, but he did track down missing children, having fallen into the business by accident after he'd lost his aerospace job just as the whole industry was drying up in Southern California. He'd been at the tracking-down for several years now and he was pretty damn good at it. He liked it, too, something about searching for the lost and protecting the innocent—indulging a sentimental bent in him—and it paid more than delivering pizzas, but just barely.

The billboard along the freeway was his first indication he was getting close: THE CALIFORNIA DREAM IS ALIVE, it said. It showed a cheerful white professional man in jogging attire beside a cheerful white professional woman in a sports bra watching a cheerful white professional child tricycling hard down a sylvan pathway. IN MISSION VIEJO.

If you liked a dream, he thought, in which all the people were white, the rough edges were all sanded away, there was no urban center, the stores and restaurants were all national chains, and the carefully platted roads wound *just so* between mini-malls, identical tract homes, and tame imitations of forest strips. In an earlier and less examined life, he might well have liked it a whole lot, too, secure in his aerospace cubicle with his conscience assuaged by a few rebellious Dilbert cartoons on the walls, at ease with his first wife and daughter. Layoffs, drink, and legal papers had seen to all that. Now he wasn't sure what he liked any more, though a less random universe and a little relief from the burning in his prostate would have been a pretty good start.

He passed a long chain-link fence with wild chaparral behind it. For some reason unkempt young men had lined up shoulder-to-shoulder behind the fence, staring out at the road with dead eyes, like a race of primitives who'd come out of the wild land and were waiting there to rush out and occupy the town once it was abandoned by the higher civilization. It made no sense he could discern. Then there was a nude man wearing only an orange visor who waved gaily to passing cars from the freeway median—it was all just L.A. saying good-bye, he finally realized—and the freeway passed over Coyote Creek as he actually entered Orange County. He had just passed through what L.A. people called the Orange Curtain. He was into *terra incognita*, and considering the address he'd been given by the Asian voice on the phone, he was heading for a lot more *incognita*.

Maybe it was just his sixth sense misfiring about the door. He knew he was highly tuned to things other people missed. In the single big room inside, things seemed all right. The green desk under the front window was spread with the books and papers for a calculus problem that was all but solved. He liked to work out his approach and make all the intermediate calculations and then walk away, savoring his mastery, to come back triumphantly later and nail down the final answer.

The desk was one of three identical tiny oak desks he'd bought from a used office furniture store in Santa Ana that was liquidating the old post office, and he'd stripped them and bleached the wood and then stained each one a different translucent finish. The red desk on the side wall held a stack of books in French by Paul Baudrillard and Roland Barthes, plus a French-English dictionary and a spiral notebook. A journal in plain yellow paper binding, *Analyse structurale et exégèse biblique,* was open to an essay by Barthes that contained a number of underlinings.

The third desk, stained blue, held a propped open copy of *The Decline and Fall of the Roman Empire*, plus several volumes on modern history and historiography. He just had time to ascertain that the desks were undisturbed when the telephone rang.

"What's the matter with you?" the sharp voice skirled in his ear. "You know I worry. You're ten minutes late and you didn't check in."

Involuntarily he pictured her—the small pouty mouth, rumpled housecoat, and those legs sprawling across the old sofa, blousing their fat over calf-high support hose. He listened with equanimity and answered promptly.

"I'll be right over."

"I don't know how you got to be so thoughtless. I gave up everything for you. What's the matter with you?"

"I'll get us some lunch in a few minutes. There's meatloaf left over and I bought some carrots I can glaze before I leave."

"Be sure to use up the old brown sugar before you open the new one. Hurry up, Billy. I'm hungry."

He smiled a curiously benign smile as he hung up. He was indeed lucky, even if it wasn't the toadstone in his head that marked and conditioned his good fortune. There couldn't be many people with a mother as loving as his.

He lingered over the red desk, fingering the spiral notebook where he was translating a passage: *What interests me the most is the abrasive [rubbings?] frictions, the breaks [ruptures?], the discontinuities of readability, the juxtaposition [overlay?] of narrative entities which [somewhat] [can run free] from an explicit logical articulation.*

He would sauté the carrots, he thought. Use just a little butter.

"*A toadstone—a celebrated amulet. It was sovereign for protecting new born children and their mothers from the power of fairies, and has been repeatedly borrowed from my mother, on account of this virtue.*"
—Sir Walter Scott, letter to Joanna Baillie (1812)

* * *

Jack Liffey hopped off the freeway at Beach Boulevard and turned north to Bolsa, then east deeper and deeper into a strangely familiar forest of warm colors, uptilted tile roofs, and diacritical marks over the vowels. He had truly entered the somewhere-else, and his forehead began to bead up with sweat. He parked his beat-up old Concord in front of a mall that was all gold and red and dragons, and he felt that strange stirring at the base of his spine that he remembered all too well. As if a bullet was about to penetrate *right there*. For several years now, an unforeseen premonition of death had been ambushing him out of the blue—a sudden sense as he drove toward an appointment that it was a shame the person he was meeting would sit there waiting for hours and not know he had died on the way. But the present sensation was a little more concrete, tied to real memories, and just to nail it down, a V of four Marine F/A-18 jet fighters came over low, booming all of a sudden on the air.

There was a peculiar impression of safety in the immediate area of his car, maybe just the familiarity of the Concord or a promise of quick getaway, and it was hard to force himself to walk away from the car out into this other world. The first sing-songy voices he heard sent his palms clammy and then the smells—sesame oil, mint and that fermented fish sauce called *nuoc mam*.

He strolled rigidly through the crowds, past a middle-aged woman in an *ao dai* and younger ones wearing jeans, young women with beautiful features that were perfectly symmetrical in their small faces, a thin old man in an outsized homburg, teen-agers with their hair cut into extreme fades who offered him the same sleepy contemptuous eyes as the cowboys—pronounced cow*boys* with a lilt— who'd haunted Tu Do Street a generation earlier, and he thought, If I stick around long enough, I'll find the guy who stole my watch. It had been done from the back of a motor scooter, snipped right off his wrist as they gunned past with a proficient bite of something like a bolt cutter. It was a mean thought, but he knew damn well that a lot of the refugees who'd come over in the first wave were the same people, by and large, who'd fed off the American troops in Saigon.

He found the East-West Bookstore between the Viet My Bakery and Bao Tram Cosmetics. Paperbacks on shelf after shelf were as brightly colored as the storefronts. There were two dozen newspapers, scores of magazines, even girlie magazines. All the titles were in Vietnamese, except for two wire racks out in the middle of the store with romance novels and self-help books and a few classics. A distinguished looking man in an open-necked blue shirt watched him from the glass counter. His temples were just beginning to gray.

"*Ong Minh*?" Jack Liffey asked.

The man smiled tightly and Jack Liffey got what he deserved for showing off, a flood of Vietnamese washing back over him.

"*Xin loi.* I'm sorry. I only remember a few words."

"It's not an inflected language," the man said didactically. He spoke with an almost mincing precision and a strong trace of a British accent. "You cannot make a question by changing your tone. More likely, it will change the meaning completely. You might set out to say, Do you think it will rain? and end up saying, I want to eat your elbows." His voice shifted gear. "Yes, I am Mr. Minh. Ong Liffey."

"Pleased to meet you." The man shook hands with that unnerving limp grip Asians used.

"Let me close up here and buy you a cup of coffee."

"Thanks."

Minh Trac did something beneath the counter, locked up the register and led him along the lane of mini-mall shops into the covered mall proper where Asian pop music was blaring away, a cover of some American tune he vaguely recognized. The white plastic bucket chairs from a *pho* shop spilled out into the atrium, facing a record shop, a dress emporium and a gridded-shut jewelry store. A group of middle-aged women with shopping bags sat and laughed and gossiped, and toward the back a number of sullen male teens in flat-tops eyed the world resentfully. There were no Anglo faces anywhere.

They sat at a table out in the mall atrium and a woman in fluorescent blue pedal pushers appeared instantly, bobbed a little, and spoke softly with Minh Trac before gliding away.

"So you were in Viet Nam, Mr. Liffey."

"I was stationed in Thailand, but I went to Saigon several times for R and R."

He raised an eyebrow. "The traffic was usually in the other direction."

"I was sent all that way because of a war," Jack Liffey explained. "I figured I ought to see what it was about."

"Are you one of those Americans who feel it wasn't worth the candle?"

Jack Liffey considered for a moment. It wasn't hard to guess the politics of anyone in Little Saigon but he wasn't about to sign onto a doomed exile crusade, even for conversational purposes. "Every country is worth it," he said. "I think what people mean when they say that is more complicated. It was a civil war and America was a big clumsy oaf who did more harm than good, and it probably couldn't have been any other way."

The *café au lait* arrived, with a lot more milk than he liked, but he could go that far for politeness' sake. The waitress gave Jack Liffey a curious look before leaving again. The boys at the back asked her something as she passed and she shook her head.

"I agree with you, Mr. Liffey, but not many people here in Little Saigon would do. Actually, that is an understatement."

"Yeah, I get it. Most political exiles are a bit sensitive." He stirred a spoonful of sugar into the fat cup and sipped at it. "*Worth the candle*. Your idiom seems very British."

"I learned in a language school run by British, and I taught English at a lycée in Saigon. That fact alone made it necessary for me to evacuate as soon as I could. In the days after a victory there isn't a lot of subtle discrimination among the victors. The children who drove the tanks into Saigon in 1975 seemed to feel if you knew *about* something you must have supported it. In fact, I had opposed the government. I was advisor for a student newspaper that was regularly shut down by the censors, but I was put into a reeducation camp for over a year. We survived on cassava and singing communist songs."

"Are you bitter?"

"Not really. There was so much injustice and pain—for centuries—that my meagre share was nothing. And we have become quite happy here. My wife and I bore a daughter as soon as we got out of the tents down at Camp Pendleton and I am very proud of her. My daughter was valedictorian at Westminster High School, and she just completed a university degree at Irvine."

"And she's disappeared?"

He nodded and fell silent.

"You know, I'd be hopeless asking questions in your community. Completely useless."

"I know that. She isn't in our community. I would know."

It was amazing what parents didn't know, Jack Liffey thought, but he didn't offer the opinion. "How do you know she's gone?"

"She is a good daughter and even though she has her own flat she comes every day to see us. She stopped coming a week ago and she has not been home either. Her landlord checked inside at my insistence. Bread on the counter was turning to mold."

"Did you tell the police?"

"Yes."

"Are the police here inclined to help people in your community?"

He gave a small shrug with his hands. "As little as possible. They have set up a Vietnamese . . . branch, in response to gang extortions and home invasions, but they are not very effective."

There was some sort of ruckus at the back of the noodle shop, and one of the boys in black threw something on the table and strode out. He brushed hard against Jack Liffey's chair, cursing once, and Minh Trac watched the boy depart with a strained composure. The boy had a checkerboard shaved into the short sides of his flattop.

"Gang kids?" Jack Liffey asked.

Minh Trac nodded. "Phuong had absolutely nothing to do with gang boys."

"That's her name?"

"Minh Phuong to her mother. Phuong Minh now. Most of her generation have reversed the order of their names and put the family name last, the way Westerners do. A lot of them even choose American names. Tommy and Johnny and Cheryl. They want to be Americans."

"Doesn't Phuong mean phoenix?" Jack Liffey asked.

Minh Trac was mildly surprised. "You might say that."

He remembered it from Graham Greene. It was the name of the embittered journalist's mistress in *The Quiet American*, and he also remembered for some reason that Greene had added, *But nothing these days is fabulous and nothing rises from its ashes*. "Did she have a job?"

Something about the question seemed to disturb the man, but Jack Liffey knew better than to try to read motives across cultures. "She was going to go back to get an advanced degree, but in the meantime she has done several odd jobs."

"What's her field?"

"Business. We've become a very practical people. Will you agree at least to look for her in the wider community?"

"It's my calling."

The man checked his wristwatch and Jack Liffey noticed there were no numbers; it was something Swiss and expensive. "It's three now. If you come to my house at five-thirty, I will give you a photograph of Phuong, and a list of her friends and jobs." He handed Jack Liffey a card with his address.

"Do you have any problems with me talking to the police?"

"Suit yourself. You can ask for Frank Vo." There was some unreadable emotion that pertained to this name too.

The women nearby stirred and a gust of laughter swept around their table. One nodded in a way that might have been indicating him, but that was just too paranoid. They brought their soup bowls up to their mouthes to eat, and one seemed to be chewing betel. He noticed on the table a big fruit tied up in its own string bag, spiky and half again the size of a cantaloupe. "Is that a durian?"

"It is indeed."

They were a fruit from Malaysia or somewhere like it. The flesh was very sweet but when you cut into it the smell was so putrid and so enduring that none of the hotels in Bangkok had let GIs bring one even into the lobby.

"I never thought I'd see one again."

"It took a long time to import them. Nostalgia is becoming an epidemic in Little Saigon."

Late the previous evening, a dog being walked near Irvine Lake had nosed up two decomposing bodies. They were in various states of decay, and the county sheriff's Crime Scene Supervisor gave a preliminary guess, behind the orange tapes and under the chugging porta-lights, that one was two weeks dead and the second was only about forty-eight hours. The badly decayed body was a male, and coyotes had eaten some of the soft parts of the other one, an elderly female who lay tucked under a lush green sumac bush the size of a small tree.

The TV reporters spent a good half hour trying to goad the police into saying that there was a serial killer on the loose and then arguing over a newsworthy name for the killer. Something to do with Dahlia would have been great, or a Stalker or some other tabloid-worthy noun. *Hillside Strangler* had been used, and anyway these had apparently been shot, not strangled.

two

Incoming

It was the haircuts that caught his eye. He parked up the road across from the high school where he had a good view of the four boys who sat on the window flower bed of a boarded-up storefront. *Only Carp Carp Only*, a sign said. He wondered if part of the sign was missing.

The board-ups over the door and window had been plastered with posters that said *Stop the Airport Ripoff! One public bankruptcy is enough!* over and over. But it was the boys who interested him. They all wore floppy black shirts buttoned up to the neck and they all had the same checks cut into the sides of their severe flattops. The boy on the end seemed to be the one who had pushed past his chair at the noodle shop. Jack Liffey wasn't certain but they seemed to be tearing the cello wraps off packets of ramen noodles, discarding the spice packs into the litter at their feet, and crunching into the noodles like Asian Fritos. One of the boys was flipping a coin and then walking it along his knuckles like George Raft.

In the past he had found that by treating black and Latino gang kids with elaborate and bona fide respect, he usually got their grudged tolerance, but, in his experience, Asian toughs always seemed to have a little something extra to prove. He strolled up the road and sat on the wall beside the kid from the noodle shop.

"Hello, gentlemen. I hope you don't object to my sitting here with you for a minute or two."

Only the boy who was farthest away glanced at him but immediately looked away. If they had been speaking English before, they were into Vietnamese now, sing-songing gently and nonchalantly. There was a big carton of ramen in the flower bed, like something stolen off a truck, and the boy one over from him reached in for a packet which he tore into. The packet had very pink shrimp on it.

"You look like the people who know what's actually going down around here."

The boy shook the spice packet onto the ground and broke the big block of dried ramen in half with a crackle like stomping a plastic toy. He began chewing off bits of one of the halves. Jack Liffey looked away, watching an old Asian woman in canvas slippers walk up the other side of the street carrying a frayed paper bag in her arms. She reached a bus bench, but instead of sitting she squatted down at the end of the bench to wait.

"I'm a stranger in these parts," Jack Liffey offered. He hadn't expected the humor to work and it didn't. "But I guess you already figured that out." The boys spoke a few lilting words to one another, then fell silent again. The silent treatment was probably supposed to worry him and make him nervous, but it didn't. Sooner or later though he'd have to cut his losses.

"You see, I'm looking for a missing Vietnamese girl and I thought you might be able to help me."

That stilled any fidgeting. Another boy tore into a ramen packet. Actually he found all the testosterone nonchalance rather touching, just boys really, trying to face down a world that probably seemed a lot more hostile to them than he'd ever know. On Tu Do Street he'd been the vulnerable outsider, guarding what he carried against a snatch, but here they were the prey to a big busy Anglo world that by and large probably didn't give a damn what happened to their self-respect.

The boy next to him finally turned and met his eyes. "*Diddy mao,* big cunt."

He knew the Vietnamese words, though he did not know their literal meaning. Anyone who'd been in Saigon for long had heard the GIs telling the peskiest of the pimps and touts to fuck off in no uncertain terms. He imagined if Gandhi had stayed long enough in that corrupting environment, even he might have broken down and used the expression. Right now, coming from a boy who was seven or eight inches shorter and fifty pounds lighter than him, it made him want to laugh, but he didn't.

"Minh Trac asked me to find his daughter," he said equably. "Phuong. Am I pronouncing her name right?"

The boy looked away again. They seemed to be inhibited by his presence now and didn't even speak to one another. People were accumulating at the bus stop, including a Latino in an electric wheelchair who kept gunning it a few inches forward and back.

Far away a police siren whoop-whooped and an armada of seagulls came over low. Finally the bus showed up. He'd never actually watched a kneeling bus do its trick. The front hissed downward as if the whole vehicle were deflating so the wheelchair could roll straight on. Then it pumped itself back up and drove off. The old woman was still squatting at the end of the bench as if waiting for a better bus.

"My mistake, gentlemen. I thought you might know what's going on around town." He got up and started away.

"Hey, mister."

It was the boy from the noodle shop. Jack Liffey waited while some war went on in the boy's psyche.

"We like Phuong. Most college girl stuck up, treat us like shit. They walk past with hard feet, bam bam bam, you boys all bums. Not Phuong."

His English was not very good for some reason and Jack Liffey guessed he'd come over fairly recently from one of the camps, probably even born in the camps. Maybe that was the only real social distinction between these boys and the computer wizards getting their straight-As at Berkeley.

"See this watch, real Rolex, not knockoff. I know where to get it at good price. Phuong show me last year. What you want to know?"

"My name's Jack Liffey," he said, and he sat back down. "Phuong has been gone for a week. Do you know where she might be?"

"She work for Frankie the Man. Big Chinaman from Saigon, Frankie Fen, big bossman, he build malls. You ask him."

"What's your name?" he asked the boy.

"Loc."

"Where would I find these people?"

Loc offered him a ramen pack, and he took it and turned it over in his hands. It was shrimp flavored all right. He decided to give it a try.

"He got office on Bolsa, next to Asian Garden. Some people like Frankie, some hate."

"Do you like him?"

"You can't never trust Chinese. They learn to cheat when they baby. Sell you old stuff no good. Plenty crap, and tricky, too."

Racism everywhere, Jack Liffey thought sadly. But it was no time to be insisting on moral lessons. He tore off the wrap and bit a corner of the hard block of noodles. It was remarkably like eating a plastic toy. He pretended to like it.

"I like your haircut. It looks great," Jack Liffey said.

When he looked up, he saw they were in no mood for compliments; their eyes were elsewhere. A lowered and blacked out Honda Prelude was coming up the street slowly and it was worrying the boys. The windows, the chrome, even the wheels, were blackened, so the car looked like a little rolling nugget of death.

"Where could I get a haircut like that?"

He felt the movement before he saw anything. Loc was up and fleeing down an alley as fast as he could run. The others were going in three different directions. Then he heard the horrible nearby rat-a-tat of automatic weapons fire. His head snapped around in time to see the Prelude drift past, one window rolled down and a boy in a black balaclava holding a little Ingram spray gun skyward, his grin a disembodied Cheshire cat in the darkness within the car. He pointed the gun at Jack Liffey.

"Bang-bang-bang!" the Cheshire grin shrieked, and then the car accelerated away and Jack Liffey was alone on Golden West Street, a profound chill spreading up his back. He hadn't even budged. He'd never been close enough to the war, stuck at his radar screens in his air-conditioned trailer off in the forests of Thailand, to get the right instincts.

"Incoming," he said softly to himself.

Billy Gudger parked his 1962 Beetle right under the big red neon hand. He liked the 1962 because it was the last one with the 1200 engine. It wasn't that it was any more durable—all air-cooled engines were designed to wear out through heat erosion and be rebuilt often, a kind of grudged tribute to entropy—but the 1200 was still the cheapest to rebuild. *Sonya Gudger,* it said inside the neon hand. *Palmistry, Bibliomancy, Tarot. Genuine Rom wisdom. Se habla Espagnol.*

There was an old Buick in front so he went in the back door and sure enough, the heavy curtain was across the foyer and she had a sucker in there. He hesitated by the curtain to listen.

" . . . Right here on the mount of Venus, see that grid of lines. It means you've walled off your heart and caged it up because you aren't sure you can trust someone in a close relationship." There was a gasp and a little hiss of emotion. "Here, too, you can see how your little finger ends before the top joint of the next finger. That means you're not comfortable sharing your emotions. *But* you're very lucky. See this cross, right under the Jupiter finger. It means you'll definitely find a happy marriage in this lifetime."

"When I going to find him? Goddam tired all the wait and all the shmucks."

"I can't say exactly, but let's look at your lifeline again. It's an indication of the force of your enthusiasm for life." She dropped into her don't-trust-quacks speech and Billy withdrew and went on into the kitchen and shut the door softly. If anyone ever tells you the lifeline indicates an exact number of years that you have to live, his mother was about to explain, you mustn't trust them at all, he's a quack. You always need three indications, and, in fact, the actual length of your life is a bargain between your life force and the world force, and no one can work that out for you in advance. But what I can tell you. . . .

He got down the big six-quart pot to begin boiling the macaroni. It was her favorite, ordered up to compensate for some transgression he'd committed at lunch that he couldn't remember, and it was a little too rich even for him. Two pounds of extra sharp cheddar shredded into the macaroni and followed with fried chunks of spicy pork sausage, canned onion rings, and bac-o-bits. It gave him heartburn just to think of it but she insisted on having it at least once a week.

The pot was just coming to a rolling boil when he heard the front door slam and Sonja hobbled into the kitchen on her four-footed cane.

"You doing macaroni and sausage?"

"Uh-huh. Good customer?"

She opened the cupboard and got down her bottle of cheap Gallo cream sherry. "Enh," she said dismissively. "Not much of a tip. A brown person of mixed background. She didn't really appreciate the real thing. She'd rather have one of those charlatans waving a chicken bone and telling her how very *special* she is."

She sat heavily at the Formica table with its little flying kidney shapes and poured a generous juice glass of sherry. "It's just more of your curse," she went on. "Marigold was right, I should have strangled you at birth and saved us all a lot of trouble."

Marigold had been his grandmother, who had claimed to be the seventeenth in a line of great seers, stretching back to the legendary Rom homeland in the Punjab. It might have been true. All the names were written out on the front page of a tattered old Latin Bible that Sonja Gudger used for counting letters and chapters and finding hidden meanings.

"Good luck for you, because of that damn toadstone in your head, and bad luck for everyone around you."

He smiled warmly. It made him happy whenever she mentioned the toadstone and praised him like that. "I had a good day at work," he said. "They let me open up the cassettes for the Betacam and put on the labels and number them. It was a whole box of ten, and if you get them wrong it's a real mess later when you go to edit."

"I'll bet you fucked it up."

"Then I took down numbers while they were shooting. They're on the side of the camera, and you look real quick right after the director calls cut and you put the number in a log where it says 'tail.' It's called the time code. You put a star on the best shots when the director tells you so he can find them again. It's a very clever system."

"Put in some salt!" she shouted. "What's wrong with you? Don't you know salt drives the evil spirits out of the pasta?"

A jewell containing a crapone or toade stone set in golde.
    —Nichols, *Gifts to Queen Elizabeth* (1558)

Jack Liffey waited on a hard bench in the lobby facing a large blue digital clock, as policemen and various people with problems came and went. He'd never liked the way digital clocks measured time. Time was circular and gradual, a slow analog losing bargain with the universe. In fact, in his current mood, he didn't much like the passing of time at all. The pace of things had begun to worry him a lot— his daughter growing up too fast and filling out a real brassiere, his life whisking by, all the tubes of toothpaste and boxes of Kleenex you were constantly buying, even the way the geraniums on his patio ran wild.

A week earlier, driving to the supermarket, he had heard a smug voice on the radio news say something about how everything would be made right after death, and idly he had replied aloud, "Oh, no it won't," and his own words had filled him suddenly with a chill of winter. Oh, no it wouldn't. Death was real. He would simply cease to exist one day, not some imaginary faraway day either, but Poof, he'd be gone. He had broken out in a sweat and stopped the car at the curb and sat in paralysis for a half hour, unable to find a way to stop imagining extinction.

A little of that shudder stayed with him now. He recalled Tom Mercer turning from the book he was reading on his bunk in Thailand one night and saying, "Man, what's worse? A contingent universe, where you can't even choose which nostril to pick, or total free will? You know what makes them both so poignant, absolutely fucking poignant, is the thought of death."

Young men dragged out of college to go fight a war and then given enough of a reprieve to land 500 miles away from the fighting to stare at radar screens tended to talk like that.

"The good part of death," Jack Liffey had replied, "is that I'll never have to hear you argue about shit like this again."

"Listen to the Philistine. I happen to know you shook the dust of religion off your heels and you stand square in the middle of the modern world."

He wondered where Tom Mercer was standing now, if he was holding down some tech job somewhere, or teaching Philosophy 1A in a junior college, or long dead of his flirtation with heroin.

Two policemen dragged a struggling woman across the lobby and distracted him.

"You'll hear from my lawyers about this!" she squealed.

"Oh, no, not the *lawyers*," one of the cops mocked.

"Mr. Liffey, Lt. Vo will see you now."

The earliest edition of the next morning's *Register* was out by late afternoon. Orange County was a land of car commuters, and street editions had almost no relevance, but the *Register* editors liked to think of themselves as neck-and-neck with the *L.A. Times*, and they maintained all the old journalistic traditions by sending a dozen sad boozers out in old pickups to fill the street kiosks with a vestigial early street edition of the next day's paper.

TWO BODIES FOUND
AT IRVINE LAKE!

A few paragraphs down, the reporters quoted an unnamed source in the Sheriff's office who'd dubbed the perpetrator with the uninspired name, *The Sagebrush Killer*.

"Wyoming," Frank Vo said in a bemused way, with his mouth full. He leaned back in his chair away from the round rice cake on a big square of wax paper on his desk. "I don't know what on earth they were thinking of. Hey, these people come from a tropical country so let's send them to the high plains where the wind freezes you into a statue and the entire growing season is six weeks long."

Jack Liffey nodded. "Nobody likes it there. I don't know why even the Norwegians stay."

"You know what they say? One day the wind stopped in Wyoming and all the chickens fell over." He laughed. He was a short man, even for a Vietnamese, in an impeccable dark suit and tie. A map of north Orange County was on the side wall of his office with different color pins stuck into it. "Want some? It's *banh chung*, usually only for Tet, but I love it. There's ground pork in the middle."

"Thanks, I ate." Jack Liffey hadn't eaten but the look of the gooey white ball didn't appeal to him.

"I finished college in Laramie but I got out as soon as I could. I don't even like the memory of those rough brown stone buildings." He shrugged it off. "I study sociology. So I end up a cop."

"You don't like it?"

He smiled. "I love it; I mean it. I want to stop all the gang nonsense and extortion. We're not like that. Really. We're a gentle and decent people. But you take generations of war and then you cream off a lot of the riff-raff and put them in refugee camps for a while and you get a mess anywhere, a few percent. You'd be like that, too."

"Sure. Mr. Minh said he was sure Phuong had nothing at all to do with the gangs."

The man shrugged. "In my experience parents don't know very much about what their children are up to."

"My experience, too. Except my own daughter, of course," he added quickly.

Frank Vo smiled again. "And mine, but she's only four. The boys you saw with the hair, they're a gang of wannabes called East Wind. Nothing serious, petty theft and stealing lunch money. They may dress hip but they're schoolkids. I'm more worried about some of the heavier FOBs. That means fresh off the boat. These are the guys who were in the camps for boat people in Thailand or Malaysia until it was too late to learn anything. Some have been here a decade now and I don't think they'll ever catch up the schooling they missed. You know, even their Vietnamese is lousy, Camp Vietnamese. Imagine. They may never have even one good language."

There was a thermos on the filing cabinet, with the big word LUCKY on it. Jack Liffey remembered ones like it from several billets in Southeast Asia, a genuine artifact of another time and place. It made him feel strange, old. It was as if a chunk of his life had been ripped out and discarded, wasted.

"What about the car?"

"Blacked out Honda Prelude, a rice rocket. They'd be older and more established boys, men really. Could be the Numbah Tens, the Bolsa Boys, Westies, Gardens. Blacked out, whited out. . . . " He shrugged. "They all do that to cars. Ordinary kids do it, too. Too bad you didn't get a license number. My money would be on the *Quan sat*. It's short for *Quan sat vien chien truong*, which means body count. You're familiar with the expression."

"Not intimately. I was an electronics tech in the war. That war's been over for a *long* time."

"Not for some of our citizens. You can be blown up here for advocating good relations with Hanoi. *Quan sat* have a peculiarity. They pick on the ethnic Chinese, just like Hanoi does."

An Anglo cop in uniform looked in the door. "Vo, there's a whole bunch of Viets here gabbling about some kin who's subletting an apartment. Can you deal with it?"

"Ask them to wait, please."

The cops stared at one another and something angry passed.

"Sure thing," the Anglo cop said laconically and shut the door.

"I'm surprised he didn't say *slopes*," Frank Vo said, then shook his head as if waking himself. "I didn't say that. Where were we?"

"Fighting the war."

"Don't you want to ask about Phuong?"

Jack Liffey nodded. "Phuong."

"I haven't had time to do anything about her," Frank Vo said. "I know her very well. She's very bright, a very good kid. I don't think it's serious that she's gone for a week. She'll show up with a boy somewhere, an honor student, skiing or going to lounge acts in Vegas. We've all got a few wild oats."

"What else was she like?"

"She wasn't like a lot of our more ambitious young people, who are usually very single-minded and focused. She had a streak of fun, and she was taking time out of school to learn practical things. She attached herself to one person after another to learn. She was closest to an older businesswoman named Tien Joubert Nguyen. Joubert is a married name she kept."

He'd heard the name Nguyen enough to be able to pronounce an approximation of the sound, *whin*. "What does Mrs. Nguyen do?"

Frank Vo puffed at his cheeks. "You might say she is a wholesaler. Or an arranger, maybe. I probably don't want to know exactly what she does all the time, but on balance she's a good woman and I think you'd say she was Phuong's mentor. Talk to her. She's a real character, more energy than a B-52. Now I really must go, I'm sorry. It seems the natives are restless."

Jack Liffey rose and shook the man's hand. The grip was surprisingly firm. "You're the politest cop I've ever met," he offered.

three

A Constant Heart Wins Out

"Is this a Vietnamese area?" Jack Liffey asked. They had already settled in and disposed of a number of stiff pleasantries. Driving into the tract in the dusk, the place had looked like any other Orange County suburb of gimcrack ranch houses. He hadn't expected something like Chinatown, but there wasn't even a hint that Vietnamese people lived here, not a single curly-haired stone lion guarding a porch, no indications at all that it was anything but what it looked like, another Southern California bedroom for the white working class in flight from L.A.

The woman in her *ao dai* offered him a porcelain smile as she set the tray of tea down on the low table. She poured and retreated quickly.

Jack Liffey took the small warm handleless cup from Minh Trac. He got the feeling the Western furniture wasn't used all that much. It had been pushed back into groups against the walls, like display areas in a big furniture store, though they were using some of it now, a leather sofa, leather easy chair, and the low laquered table. A small bookcase full of Vietnamese books faced them on the far wall, with a giant television sitting on the floor beside it. The only wall adornment was an elaborate golden plaque with a line of Vietnamese written on ribbed velvet.

"Actually there aren't any Vietnamese areas, if you mean in the way there are black or Latino areas up in L.A. We bought houses as they became available. And I think a lot of us who got the money together to buy wanted to be Americans." He shrugged. "We're scattered all through Westminster, Santa Ana, Garden Grove, even Anaheim. Maybe 100,000 of us now, but even here in Westminster I think we're less than a third of the population."

Jack Liffey sipped at the thin tea. There seemed to be some baffling protocol in Vietnamese culture between when to offer the watery tea common in Asia or the strong coffee the French had brought into their colony, but it wasn't worth asking about.

"I spoke with Frank Vo. He hasn't done much yet to look for Phuong and he didn't seem too concerned." He decided not to mention the boys of East Wind and the burst of gunfire. It didn't seem to have anything to do with Phuong.

"Smoothing things over is Vo's profession. If you were on fire, he would try to convince you not to cry out because fire is a good thing that warms up those in the community around you. *I'm* concerned."

"I understand."

Mrs. Minh glided back in with a 4-by-5 photograph that she presented to him on two hands, as if it were very heavy but very delicate. It showed a beautiful young woman, her long glowing black hair cascading over one shoulder as she turned to smile so brightly it seemed she'd just won the lottery.

"We have other copies," her husband said.

Jack Liffey took the flattering studio photo, wondering if it looked much like the girl, and the woman sat uneasily on the far end of the sofa, perched on the very front edge of the cushion as if ready to leap up at the slightest craving anyone expressed. Minh Trac spoke for a while of Phuong's exemplary childhood, but the things he was inclined to relate were all so ordinary, so seamless and unexceptionable, that Jack Liffey hardly listened. He'd had enough hints of the tensions in the Vietnamese community that he couldn't quite dismiss the possibility that some political rivalry in Little Saigon might have played a role in her disappearance. At least, it was something to eliminate.

"You said you were never a great supporter of the Saigon regime. Doesn't that put you in an awkward position here sometimes?"

The man smiled suddenly as if finding one bright pupil in a dull classroom. "The future changes the past, Mr. Liffey. And that's not cynicism, it's epistemology. I don't get a chance to talk about this very much these days."

I'll bet you *don't*, he thought. Clearly, the man longed to be back in the classroom. Jack Liffey settled in for whatever it was Minh wanted to expound. He was paying.

"Let us imagine my cousin Hoa, living in 1970 in an ordinary village up-country called Bu Noi. It's 300 souls farming a big clearing along a tributary of the Dong Ngai River. The village chief was appointed by Saigon, of course. They paid taxes to Saigon, when they had to. They tacked up government notices when the armored riverboat came up once a week and they cheered dutifully whenever a general flew in on his American helicopter. Like a thousand other villages.

"There was also a Viet Cong committee in the village, most of the same men who sat on the chief's council. They paid a fish and rice tax to the N.L.F. cadres when they came. When they were sick they went to N.L.F. doctors in a tunnel in a liberated zone up the river and they sent a few of their boys to fight with the Front. The village could have turned over at any time if it was to their benefit."

The tidy house was suddenly assaulted by the noise of a helicopter, as if the war had come back all at once. It circled the neighborhood once, and a bright light played in a window for a moment. Jack Liffey's hair stood on end, and no one in the room spoke until the ugly hammering sound faded away.

"Tell me the truth about Bu Noi," Minh Trac said finally. "Which side did the village belong to?"

Jack Liffey shrugged. "The Front."

"Really? Say the U.S. wins in the end—or Saigon wins, if you prefer. The Front sympathies, however deep or shallow, melt away without an objective sign they'd ever existed. The tree didn't fall in the forest. By any measure, most of the village stayed loyal to the government all along."

"Okay."

"What I'm trying to say, Mr. Liffey, in a fluid world, you don't find a truth like that under a rock. What I do now, or what somebody else does *today* can change the meaning of what I did last year."

He had fidgeted and Mrs. Minh shot up to pour him more tea. "What does your past mean now?" Jack Liffey asked.

"Since I was sent to a reeducation camp, and since I came to America, ipso facto, I was always on the right side. Even if I told people differently, no one would even hear it now. *And* what's important is that it's not just the philosophers here who believe that, but also the ex-paratroopers who run the committees and banks and welfare organizations. To all of them I am an objective anti-communist because I'm here."

Jack Liffey frowned. "Your theory would make it pretty tough to be a journalist."

"Yes, indeed. You report what you think is true, and it changes under your feet, *really* changes. The only guarantee I know for never being wrong is never trying to say anything that matters. There's a lot of that going around in Little Saigon."

And everywhere else, Jack Liffey thought, but he didn't want to encourage any more philosophy.

"Do you think Phuong subscribes to your theory?"

"She is as nonpolitical as a songbird. All the children are. It means they are Republicans, of course, and water skiiers, and business majors."

It was hard to discern his attitude to this depoliticization. "Of course."

Minh Trac gave him a list of his daughter's friends and their phone numbers, and a check for the retainer he had asked for. The check was written on the account of East-West Books.

"Not your personal account?"

"Most of us prefer the liquidity of cash."

Jack Liffey rose and came face-to-face with the golden scrollwork. "What does this say?" he asked politely.

The teacher nodded. "Usually plaques like that in Vietnamese homes just say Good Luck; the idea of luck is very important in our culture. But mine is different. Every Vietnamese knows that line of poetry by heart. It's one of the first lines of the masterwork of Nguyen-Du, our Shakespeare. Let's see if I can do it justice. 'Talent and Destiny are poised in bitter conflict.' "

He took Jack Liffey's hand limply at the door.

"Which do you root for?" Minh Trac asked. "Talent or destiny?"

"Beats me."

"Don't worry. There is much suffering to go through, but at the end of the epic, a constant heart wins out. Please find Phuong for me, Mr. Liffey."

As he left Trac's house, he saw a car with blacked out windows following him. It stayed back, and once he got onto the 5 and headed up toward L.A. it dropped away. He passed the small absurd replica of the Matterhorn at Disneyland, all lit up on the horizon, then glimpsed the tip-top of the bell tower of Philadelphia's Independence Hall at Knott's Berry Farm, and then he burst over Coyote Creek and back out through the Orange Curtain smack into that overwhelming aroma of potato chips from the plant in La Mirada. He wondered if northbound commuters came to associate that smell with whatever L.A. meant to them. A cubicle job they loathed that waited in the little visible island of skyscrapers downtown that was still far ahead, an exhausting ill-paid job in some decrepit bucket shop with wired windows over the old machines. Or, in the worst case, just a forlorn search at the margins, at the exits from do-it-yourself centers, for day labor.

Dropping off the freeway finally, he saw two men standing in the bed of a stake truck dueling with shovels right under a bright yellow streetlamp. They were taking wild angry swings, clanging against one another, but he was too tired to think about it. It was just L.A. welcoming him back.

He passed up checking in at his old condo, which now served as his office, and headed home. When he'd moved in with Marlena he'd turned his condo into a de facto office because he couldn't have got rid of it even if he'd wanted to. He'd bought it at the very peak of the market in 1989, like all the other lame-brained economic decisions of his life, and after the real estate collapse of the early '90s, he still owed the bank more than the two-bedroom apartment was currently worth.

He parked in front of Marlena's little bungalow and saw movement against the light at the gauze curtains. He didn't quite think of the pleasant little shingled bungalow as his. Their relationship would have to show more signs of taking before he did that.

Before he could even get fully out of the car, the front door slammed open, and he was surprised to see his daughter sprinting happily across the scraggly lawn.

"Daddy!"

"Punkin', what a nice surprise."

She drew up when she saw the car and scowled. "I thought you were going to replace Hylton."

Hylton was her nickname for his 1979 AMC Concord with one primered fender, red cellophane over the taillights, and the smashed-in doors and windows on the right side covered with plastic and duct tape. The doors were held shut with rope that was wound around the window pillars. The car did run, sort of.

"You have to special-order Ferraris. It takes a while to get one."

Maeve giggled and hugged him. "And Mom wonders where I get my dry wit."

"She's wrong. Your wit's as wet as it comes."

She pounded a bit on his shoulder and then hugged him like a spider monkey. He was a bit embarrassed by how easily he felt her prominent new breasts pressing against him. He was so pleased to be talking to Maeve that he tried to delay the going-inside.

"To what do I owe the surprise visit?"

"Mom and Brad had a hot date, I guess. I'm here for the night."

"Good for her, or should I say good for him?"

She took his arm and began steering him toward the house. "*I* had a hot date last week."

He went very stiff and something chilly fell through from the top of him to the bottom. She was thirteen years old, and had only been filling out that brassiere for a few months.

"See, my wit *is* dry. You can relax, Daddy; it was a sock hop at school and Jason just held my hand. That didn't count as first base even in your time."

"I don't even like to think of boys in your on-deck circle, hon." Especially boys named Jason, but he let it go. That terror would all come to roost soon enough. "Getting along with Marlena?" he asked.

"Sure. I like Marlena a lot."

"So do I."

"But not for the same reasons," she suggested wryly.

Jack Liffey smiled as they came up onto the wide bungalow porch. He thought of some of the things Marlena did in bed that he liked a lot and was perfectly happy their reasons differed. Beyond that, there were a lot of real problems they hadn't worked out yet.

"Would you wait out here for a minute, hon?"

"You two gonna fight?"

"I hope not."

He found her in the kitchen, fussing over a big pot of something as she peered under the lid. She had actually lost about fifteen pounds recently, just for him, she said, and she looked a lot better for it. Another fifteen would have got her back to the regular dress sizes.

"Hi, Mar. I'm home."

"Jackie, you didn' call."

"I said I'd probably be late."

She nuzzled and clung to him when he kissed her and he could

sense her sniffing him for foreign perfumes. Then she took his hands
and smelled at them too, one after another. Finally she wormed a
hand down into his pants and grasped his penis and manipulated it
in a way she had. She claimed to be able to tell if it had been used.
There had been a little jealousy before he moved in, but the pathological aspects had developed after.

"Feels okay," she said. "You know what I want to do with Big
Jackie later?"

"I can think of a number of things," he said. "Maeve's right outside," he added quickly.

She gave a last squeeze. "You be thinking of one you want special
for Big Jackie. I got some ideas for Brown Betty, too." Her little dog
leapt between them and got his own ideas and started vibrating on
Jack Liffey's foot. "I'm steaming some tamales. You hungry?"

"Sure, thanks. *Love* it." He used his other foot to shoo the dog
gently away and it yipped in complaint. "Hello, there, Fidel. Are we
happy, tonight?"

"He loves Maeve bein' here."

"It's mutual, I'm sure." Just about every evening, he had the same
thought at least once—how easily the chihuahua would fit into the
microwave. He could see the door closing and the light coming on,
the turntable starting up as the tiny brown eyes got much bigger and
the mouth opened soundlessly. His own dog, a big incorrigible half
coyote, was confined out in the backyard. Loco would have eaten
Fidel for a canapé.

"So how were *The Young and the Clueless* today?"

"*Restless*," she said in a huff. Normally he was careful not to joke
with her like that—she tended to react to his irony as if he were
speaking a secret language in order to make fun of her—but Maeve's
appearance had led him to relax a little too much.

"Sorry. Of course." Marlena had had a hard life, she had a real
core of human decency to her, and sometimes he felt such tenderness
for her that he got woozy with it. Other days his own temper would
snap out uncontrollably at something untutored she said that he felt

reflected back on him somehow. It didn't make him like himself much, and he hoped time would sort it out.

"Baker, the tall lady with the sports car that owns the gift shop, and her old boyfriend, the intern, are getting back together," she explained, as if they were all real people who lived right down the road and came to Sunday barbecues.

"Great."

The front door creaked and the dog yipped and tore out of the kitchen toward Maeve. Jack Liffey looked forward to going out and giving Loco a big hug later.

"Stop that!" he heard Maeve say sharply, and he pictured the little dog humping away on one of her fuzzy brown shoes.

A Santa Ana was blowing, scouring the sky with hot dust and filling the dry night air with anxiety. Billy Gudger saw a couple of tall palms lean west and then lurch even farther in a gust. His old VW ran better in damp air, but it never got much of a chance for that. A family from somewhere in the Midwest scurried away from Disneyland toward one of the cheap motels, the father in a flapping sport coat bent forward in the lead with the others towing behind. Other than that, Harbor Boulevard was almost deserted.

Then he saw one at last standing by a bus stop. Sometimes the cops swept through and drove them all over to Knott or Beach. A willowy black woman in a tight bandeau and scarlet hot pants, it was unmistakable what she was doing there. At least, that's what he figured, but who could ever tell for sure?

The third time past, she noticed his beat-up black VW and she met his eyes and winked in a friendly way. Her hair was straightened and her lips were a lurid red. The engine missed a little, the famous VW hesitation, before Billy Gudger could accelerate away. If only he knew what to say, he thought. If only he'd read in a book or seen in a movie exactly what to say to a prostitute when you were hiring her, he might have been able to do it, but he hated doing anything for the first time. There was too much chance you'd get it wrong, be conspicuous, do something they would think ludicrous and have them laugh at you. Some day he'd buy one of those dish microphones and set up a block away and listen for a while and then he'd learn how to do it. Or—he had an inspiration—he could borrow a shotgun mike from the prop room at work without even asking.

A tumbleweed crossed the road ahead of him in two rolls and one big hop. He wondered where that one's journey had begun. Its true name was *salsola kali*, or Russian thistle, a pest that had been introduced into South Dakota by accident in a shipment of animal feed in 1877. The offspring had spread uncontrollably by dumping as many as 200,000 seeds per plant as they rolled. A year earlier, 1876, Japanese kudzu had been imported into the South to grace and shade the verandahs of the old mansions, and before long they'd discovered to their horror that kudzu grew as much as a foot a day until it had ruined millions of acres of cropland.

Billy Gudger liked the concept of introduced species that flourished, outsiders who wormed their way into niches where they had never been and where they knew they didn't belong.

> *Sweet are the uses of adversity,*
> *Which, like the toad, ugly and venomous,*
> *wears yet a precious jewel in its head.*
>   —Shakespeare, *As You Like It* (1599)

four

Go See Wyatt Earp

Not a soul was out and about when they pulled away from the curb, no cars passing on any of the crossroads ahead, and it felt like they'd fallen through into some post-apocalyptic world.

"Could everybody be in eating lunch at once?" he said.

"It's SC against UCLA," Maeve explained. "It's on TV."

"What, a spelling bee?"

She smiled. She knew his taunts against sports were wide and frequent but they were not very deep, just a mild fever that had to roll off him whenever the subject came up. "They're parsing Latin verbs."

"Conjugating," he corrected.

"You've got a real 'tude today."

"Whoa. *Tude*. Twenty-three skidoo," he said.

She refused to rise to the bait. "How are you and Marlena doing?" she asked.

"Pretty good between rounds." It had turned out to be a terrible night, with Marlena so upset about something that despite trying everything he could think of, including the goofy little vibrator they'd bought, he couldn't get her to come, which was so unlike her it surprised both of them, but she wouldn't talk about it. "Which way?"

"Up the side street there, by the yellow house," Maeve directed.

"Is it me being at the house? Does she mind when I come to visit?"

"I don't think so; she seems to like you a lot, but you could ask her what's eating her if you're curious. Maybe she'll tell you." He parked where she pointed.

"I will. Men never know how to talk about stuff like that."

He wondered what she thought *stuff like that* was, but she was already cranking the window down and grinning. The house had probably started as one of the Culver elf houses that had been built in the 1930s by bored sceneshop guys from the defunct Willat Movie Studio. There were five or six of them scattered around town with witch eaves and gnome windows and gurgling pools.

"Gnarly," he said, but she wasn't giving him any credit at all for slang.

The house was basically a bungalow in river-bottom rock, but someone had found a way to insert cacti into all the pointing between the rocks, and the structure now bristled with little flowering beaver-tails and fat barrels and phallic stalks craning upward from their niches, and spiny cholla and deep green woolly kegs. The yard too had been pared down to dirt and then covered with rock and cacti so it was hard to see how anyone could get to the door. As a final touch, the roof sloped gradually and it too was a rock garden beset with cacti.

Despite the unconventional exterior, he could see a blue glow through the oddly shaped window and somebody in there was watching the game.

"I'm not sure it's weird enough for a full point."

"Daddy! I gave you a point for all those plastic palm trees the city put on Venice Boulevard and that's not very weird at all."

"Especially since they're all gone now. Okay, you win. We'll go get some lunch if you don't mind a quick stop at Mike's first."

"Mike Lewis? I thought he lived up in Pasadena."

"When Siobhann left, he took an apartment in Mar Vista that's closer to the architecture school."

Mike Lewis was a social historian who'd had a big vogue five years earlier after releasing a book that had tattled on a lot of L.A. power brokers, but had fallen on hard times and was eking out a living teaching part time at art schools while he waited for the next vogue.

"You're grumpy today," she said.

"Sorry, Punkin. It's just lack of sleep. I'll perk up when I get some coffee. I really am happy to be with you."

One Gold ring with a large counterfeited Toad stone.
—*The London Gazette* (1679)

"Have one." Billy held out the juice glass half full of the amber Gallo Cream Sherry she loved. He knew enough to offer only half, because the point was to get her drunk enough to be voluble and then nudge her toward the subject of his father, but if he made the campaign too obvious she'd talk about the stars in Orion or the wisdom of the Tarot just to spite him.

She squeezed the glass between her fat palms and took a big sip. It was too strong and too sweet to do more than sip, even for her. In the corner of the living room the old TV was murmuring away with some football game. He had no idea why she had it on. She didn't know football from lacrosse.

"I'll bet nobody with the circus ever watched football," he said, as if idly.

She squinted suspiciously at him for a moment and then shrugged. "A few of the muscle types did. Circuses always divide into muscle types and art types and the two don't usually mix much." She readjusted heavily on the old sofa and grimaced at some memory of pain in her back.

"Can I get you something?" he offered quickly.

"Stop it. You're always making me feel old."

"You were one of the art types, I'll bet." He settled onto the leather ottoman with the stars and crescent moon embroidered on it.

"Most of us in the carny end were artistes. We were attached to the Colonel Wills Foster Mid-American Extravaganza and Circus, but we weren't *of* it. Even the circus part was a merger of the old

Robert E. Wills Traveling Circus and the Colonel Tom Foster Wild West Show and Fierce Animal Exhibition—they just slapped the colonel part up front for the hell of it. The carny started out as a side show to one of the two. It was before my time, almost back to the Chautauqua circuit. Everything was separate checks, the circus was one account and we had to pay our own nut. Hell, I bet you don't even know where that expression about the nut comes from."

He shook his head, even though she'd told him a dozen times.

"In the real old days the circus would roll into some podunk town and rent a big vacant lot on the edge of the place from some farmer or townie which was big enough that they could throw up all their tents and booths. They'd hold their show a few nights or a week, depending on the population thereabouts, and once in a while, circus people not being your super affluent types, they might not make enough to pay what they promised the farmer and also go on eating that week and they'd fold up their tents and skedaddle in the middle of the night without paying."

She took a long sip of the sherry and let a shudder wriggle her shoulders.

"Oooh. So the small-town sheriffs took to pulling the big nut off the wheel of the biggest circus wagon. Sometimes it was off the circus owner's live-in, or maybe a wagon with the big cats in it, and if they was to try to abscond without paying up, the wheel would fall off. So when you made enough to pay off the land owner and anybody in town you bought provisions from and actually paid the bills, the sheriff gave you your nut back and said you'd paid your nut." She looked up proudly and he smiled back in appreciation.

"That's good."

"The expression comes from way back in the horse days, of course. In my day, the old circus wagons were all gone and everything traveled in semis. Sometimes a sheriff would pull a distributor head out of the engine, but who wants to say you paid your distributor head? That's no good."

He waited a moment while she drifted in some sort of nostalgic reverie. "Did you and the sideshow people travel in a different group from the circus?"

"I got everything I needed in my old woodie wagon and a little Airstream 16-footer."

The TV roared for a moment and she glanced at it, as if something had landed from outer space and then she dismissed it from her world.

"The carny owner, a gent by name of Cordell Blossom, had this super-long tent with a lot of separate partitions that I rented space in. I usually got set up between Missy Araby, the hootchy-kootchy dancer, who was really Ruthie Benjamin from the Bronx, and Gilly Kwitkin, the glass-eating geek. Damn if Gilly didn't actually crunch down on bottles and eat them. He had a stomach of iron. Between that hootchy-koo music on Missy's Victrola and the random crunches on the other side, it could get to be a real devil to concentrate on reading palm."

He'd heard all of this a hundred times. She never seemed to remember what she'd told him before and what she hadn't.

"Did you ever get to go in the big tent and see the main circus?"

She looked straight at him and smiled a mean smile. "You mean, did I watch the lion tamer? That's what you want to know, isn't it?"

He didn't know what the right answer was, so he didn't reply. He poured her another half glass of sherry and she accepted it grudgingly, but then swigged it down and hissed for a moment. "Okay, I'll tell you something you don't know about him. Just to show your mommy's got a heart, after all. One of these days you go downtown in L.A. and across from Union Station there's an old restaurant called Philippe's. You been there?"

He shook his head.

"It's about a hundred years old and it's been a place for working folk for most of that time. There's sawdust on the floor and all that, and once a month a bunch of old retired circus folk meet there for breakfast. It's a big place on two floors, but you stay on the ground floor and you go out into the big room toward the crappers and you'll see photos of circus people all over the walls and on all the snugs around the booths. One of those you'll see a man with his hand on the haunches of a tiger and that's your daddy. He always said tigers were the bigger challenge because they were more unpredictable than lions."

She shook her head in some reminiscence and laughed. "Fucking tigers. What do they know?"

"What else do you remember about him?"

She drank off the rest of the sherry and wouldn't accept more.

"What do I remember?" she said pugnaciously. "Your daddy never knew this, you little punk, and I guess I have to teach you, too. The difference between me and an idiot is I'm not an idiot."

"What was his first name?" he asked.

"Mister," she said. "That's enough for a lifetime."

A young brown-skinned woman with a single black pigtail opened the door with an Exacto knife in her hand. She was startlingly beautiful in jeans and a blue work shirt, and she had a turquoise belt buckle the size of a toaster.

"Yeah?" she challenged.

"I'm sorry. I thought this was Mike Lewis' place."

"Mike!" she yelled and she opened wide and walked away.

A pinch hitter for Siobhann, he thought. He guessed she was a student. Soon, Mike showed up in a shorty bathrobe with a fat book in his hand.

"Jack! Maeve! How engaging. I want you to meet my friend Anna Cochise Preciado. She's almost 100 percent Chiracahua Apache." He craned his neck but she'd left the short hallway, and he shrugged. "Anon."

They came in off the runway balcony. It was a 1950s stucco apartment building with all the doors off a landing like a motel, and a spiky carriage lamp like a big exploded insect above the half-sunk garage. It was a real comedown from his place on the Arroyo in Pasadena.

Anna Cochise Preciado was kneeling in the living room in the midst of a dozen cardboard and balsawood models of buildings, and he introduced them. She was at the architecture school, about to graduate, and she already had a commission to work on a school auditorium in San Carlos on the Rez. Maeve took to her immediately and squatted down to ask about the maquettes she was working on.

Even here the TV was on faintly, with a cheerleader dancing and kicking.

"You into football, Mike?"

"In a way. You realize American football is by far the best spectator sport in the world. Unlike soccer, it stops and starts so you can match your strategy against the coaches', like watching a war and second-guessing Patton. Every series builds up dramatically to success or failure. And it's a decisive game. No penalty kick-offs to decide 1-to-1 games. The best team on that day wins."

"In some cultures I suppose that would all be considered normal. Can we go for a walk, Mike?"

"Sure." He threw on jogging pants and they left Maeve chitchatting happily with Anna Cochise Preciado and strolled out into the neighborhood. Mar Vista was a no-man's-land between Venice and Culver City, with no real center and no identity other than as another tattered corner of L.A. where poor whites and poor Latinos shared their fears of an uncertain future. Toppled tricycles and shaggy aloes lined their path as a familiar gloom emanated off Mike Lewis.

"How's the thing with Siobhann?"

"The 'thing' is probably fine, but *we're* not so hot. I guess you can tell I'm not counting on her coming back soon. Anna's great but she won't be here very long."

"I'm sorry."

He shrugged. "That's life in the big city. And Marlena?"

"The jury's still out, but I didn't come to talk about that. I've got a job down in Orange County. New job—I always need an edge, it's what I count on. Your work on L.A. has always helped me sort out which one's the big dog and which one's going to go hide under the porch."

Mike Lewis sidestepped a buzzing radio controlled race car that a little boy was aiming at their feet and he smiled. "That's so like you, Jack, reduce all social history to dick-waving contests. Watch out, kid."

The toy car spun around nimbly and headed away.

"Orange County," Jack Liffey said. "All I know about it is it's a big white-flight bedroom for L.A."

"All you know about it is wrong. It may have started that way after the war but it graduated a long time ago. I might even write about it one of these days because it's become a really fascinating new social formation. It's not a city in the old sense and it's not a suburb, either. People have been trying to make up names for it like 'technoburb,' and 'edge city' for ages, but most of the names are off-base. There are maybe 20 of these strange entities scattered around the country, all outside the bigger cities, like Suffolk County in New York, Oakland outside Detroit, Broward in Florida and Silicon Valley up north."

The buzzing swelled again and Mike Lewis glanced back as the tiny race car bore down on them. "This is folly, son," he said darkly, keeping his eye square on the car.

"Dig it," the kid called, and the car swung away and leapt off the curb to spin around in the street a couple of times.

"It couldn't have done us much harm," Jack Liffey said.

"Unless it was full of C-4 explosive," he said. "I don't trust children. Where was I? Oh, yeah, the post-suburbs. They're nowhere near as bedroomy and whitebread and family-heavy as first-generation suburbs, and they've got centers. It's just, they've got more than one. The traditional city tries to stuff all its cultural and financial wonders in one place, but these things have several cores spread around, like the lumps in plum pudding. In fact, I'm thinking of calling them plum-pudding cities.

"Take the big Orange. It's got the old government center in Santa Ana, a new cultural center with a theater bang on the border between Santa Ana and Costa Mesa, education centers in Irvine and Fullerton, a sports center in Anaheim with the Angels park and the Pond, all the amusement parks up in Buena Park and North Anaheim, a financial center in Newport along the freeway and, believe it or not, one of the world's biggest light industrial complexes squashed in between Irvine, Santa Ana, and Newport. And this is just off the top of my head. I'm no expert."

"False modesty becomes you."

A faint cheer rose on the air, ghostly and ill-defined, apparently from TVs in several houses on the street. Somebody at the football game must have scored.

"Look, all of this has been debated for years. Where you been?"

"While you were writing *The Underground History of L.A.* I was busy pedaling the corporate hamster wheel, writing things like *The Deposition of Rare Earths on Silicon Substrates.*"

"Sounds super. Did you actually know that stuff?"

"I was always a bit over my head. The trick was leaving your prose just exactly murky enough. If you made it too lucid, the engineers assumed you couldn't possibly know what you were talking about."

"Look at this." Mike Lewis pointed to a small stucco house. In perfect silhouette within, there was a man sitting in a lounger trying to watch TV and a woman standing between him and the TV waving a frying pan. "It's a wildlife short. The American Working Class."

Jack Liffey laughed. "Too emblematic for belief."

"Yeah. Like an Irish drunk or a German bully, it puts the fork right in the oyster for you."

"Can you tell me anything else?"

They resumed their measured stroll. "I can tell you that the other characteristics of the plum-pudding city revolve around a lot of high-tech jobs, mostly in information and medical technology, a really galloping consumer culture with malls every few miles and a me-me-me display of goods like exotic old cars or boats. There's also a rejection of any public life at all—you can see that in the way the design of the houses has shifted, with the big porches contracting into little stub slabs and the living rooms all facing the backyard now. Oh, and strangely enough there's a bit of cosmopolitanism diffusing through it all. They've got a lot of immigrants scattered around and all the new restaurants, Indian, Thai, Greek, Afghan. But that's all abstract stuff, typical of my long-range view and my limited info on the ground. What you really want to know, I can't tell you. You want to know whose ox is getting gored and who's really running the show."

"Uh-huh."

"Talk to my pal Marty Spence who teaches at Irvine. He knows Orange County like I know L.A. And there's one other guy you ought to meet. You know, the most amazing people turn up in L.A. Did you know Wyatt Earp lived for years just off Slauson?"

"No, Mike, I didn't know that. You're not going to tell me to go see Wyatt Earp, are you?"

"He died in '29. No, but it's almost as amazing. Up one of the canyons in Orange County is the most famous detective L.A.'s ever had. He's 93 and long retired but he always keeps a finger on the pulse. Philip Marlowe."

"Thanks, Mike. That's exactly what I need, a mythical old fart."

Back at the apartment, Maeve was lying flat on her stomach holding two thin stringers of balsa wood against a model as Anna applied the glue. The TV game whickered and hissed in the background, then it roared suddenly, a strange roar that didn't sound anything like the reactions of a sports crowd.

"Who's winning?" Mike Lewis asked.

"Frank Lloyd Wright," Anna said.

No matter what he did she wouldn't tell him anything more about his father. The clamor in the corner had stopped and when he finally looked up, the picture on the television was gone, to leave only an even blue and a band of type scrolling across the bottom.

PICTURE INTERRUPTED AT POLICE REQUEST. USC QUARTERBACK BUDDY HARRIS HAS APPARENTLY BEEN SHOT FROM THE STANDS. PLEASE STAND BY.

"How come you had this on anyway?"

"Don't you know? USC has more Romany kids enrolled than any other college in the country. It's our school."

five

The Welcome Bridge

He held back the big rectangular metal block called the receiver and poked out the locking lever to release the whole assembly. One twist and the 9mm barrel was out. He explained it all as he did it, so his Martian friend would understand. He sniffed at the barrel and then set it on a newspaper on his red desk, wrinkling up his nose. You could sure tell it had been used. It was only a crummy Spanish-made Star auto that he had bought years ago at the unofficial swap meet in the alley behind the Santa Ana gun store, after working up his courage on a dozen dry runs. It had been very cheap because the alley was mostly a Latino marketplace and Latinos really only wanted revolvers, maybe from seeing all the posters of Pancho Villa.

Billy Gudger screwed the handle onto the jointed cleaning rod and then threaded a little square of cotton into the hole at the top end. He told the Martian that it would take five or six of the patches doused with Hoppe's Powder Solvent before one came out clean. If you didn't clean up after you had to use a pistol, the barrel would start to corrode from the residue of the gunpowder gases. His friend always appreciated lucid explanations.

For years Billy Gudger had been offering his Martian friend explanations of everything, from how the muscles of the body worked as you walked along to the store, to the characteristics of the postmodern in architecture, to how an internal combustion engine sucked in a fuel-air mixture when the intake valve opened. His friend was attentive, polite and unfailingly grateful for the explanations. Of course, Billy Gudger knew perfectly well there wasn't actually a Martian visitor floating alongside him to keep him company—he wasn't crazy—but it was a comfort nonetheless.

I wish people would stop making me use the pistol, he told his friend. It makes things complicated.

> Or were you enamour'd on his copper rings,
> His saffron jewel, with the toad-stone in 't.
> —Ben Jonson, *Volpone* (1605)

He had left his mother snoring away on the sofa and covered her with the threadbare quilt that she said her mother had made for her. He figured it was probably just another of her bogus memories. It was hard to tell when she was spinning out one of her fibs. Denny at work had said, "Women, man—when the lips are moving, that's how you can tell they're lying," and he had pretended to like the joke more than he did. Lies were never a good thing, he knew that, even when they were necessary. They just never went away once you sent them out into the world. Lies were like wild animals running in all directions. You couldn't tell who they'd stir up.

One day soon he'd go check on the tiger-man at Phillipe's and see about that.

On his way east on Bolsa, an Asian woman driving a brand-new Toyota did a left turn right across his path from the far right lane at about 10 miles an hour, and he had to cram on the brakes. Jack Liffey tried very hard not to think in stereotypes for the next minute or two. He tried, instead, to imagine the fears that beset a woman who had grown up in a rural Asian village and had never directed a big chunk of steel machinery along an urban street, learning one day to her horror that it was the only way to get to the store to buy what she needed for dinner. The rest of the cars seemed to be driving at normal speeds and making the accustomed maneuvers.

That morning he'd got Maeve home in one piece, only a few minutes late, and he had even had a few pleasant words with Kathy at the door. It reminded him a little of what it had been like caring for her at one time, and then the question of money came up and he was reminded of the rest, the whole grand opera.

The little stucco building fronting Bolsa had two tenants, at least judging by the parts of the sign he could read. *Frank Fen, General Contracting and Engineering, Fast Track Work a Specialty* was one, and the other was *Sleepy Lotus Import-Export, Tien J. Nguyen, prop.* Both parts of the sign were duplicated, or maybe amplified, by Vietnamese phrases that didn't do him any good at all.

There was one big room inside the door with a number of rooms off it, but it was not immediately apparent which related to general contracting and which were import-export. Five desks sat out in the middle and a dozen hard chairs along the walls were inhabited by an exactly equivalent number of patient Vietnamese women of various ages. A couple of the women wore loose cotton trousers, but most wore Western skirts. Only one desk had an occupant, a young Vietnamese woman so over made-up she looked like she was headed for a Kabuki play.

"Hello," Jack Liffey said. "I'm here to see Mrs. Nguyen. I was sent by Mr. Minh Trac, about his daughter."

The young woman finished putting nail polish on a pinkie and looked up but made no indication she had heard him. It was a neutral reaction he remembered well from the service—as if by simply waiting out anything unusual you could make it go away. It was a simple enough method that in his experience had come very near paralyzing an entire foreign-imposed administration.

"I'd appreciate it if you'd let her know I'm here. About Phuong Minh." He wondered if he should have left the name in its accustomed Vietnamese order, but she budged at last and pressed a button on a fantastically complicated digital console and spoke into it in Vietnamese. At least, he thought, this receptionist would only see another *thong miao*—the expression meant *gook* in Vietnamese—whose existence had no import at all, and she wouldn't be judging him by the cost of his shoes and his wristwatch, which in his experience was a whole course in most American receptionist schools.

A little boy squealed and jumped off his mother's lap, then thought better of it and climbed back on. The women seemed pure emblems of patience, neither reading anything to divert themselves nor talking among themselves. They were trying hard not to stare at him, but he had the feeling that the moment his gaze drifted away, two dozen eyes would be fixed on him in flinty attention.

"You wait," was the whole message, translated back selectively from a long run of tonal Vietnamese that had come out of her machine.

He nodded and for want of anything better to do, he went to the side wall of the room where a number of architectural blueprints were on display under a signboard that said *The Harmony Gate*. They were apparently alternate designs for an Asian-themed pedestrian bridge between the two big malls that faced one another across Bolsa, somebody's idea of a welcoming arch for the whole shopping district, and each design said "Welcome to Little Saigon" on it. The biggest drawing was in perspective and showed an arched bridge that ran between a pagoda at one side of the street and a similar looking clocktower on the other. Spaced away from this on the wall were variant designs with much sketchier detail. *Contemporary Style* looked like an elevated international style factory with some Asian details larded over it, a few Chinese characters and medallions. After this there was *Chinese Style*, with curlicued pagoda tile roofs at the middle and both ends. His eye drifted on to *Thai Style*, with a much more elaborate pagoda in the middle and dragon designs on the walkway.

A door slammed somewhere, but no one seemed to move. One child started to insist on a word, growing more and more emphatic.

Vietnamese Classical Style had a flattened tiled roof and the pagoda and clocktower at the ends were reduced to embellishments, and finally *French Colonial Style*, the roof without curlicues at all and the clock tower moved to the middle of the bridge. That was one he recognized right away—on R&R trips to various French colonial outposts he and his friends had dubbed the style Babar the Elephant Colonial. His eye went back and forth, and despite the obvious variations, he had trouble seeing all that much difference—like minor mutations in the shape of a sweet pea. Even the *Contemporary* had so much Asian detailing that its pedigree was unmistakable. A news article was taped up beside the designs:

Frank Fen's Harmony Bridge
Rejected as Too Chinese

Rejected by whom, he wondered.

"You come," he heard, and when he looked up, a strikingly beautiful Asian woman stood in an open doorway looking straight at him with spooky dark brown eyes. Ages were always tough to guess across cultures. She was probably in fact about his own age, but she was someone who would always be described as looking half her age. She wore a navy blue business suit with a ruffled white shirt billowing out of it, and her offered hand was frank and mannish in his.

"I'm Jack Liffey," he said.

"Come in. I am Tien Joubert." She shut the door, a little harder than necessary.

"I hope I'm not jumping the queue."

She shrugged. "They're Vietnamese. They like to wait. You need to get better shoe, Jack Liffey. I could get you Italian shoe at half. Good soft leather, like butter, and very thin sole."

He suppressed a laugh; he hadn't come there to bring her up to speed on his theories about receptionist school. He twisted up his wrist to show the Timex. "This is junk too. I leave my Rolex home in the Bruno Maglies. I bet the Vietnamese people out there don't like to wait anymore than I do."

"Well, they got no choice. Their paperwork coming across town by slow boat." She showed no inclination to smile as she motioned him into a chair and sat herself at an elaborate antique desk. Her movements were very graceful and he thought once again how striking she was, like some idealized mannequin of Asian beauty.

He explained that Minh's daughter seemed to be missing and that he'd been hired to try to find her.

She nodded. "Real good kid, Phuong, smart girl. Phuong can go far in business if she get over fear of mistake. Mistake is the start of all opportunity for people with lots of luck, and Phuong got good luck, better than me even, and I got great luck. I didn't leave Saigon until May of 1975, and I have to leave all my property, and one husband die in Saigon there in final days and another husband no damn good in Paris, but I doing very fine now, thank you very much."

The whole life story in one punch, he thought. "I heard Phuong worked for you part time."

She stabbed at a device on her desk and spoke into it, then looked up at him. "You like coffee or tea, Monsieur Liffey?"

"If I'm *Monsieur* Liffey, it must be coffee."

Still no smile. She completed her order and then went on as if nothing had intervened. "I doing so good I don't need no husband number three at all, but maybe I take one to make mummy happy. Maybe I take big hairy American like you this time."

She didn't smile, didn't wink. He had no idea what was going on. He studied his palms and then held them up to show them to her, as he had his third-rate watch. "There's no hair on my palms."

Finally her expression cracked and she smiled just a little. "I like hair. I like everything American. I like your American smell, too, though mummy says it's like spoil butter. If I start over, I go to a very good doctor and get nose job, I get round eyes, I get big falling tits, the whole American thing. To me look delicate means defeat and weakness. I want to be big and powerful."

"You seem to be doing okay as is," he offered.

"You married?"

"I'm not much of a catch, and I dress badly, too."

"That for sure. I can get you good suit, Italian, very good wool blend, nice cut. When we through, I take you to Tri's Hong Kong Tailor in the Plaza. He a friend of mine and he'll dress you up good."

He smiled. "First, could we talk about Phuong?"

The coffee came in, a silver salver with a double-deck French porcelain drip pot and delicate porcelain cups carried by the Kabuki actress. She set it down and Tien Joubert shooed her away. She poured the coffee and handed him one, hardly more than espresso size. He sipped and it was strong and good.

"My English bad, I know. It don't mean I'm stupid, Jack Liffey. I been to the Sorbonne two years and I'm pretty fluent in six languages. I been to French Institute of Commercial Studies, and I run big import house in Rouen for five years. I got property and stuff worth more than five million bucks. I only been in this country since three years and I'm still with one foot in Europe and foot two in Asia." She slapped herself in the stomach. "I got the body of young girl and I'm from a good family, all got education."

He felt like asking to check her teeth, but decided he wasn't really in a buying position. "How did you end up in France?" he asked to be polite.

"My father and husband were generals and they fix it. They had a saying in the Army in '75—sergeants to America, officers to France. But it was more complicate than that. It was not only a matter of rank but of . . . we say in French *noblesse*."

"Maybe *tone*," he suggested.

"After all, Ky was a general and he came here, the horrible little man, and he ran a damn mini-market and didn't even pay off his loans and went bust. He manage a shrimp plant in Texas now, not even own it. *Shrimp*. General Thieu went to Paris."

"With a lot of the gold from the treasury, I hear."

She shrugged.

"What did Phuong do for you?"

"I teach her about business, but she not really interest in things I know, all how deal really works. She want to know about *market research* and *demographic*, whatever that is. She say she like big business stuff, not little." Tien Joubert said it all with distaste, as if holding a rodent out by the fingertips.

"All real business is little stuff, she don't learn that yet. So I get her what she want, I take her to Orange County Industrial League, and she get to do research on real big stuff. She love it, like cat in clover."

He didn't think cat was quite the right animal but he let it go. Curiously he found himself liking her artlessness and candor. It was like being in one of those experimental plays of the '30s with the actors speaking their Freudian subtexts aloud.

"She still good kid, I like her. Big heart. Like American."

"Do you have any idea why she might have taken off for a while? Or where she'd go?"

"No, but she big girl. Maybe you talk to her boyfriend Tommy Xuan."

It was pronounced Swan, or thereabouts, and it was the first he'd heard of a boyfriend.

"Or you talk to Frankie Fen. I get her job with him, too, on his big cuckoo bridge idea."

"I saw the designs out in front."

She poured herself some more coffee and he held out his cup. It was the first time he'd asked for seconds in a long time. He'd have to find out her brand of beans and tell the ad people.

"The newspaper said people found the design too Chinese," he suggested.

She snorted. "I tell him right in beginning it not going to go flying. Not 'cause the design too Chinese, 'cause Frankie Fen too Chinese. He build all two of these malls here and he call himself the Godfather of Little Saigon. He got one big head."

"Isn't he from Viet Nam?"

"I got bulldog from England, too, but it not Englishman. Frankie Fen could draw that bridge like ding-a-ling French castle at Disneyland and it still too Chinese because Frankie Fen draw it.

50

Vietnamese don't like Chinese deep down, that just the way it is."

"You think he's in today?"

"No, he working on apartment building in Fullerton. I get you address. You go see Tommy Xuan and then you go see Frankie Fen and then you come back and we talk about *me* some more. I'm pretty interesting."

"You can say that again."

"I'm pretty interesting," she said, absolutely without irony. It would be fun to introduce her to a Marx Brothers film, he thought, and see what happened.

He found his car in the mall lot, between a new Honda and a new Toyota. His beat-up Concord was probably the oldest and ugliest car in the whole lot. It had one other distinction over the others, it had a note tucked under the windshield wiper, facing in to the driver's seat.

GO WAY BIG CUNT, OR ELS, it said.

"Must be for someone else," he said aloud, but he folded it and put it in his pocket.

It was just about the ugliest animal he had ever seen and it was growling at him and kicking stiff-legged in the dirt like an angry bull. The dog was the size of goat but the skin was the size of a pony, and there was nowhere for the extra flesh to go except to bunch up.

"Must have got a whiff of my dog," Jack Liffey said. "He's half coyote."

"Attila doesn't have to have a reason. The shar-pei is notoriously protective. He started out with my wife before we married and he wouldn't even let me get close for months. Heel!"

The leash went slack and the dog finally decided to lead up the trail into the yellow hillside.

He smelled sagebrush and something else, sweet and clean, on the breezy air. There was a shrill scream from below and a Marine F/A-18 swooped up off the runway and into a little show-off turn and then climbed away. He braced for the sound of the second one. They always traveled in pairs. It came, and the dog didn't like it much either.

"The dog's got short-man's syndrome," Marty Spence said when they could talk again. "Challenges anything that moves. I think it's overbreeding. They only brought seven of them over from China and that's a pretty small gene pool."

Marty Spence certainly didn't have short-man syndrome. He was graying a bit, but he was tall and lithe, like somebody who played tennis three times a day. Jack Liffey had called him from a pay phone, using Mike Lewis's name. They'd agreed to meet on a dirt pad off a country road behind the Marine Air Station, the unofficial trailhead where he walked his dog on his afternoon off from teaching.

"Be careful if you pet it. Their skin isn't like other dogs and a lot of people are allergic. It's oily and the hair is brittle, like horsehair."

"Why do people have them?"

"Why did we wear platform shoes in the '70s? You'll have to ask my wife."

"I didn't," Jack Liffey said. "But I did have a chartreuse Nehru shirt."

"My point exactly. So you're interested in the Industrial League?"

"Uh-huh. Sounds like some socialist party back at the turn-of-the-century."

"Odd name, isn't it? Heel!" The dog had scampered hard off the path toward a big sumac that was crackling, and then the animal started making a peeved sound from the back of its throat. "Probably a rabbit. You're going to need a little background first."

"That's why I'm here."

"Before the war this county was a feudal kingdom, with a few villages like Anaheim and San Juan Capistrano scattered between the big ranches of the landed gentry. The Irvines, the O'Neals, the Segerstroms, a few others. The ranchos all started as Spanish land grants but Anglos moved in, married the older daughters and the rest is history. With the post-war boom, the bean fields and orange groves turned into tract homes, and power slowly shifted to real estate and chambers of commerce. Nobody ever gives up power without a fight and in the 1950s we had the last hurrah of the landed gentry. The fights were over land-use, of course, and slow-growth measures. But growth won, as it generally will."

One of the jets shrieked past and all his hair stood on end. He'd never seen enough of the war so it constituted a sense memory out of the past, but he still didn't like it. Sweat broke out on his forehead though the temperature couldn't have been much over sixty.

"Man, I hate that." He was frozen in his tracks, and when he looked up Marty Spence was watching him. The second jet followed, just as loud with full afterburner flaring. He could understand wanting to shoot them down. In fact, he wouldn't have trusted himself with a shoulder-launch SAM right then.

"Viet Nam, huh?"

"Just a little. I only got caught in a few days of combat at Tet, but it was plenty."

"Sometimes I regret missing the seminal experience of our generation. I was finishing grad school, and then I was too old."

"Yeah, well. The principal human experience of everybody's generation is dying, but it'll keep."

He turned and watched the sleek jets circle far out over the sea of tract homes. El Toro Air Base spread immediately below with a big X of runways and a deep green golf course, the two essentials of a military air base.

"We were up to the '50s."

"Sure. That was when the big boys started moving into the county with a vengeance. National corporations, a lot of electronics companies fleeing their unions. Medical technology, information companies, warehousing, Fortune 500 subsidiaries. Some of them even had headquarters here, like the international construction giant Fluor. They don't have quite the same interests as the local businessmen. For example, there was a bitter fight over growing the county's commercial airport, John Wayne Airport down between Newport and Irvine. The big boys want the infrastructure to fly in their Japanese customers, the little boys *live* down there under the 100-decibel runways. That was probably the last gasp of the small capitalists. Big generally beats small, as we all know. What they did to win was set up extra-governmental planning bodies like the County Transport Commission to escape the fiddling of local governments and control the things they really cared about."

"The Industrial League?"

"That was where the game was played. It was set up in 1970 by executives of the big corporations, ostensibly to boost business. In fact, it was to fight the chambers of commerce, who were controlled by local business." He looked back and grinned. "I love my job. It's like watching medieval tournaments, big armies meeting out on the plain with their visors down, and trying to figure out who's wearing the black insignia on their chest armor and who's in the red."

They reached a rock outcrop near the crest of the first range of the rolling hills below Saddleback, and they sat side by side just off the trail. His heart thumped a bit. He wasn't in the greatest shape. The county spread away under them, going bluer and fainter in the haze beyond the air base. Fancy high rises were visible along the 405 and in a few scattered islands.

"So what's at issue now?" Jack Liffey asked.

"You're looking at it. Airport again. Back in the '80s, when expanding John Wayne Airport was the agenda, the county begged the Marines to give up the air base there. It was surrounded by miles of open land then and would have been a perfect regional airport. The Marines said Never-Never, Absolutely Never, so the county rebuilt John Wayne, but it only had room for one runway and it's already pushing its traffic limits.

"Then the '90s and irony struck. El Toro became a small part of the peace dividend, scheduled to close soon. Most of the big boys perked up and want this to become a regional airport, but look at all the homes that have crowded up to it in the last decade. It's the John

Wayne airport fight all over again. Though, this time, the smaller businessmen who live near John Wayne would *love* to see El Toro become the main airport so they could cut back on theirs. There's the knights in black, galloping down the fields with their lances stuck out in front. But who's in those suits?" He grinned. "It's so much fun to watch."

"Not as much fun if you've got a house down there."

"*I've* got a house down there. I'm rooting against the airport, but that doesn't mean I think of it as a moral issue. People just follow their interests. Even Marx said capitalism had a historical mission to raise the productive capacity of society."

"That's an edifying thought," Jack Liffey said. "Did he say anything about when the productive capacity would get high enough so they stop trying to eat us for lunch?"

"Not that I recall."

"Is this airport feud bad enough to get people hurt or kidnapped?"

Marty Spence made a series of faces as he ran a hand along the grooves in the dog's neck, like the folds in an outsize spacesuit.

"You hesitate," Jack Liffey observed.

"When billions of dollars are involved, who can say?"

A Squabble of Seagulls

His old car rumbled along between the forbidding eight-foot concrete block walls that were so characteristic of the county and made the road seem an autoroute into Cold War East Berlin. Perhaps they were to keep foreign spies out of the ranch homes inside there, he thought. He understood the aversion to having your front yard on a six-lane through-road, but the architects should have looked for another solution. Every housing tract for miles was imprisoned in its own game preserve, with only the roofs and a few trees peeking out at him as he passed.

On the other hand, in some moods, he found driving along these grim and eventless Orange County streets restful compared to the level of oddity he had grown used to in L.A. No one popped out of an alcove to wave a tomahawk or tapdance in a pink tutu. The Orange Curtain had pretty well penned the bizarre and the random back into the big city. He found an opening in the walls beside a sign that said *Seahorse Riviera* and it led him into the greener pastures.

It was only because the remote on his answering machine had decided to start working again, as it did just often enough to keep him checking, that he'd got Minh Trac's urgent message to come back to his home. There were no details because the machine had cut the man off after about fifteen seconds as it was prone to do with people with soft voices, and when he'd called Minh Trac's number, he'd gotten an out-of-service buzz.

For some reason Minh Trac was sitting on a lawn chair in his driveway. Beside him was a young man on another lawn chair. The younger man had neatly pressed slacks and a bright knit shirt, and Jack Liffey remembered Mike Lewis once describing a busload of Asian tourists as dressing like escapees from a golf magazine.

Minh Trac nodded recognition as he parked in front and then Jack Liffey noticed the orange crime scene tape strung across the open front door of the house. A white Crown Victoria plainwrap was parked up the driveway with the police bust light clearly visible in the rear window. Seagulls wheeled overhead, crying out now and again to remind him he was only a mile or two from the coast.

"Thank you for coming back so quickly."

"What's happening?"

The boy had risen to take his hand.

"This is Tom Xuan, my daughter's boyfriend. Jack Liffey, the man I told you is looking for Phuong. Somebody broke in and wrecked my house. Luckily my wife was at her sister's."

They shook hands and the boy ducked and glanced up involuntarily as a seagull screeched, circling much lower than its pals, then he brought his eyes back.

"Pleased to meet you, sir."

"How come you didn't tell me she had a boyfriend?" Jack Liffey asked.

Something passed between the two of them that he couldn't read. After a moment, Minh Trac shrugged, and a little chagrin showed through. "I didn't know," he said. "She never told me. He came to see me just now because he had heard she was gone and he wanted to help."

Something was still heavy on the air, and finally the boy decided to let it out. "Xuan is a Chinese name, Mr. Liffey."

"Mr. Liffey's my late father's name. Call me Jack. I know Xuan is a Chinese name. Does that matter?"

"If he were black and dating your daughter would it matter? I don't care what you think you feel about tolerance. It would *matter*, wouldn't it?"

"Not much. I'd like it a lot, actually. Without African Americans and Jews, the only culture this country would have is football."

"I believe I feel as you do," Minh Trac said. "I have nothing against the ethnic Chinese who have lived for many generations amongst the Vietnamese in Viet Nam. They enriched our culture immeasurably. I can't understand why Phuong doesn't know I feel this way. Maybe because she has seen so much animosity in the fight over the Welcome Bridge."

A cop came out and ducked under the orange tape and looked at the three of them, then ducked back into the house. Hundreds of gulls came over very low, squawking, and all three looked up at them for a moment.

"The official collective noun is a squabble of seagulls," Minh Trac said. "I taught absurd things like that in English class."

"Let's talk about what happened to your house," Jack Liffey said. "Do you have any idea who did this?"

"No. They smashed in the patio window and broke up all the furniture. It was obviously a message, but I can't understand it at all."

"I think it was *Quan sat*," the boy said. "It means Body Count, but that's just bravado. They're too young even to remember the war. Somebody wrote *coi chung!* on the wall with lipstick. It means look out or beware, and I've heard it's their motto." He laughed derisively. "It was misspelled."

Jack Liffey thought of the note in his pocket. The spelling wasn't all too hot on the note either. "Do you think they could have kidnapped Phuong?"

"I doubt it," the boy said. "Everyone knows their specialty is extorting protection money from rich businessmen, and they haven't asked Mr. Minh for anything. But they are not very bright and they are very paranoid. Many of the *Quan sats* are camp boys who had to wait for years and years to get in the country and never got much of an education. Some of them can't even dial a phone."

The cop came out again, carrying a couple of silver Halliburton cases that looked like they contained film equipment. He put them in the trunk of the plainwrap and glared at Jack Liffey for some reason.

"Don't disturb anything," he called officiously.

Jack Liffey ignored him and turned back to the boy. "Where did you meet Phuong?"

"UCI, in the Vietnamese Student Union. I've got another year to complete a physics doctorate. I'm working on a neutrino experiment with a colleague of the Nobel laureate, Dr. Reines."

"When was the last time you saw her?"

He thought for a moment. "A week ago. The student union told us a little film company wanted a Vietnamese couple to appear in an educational film about TB. Phuong thought it would be a lark. When we showed up, they decided we were too old—I think they wanted high school kids—but they used us in one scene, anyway. I had to go to a night lab as soon as we finished the scene, but she said she could get a ride so she stayed after me."

"What was the night?"

"Tuesday."

"When was the last time you heard from her?" he asked Minh Trac.

"Monday, the day before that." His eyes were looking worried.

"What's the name of the film company?"

"It was video really. They're called MediaPros, over in Garden Grove."

"Do you have any idea who might want to harm her? Enemies? Campus racists?"

"Racists?"

"Didn't you have an incident at UCI with a kid threatening Asians over the Internet?"

He raised his eyebrows. "I forgot, it was so unusual. Really, we don't have much trouble. Just a kind of silent resentment." He smiled lightly. "It's whispered we study too much and we're over-achievers. I suppose we should arrange it so a statistically significant group of Asians flunks out of school every year. Nobody's really going to hurt anybody over getting good grades."

The kid on the Internet had threatened to kill Asians, one after another, until they were all driven off the campus, if Jack Liffey remembered right. Somebody like that might well have started with an honor student like Phuong, but it wasn't something he wanted to say in front of her father.

"She's not on campus much any more," the boy said. "She's been doing a business project before starting the coursework for her MBA."

"What was that?"

The Vietnamese cop that he'd met came out onto the lawn and stared at them with a melancholy frown.

"She was working on something with a group of planners called the Industrial League. I think it had to do with plans to make El Toro a regional airport."

Frank Vo was the name, he remembered, a polite soft-spoken cop.

"Mr. Liffey," Frank Vo called.

Jack Liffey apologized to Minh Trac and the boy and then crossed half the lawn to talk to the policeman.

"Hello, Lt. Vo."

"Good day. Do you have any reason to believe this vandalism was connected with this man's daughter's disappearance?"

"No. But I don't like the concept of coincidence very much."

"Me either. Do you have anything else to tell me?"

"I just got started."

His brow furrowed up and another squabble of seagulls came over low, crying and shrieking, but he took no notice.

"My partner feels that you would be better off somewhere else right now." He didn't seem to want to say this.

"I don't want to cause any trouble. I'll go."

"Thank you. Good luck to you."

"You, too," Jack Liffey said. "I'll tell you everything I learn."

He had enough information to get started, so he said good-bye to the father and the boy and walked to the car. When he saw the Anglo cop stroll out to watch him leave, he decided to come back up the lawn for a moment. There was a limit to how accomodating he wanted to be to a prick cop.

"You can kiss my ass," he said softly toward the cop, not loud enough for him to hear but distinctly enough to read lips.

The cop's head recoiled a little, as if struck.

Jack Liffey smiled broadly. "Have a nice day," he said, quite loud.

The cop seemed not to know what was happening, and Jack Liffey walked away. It was good, occasionally, he thought, to take someone like that through a little opening into another universe.

On the way to MediaPros, he stopped on a whim for a late lunch at a tiny Peruvian restaurant, the place graced with artifacts and travel posters of mountain temples and a pyramid of cans of Inca Cola. He smiled to himself about a menu entry that translated *lomo saltado* as "beef, tomatoes, and onions fried with french fries," and idly he ran up in his head other sentences he'd read that had fractured along cultural fault lines.

I saw a lion riding in my car.

He hadn't noticed such a pedantic streak in himself in years, and he wondered if its waning had something to do with the gradual loss of his old identity. The secure tech writer job in Martin Aerospace, the marriage and the tidy suburban house with the workshop out in the garage, and the comforting feeling that things in his life were going the way they should. All gone the way of the Hula Hoop.

On a whim, he ordered the *lomo saltado* and then had a laugh at himself when it arrived and he found it actually was beef, onion, and tomatoes with french fries stir-fried in. That ought to teach him something about cultural sensitivity, but he wasn't quite sure what.

MediaPros was a featureless white building made of tilt-up concrete slabs, just like thousands of others scattered through Orange County's little industrial parks. The receptionist sat alone in an entry alcove transferring index cards from a big tray into a row of small metal boxes, screwing up her beautiful young Latina face to make a decision on each one.

"Can I help you?"

He didn't usually like to use it, but he showed her a leather ID wallet briefly. It had an ID card with a picture of a badge and a statement in fine print that he'd passed a course on investigation and dispute mediation at World Wisdom College of East Orange, New Jersey. Even that wasn't true.

"About a week ago a young Vietnamese woman named Phuong Minh came here to help make a medical video. I'd like to speak to someone who worked with her."

"Oh, wow, man." She screwed up her face again as if trying to decide which file box he should go into. "What's up?"

"She's been missing for a week." The cops were pathological about keeping stuff like that secret, but he usually liked to shovel it all out in the open and see what happened.

"Oh, wow," she said again. "I hope she's okay. The director's in the studio right now shooting, but maybe I can get you one of the writers." She played with the intercom, and it beeped back at her, startling her.

"Ken, this is Anita. Did you work on the TB video?"

"I wrote it."

"Could you come up to the desk? There's somebody who'd like to talk to you."

"Right up."

She did something gingerly to the machine and it beeped again. "New equipment," she explained. She had him sign a guest book on the counter as if he were registering for a room.

In a moment, a gangly young man came into sight and thrust out his arm.

"Kenny Dunne."

"I'm Jack Liffey. About a week ago, did you meet a young Vietnamese woman named Phuong Minh?"

"I met a Vietnamese couple during the shoot. I don't remember any names."

"She's missing and I'd like to talk to anyone here who worked with her."

His eyebrows went up. "You a policeman?"

"I was hired by her father."

"Come on."

Jack Liffey followed down a long white corridor filled with the burnt carbon smell of a Xerox machine working overtime.

"Yeah, like I actually know what I'm doing," wafted angrily out of an office they passed.

The young man bobbed his head into another office. "Have you got the call sheets for the TB production? No, of course, you don't. Billy has them on the set."

At the end of the corridor, he put up a hand to halt them at a serious-looking door. A sign over the door was flashing *Recording*. He held his ear to the door for a moment and then tugged it open slowly, inviting Jack Liffey to follow. They went down a hall and into a cavernous room with dark lighting equipment dangling from a grid overhead, a clutter of cables that you had to step over to go anywhere and big theatrical flats leaning against the walls. What light existed was concentrated on a two-wall set out in the middle of the space, done up as a medical examining room, where a black woman had her sleeve rolled up and a nurse was standing by with a syringe in her hand, stifling a yawn. Two men were peering into the innards of an opened-up video camera on a big dolly and several other people sat around on high stools and canvas chairs. There appeared to be several other standing sets off in the darkness, a bathroom, a hospital room, and what was probably meant to be a booth in a fast-food restaurant.

"Dan, you at a break?"

A husky guy with a *Star Trek* T-shirt and a graying pony-tail leaking out of his baseball cap looked up. "Until they find out why we're getting hits every time we fucking dolly the camera, I got nothing but time."

A woman nearby said, "And he says, it's only a sin if you come," in an Irish brogue and the group around her bellowed with laughter.

"This guy is a detective. He wants to ask you about the Vietnamese girl we used last week."

"*Woman*, Kenny, let's be PC here."

The director stood to take Jack Liffey's hand. "What's the problem?"

"Phuong Minh has been missing from about the time she worked here."

"No shit? I hardly used her. She looked too old to be a high school girl playing drums in a school band. Hell, she showed up in a power suit, straight from some business job. She changed into jeans and stuck around for a crowd scene, though. Helped our ethnic balance, and it looked like she was getting a kick out of watching the shoot. Billy?"

A very short young man in his twenties came out from behind the clipboard he was holding and watched Jack Liffey cautiously.

"You got the Burkett time sheets for last week?"

The short man nodded and dug into a manila folder that lay on a big steamer trunk. He stepped over a tangled mass of cables and brought across a two-part form from a modeling agency and Jack Liffey noticed the soft suspicious eyes watching him. He looked like the kid who always had to double-lock his dorm door to stop the pranks.

The sheet had *Minh Phuong* typed across the top and it listed her arrival as 3 P.M. and her departure as 7:30 P.M. She was to be paid at the rate of $150 for a nonspeaking role.

"Did the agency send her?"

"No. We just pay everybody through the agency to avoid legal problems."

"Do you remember if she left alone?"

The director looked at his assistant who just shrugged.

"Could I see what you shot with her?"

"Not today you can't. We need our one functioning Beta playback on the set. If you come by tomorrow morning, I'll have somebody dig out the tapes. Probably the last two that day. Can you set those aside, Billy?"

The boy nodded but kept his eyes on Jack Liffey, as if he were a small animal who might soon be eaten.

"Hey Dan, we found it! The glitch was just one of the leads from—"

"I don't want to know." He turned back to Jack Liffey, suddenly much more abrupt and businesslike. "How the damn camera functions is an intimacy that does not concern me. Come tomorrow morning. Kenny will take you out now."

"Thanks."

He headed out as the hubbub built behind him.

"Margie, get set to stick her."

The writer led him out the soundproof door and back to the front. "Come in tomorrow and ask for Billy Gudger. He'll set you up with a playback. If she actually left at 7:30, everyone else here was long gone except the crew and talent."

It was a toss-up. He could hit the freeway and head over to Irvine to find the Industrial League in its high rise or jump straight down Beach Boulevard or Magnolia to Little Saigon to see if he could talk to Frank Fen at his contracting office. Little Saigon was closer so he turned down Beach. The broad ugly boulevard was lined with used car lots, taco stands, RV sales centers, and abandoned storefronts. It looked like a poor Latino area but as he drove southward, the gross income seemed to rise like bread dough and the commercial sprawl got more familiarly suburban, Kmarts and theme restaurants and home centers.

Frank Fen was still away at a building site, but Jack Liffey strolled in curiosity out behind the mall on the north side of Bolsa where something big was being constructed. A huge parking lot was hemmed around by massive Vietnamese historical plaques in bas-relief on the side walls. About half had been painted up gaudily, though no one was doing any painting at the moment. In the middle of the lot, a score of towering sculptures of Asians were watching over a row of empty stalls that looked like they had just been built. "Nguyen Trai (1380–1442)," he read on one. "Great statesman, author of Binh Ngo Pai Cao (Proclamation of Victory over the Ngo), the culmination of patriotism in Vietnamese Literature." He was brightly painted, but most of the others were still white concrete.

No one was at work at the moment, but piles of cement bags, lumber, and building blocks sat around awaiting a new impetus. Then two blacked out Toyotas squealed into the empty parking lot behind him and pulled into a V to block the driveway.

Uh-oh, he thought.

The doors opened and too many young men got out, like some sort of circus trick. They mostly wore black and they weren't kids like the gang outside the high school, they were in their late twenties and thirties. One was taller than the others and he led the rest in a flanking approach that soon trapped Jack Liffey in a corner of the building site.

Here and there Jack Liffey saw a weapon in a waistband. The tall one stopped a few feet away. He had one pink eye, like some wayward albino trait, and a long whisker on the same side of his face which made him look a bit crazy and would also make him pretty easy to identify, Jack Liffey thought.

The one with the pink eye gave some order in Vietnamese and a wiry young man with a gold chain seemed to speak for him.

"Fuck you, fucker," Gold Chain said. "You come to our town and make us trouble."

"I don't mean you any harm," Jack Liffey said.

"We know you. You been to our country, fucker, take our girls and blow things up."

"You have me confused with somebody else."

"We know you ever since we were little babies."

The one with the pink eye looked around him as if counting his gang, then ended with a finger pointed straight at Jack Liffey and said something.

Gold Chain seemed to be translating. "Fourteen here. That unlucky. Got to get rid of one."

"Getting rid of me is even more unlucky, if I can prove you didn't hurt Phuong."

"This America. We innocent until guilty."

"You really believe that? Tell me the cops never hassle you."

"Bad luck is *you*, fucker."

Pink Eye gestured and five of them closed around him and all at once started hitting him with high kicks and straight blows with their hands crooked in weird karate shapes. They weren't hurting him very much, like being assaulted by toddlers, either because of his adrenaline rush or they were pulling the punches, and he was just starting to think, Thank God I outweigh them by fifty pounds, when things seemed to change gears and one blow in his kidneys hurt a lot.

"Hey there, you stop now!" It was a woman's voice far away.

Another hard blow caught his neck and he wondered if he should warn them he had a metal plate in his head from an earlier accident and they could do him more harm than they intended if they hit him there.

"You fuck, leave our town!" he heard just as a rain of really sharp blows came down on his neck and head and he lost consciousness.

seven

Betrayed by Language

He turned his head a little and stopped, but his brain kept right on moving and then banged to rest against his skull, and he cried out faintly. There was a panting sound very near him and he opened his eyes to see, three inches away, the gnarled, flattened mug of a bull-dog drooling foam. The dog made a stab at licking his nose and he recoiled, bestowing on his brain another impact.

"Oooh."

"You 'wake. Go 'way, John Bull, scatter! Here, take this."

The soft bed he lay on heaved a little and Tien Joubert was sitting beside him, holding four white pills in her tiny palm.

"What is it?"

"Panadeine from France, can't get in store here. It got codeine in it, work real good. Make you feel good."

She gave him a stemmed wine glass of water. He swallowed the pills, and as he settled back he noticed he was under silk sheets in a huge bed in a blue bedroom and he checked a little and found he wasn't wearing any clothes.

"Where am I?"

"You die and go to heaven. Heaven got me, naturally. You want the other place, you got to dress like devil."

67

"I don't seem to be dressed at all."

"Your clothes was a mess. Blood all over like crazy. I get rid of them. I get you good stuff, Country Road trouser and nice Ralph Lauren shirt. Maybe Alfani shoe. No, *I know*. I take you Di Fabrizio, get you foot model like movie stars and he make you special good shoes."

He pictured himself showing up at the end of the day at Marlena's in bright designer clothes and two-tone movie star shoes and saw the look on her face and it all took place in the achy part of his brain and he almost shuddered.

"You rest. I get you some noodles to make you strong."

He slept, he wasn't sure how long, but she was there when he opened his eyes again. It was dark outside and a garish gold lamp on the side table was on.

"Hi, Jack Liffey. Bet you feeling better."

He was. In fact, he was lightheaded on the codeine.

"What happened? I only remember the gangsters surrounding me."

"They kick you some when you fall down, but I stop them. Everybody coward when you wave gun at them. Bad boys run for the hills, and I bring you home, nurse you back to health."

"You waved a gun at them? Half of them had Glocks in their pants."

"They not dare mess with me."

"Well, thank you. It was still brave of you, even if you are too important to mess with. I've got to call my home."

"Not yet. We talk some more, it my turn." She put her hand lightly on his chest and settled into a long tale about her life. He tuned back in as she was sneaking paper money out of Viet Nam in a padded bra and girdle and then being met by a guy in Paris, a recent exile like herself and a friend of her dead husband, who offered to help her get settled. The man got her an apartment with three other Vietnamese women and talked her into investing in a new Peugeot dealership located where the rich Vietnamese lived. He took her money and a lot of other exile money and fled to Texas, where he bought a fishing boat.

"Eight year later, I got plenty money again. I fly to this Texas, Galveston, and I find this guy and tell him, give me my money back and I won't hurt you. He just laugh and tell me to go chase my tail. So I find some roundeye Texan don't like some Viet Nam fishing guy very much, anyway, and after a while he sink his big boat at the dock one night. Of course he don't got insurance. Next day I go see him, and he weeping and pulling his hair, and I say, give me my money back and I won't hurt you, and he give me my money. It not much, just the principle of the game."

"Game?"

"Well, life. You got to come out even. Just even is best. I loan money when people need it, don't ask for interest. When I want something, I get it. Big screen TV, Mercedes, house with boat dock— you got to see my view in front room. We in Huntington Harbour." She touched his head, smoothing his hair down. Her tiny fingers were very gentle. "When I waiting down in Texas for American guy to sink boat, I go sport fishing one day. On the boat, they talk a lot about 'keepers' or not. I think you a keeper. When you stronger, I love you."

He tried to sit up to protest and pain shot through his head, so severe that he almost passed out.

"I'm living with someone, Mrs. Joubert."

"Please call me Tien. I know you not happy. Your woman no good for you. I buy you things, dress you good." She glared at the Timex on the dresser, the only possession of his she seemed to have kept. "Get you good Movado. Make you look sharp."

"If my clients saw a Movado, they'd think I was stealing from them."

"You not have to work. You kick back. Go out on boat. I only got harbor boat now. We get big boat with flying bridge and lots of wood."

He tried to imagine himself dressed up like a magazine ad, flaunting his leisure, the kept man of a millionaire businesswoman, tried to imagine what various people would think. He enjoyed the outrage he imagined Kathy venting, but Maeve was another question. And his feelings toward Marlena were such a mess that he got guilty even thinking her name.

He had to call her, he thought abruptly. But there was no phone in the room that he could see, and he was so weary and sore that he dropped back onto the soft pillow and then fell into a drugged sleep.

> *These convex osseous Tubercles are of the same kind with our English Bufonites or Toadstones.*
> *—Philosophical Transactions of the Royal Society (1696)*

He parked the VW at a meter in Chinatown, though he'd seen the free parking lot for Philippe's. He never liked to use official lots. There was always the troubling sensation that the lots were for other people, for normal customers, not for him.

Billy Gudger made himself very small just inside the door to watch, and he noticed customers came in and stood in lines at the broad chest-high glass case where a dozen women made up the sandwiches and got the drinks. Then the customers carried away their brown trays and drifted across the sawdusty floor to stools at high counterlike tables spread all over the room, and around the corner in other rooms. It looked like the place hadn't changed in a long time. The sign outside had said *Since 1917*.

He waited behind an old man in a checkered shirt, and after the man said, "Beef dip and a Millers," and gave the woman a five, he said exactly the same words and gave her a five, too. It was a way you knew you wouldn't go wrong and do something embarrassing, even though he wasn't quite sure what a beef dip was. Watching like a hawk, he had seen the man ahead of him leave two quarters in the glass tip cup and he did the same.

"Here you go, sir."

It turned out to be sliced beef on a soft roll dipped in gravy, which didn't seem very appetizing, and he carried his tray off to the right and around the corner and kept going through one big open room into another where he noticed a lot of posters and photos under glass on the walls. He sat at a little round table and let his eyes drift across the pictures within his view. There were large posed groups in front of tents, women on high wires, clowns putting on makeup, men standing on ponies, and bright vintage circus posters emblazoned with words that seemed to bulge out of the paper.

A little girl in pigtails was walking along studying the pictures, so he figured it was okay for him, too, and he abandoned his tray. It took only a glance to check and dismiss them, one at a time: a group shot in a bleachers; a man kneeling beside a German shepherd with its forelegs on a colored barrel; a pretty woman with hefty legs in a tutu; two aerialists dangling side-by-side from a trapeze.

He caught sight of a grizzled old man who was watching him. He was unshaven and his hands jutting out of tattered long sleeves were so filthy they were almost black. Billy moved on into the next room, where there were more pictures. There were a lot of posters here, too: Ringling Brothers; Clyde Beatty; circuses he'd never heard of; still more aerialists; a lion tamer in a cage; bareback riders; clowns. Finally, on a cubicle wall twenty feet away, he saw a man with a tiger, and a chill went down his spine.

As he approached the picture, the filthy old man came into the room behind him. Billy slowed and pretended to study other pictures. A smiling face peered out of the muzzle of a big cannon. A bearded lady stood arm-in-arm with a man covered with tattoos. The old man came up and looked at one of the pictures, then at Billy.

"I was in the circus."

"Go 'way."

Billy hurried to the tiger picture to get a look before something could go wrong. Disasters always loomed. The tiger looked bored, and the man stood with his palm calmly on the beast's hips, square-jawed and poised and handsome. *Alton Ford, King of the Tigers with Raju, the Tiger King*, the caption said. It was wrong, Billy could see that instantly. He got no frisson of kinship at all, and he knew he looked nothing like that tall, strong, confident man.

"Do you like the circus?" The dirty old man was back, he could smell him, reeking only a foot away, and Billy was starting to get panicky. Just then he noticed a smaller photo, fading and cut from a magazine. *Will Detrick, Famed Circus Wagon Painter*. He was short and round and held a fasces of brushes upright in his fist the way someone else might hold a bouquet of flowers. Behind the man was a gaudy wagon with *Happy Time Dog and Pony Circus* painted on it and a lot of tracery and dogs and ponies. It took almost no time at all to pull out all your guts and stomp on them and make you feel like you were going to die very soon.

"Them was great days."

"Go 'way!"

Billy bent close and found himself staring straight into his own face, blurry and cherubic, and he wondered if she had wanted him to find the picture for some perverse reason, or if she had forgot it was here. He was getting more and more nauseated, and he felt his hands tremble, and he begged the gods for just a few minutes to study the picture closer.

"No jokes, man, no booze, just some money for food, okay?"

Fingers plucked at Billy's sleeve and he whirled, his hand diving into the pocket of his jacket. The ragged man took his arm with both hands.

"Just a little spare change, man. I'm hungry."

"Get back!" Billy squealed. The hammer of the pistol caught in his jacket pocket or he might have lost it right there and shot his tormentor. He ripped his arm free and ran, deprived once again of his father. He knew he could never come back because they'd be waiting next time.

When Jack Liffey woke up, Tien Joubert was in bed with him and her tiny gentle hands were passing up and down his body like thoughts.

"Ah, peekie-boo," she said. "You 'wake again. You just don't move, I take care of you."

The top covers were off and she was naked beside him, small and nearly perfectly formed, with small brown nipples on her breasts. Age showed a little in her belly and thighs, and the way her breasts fell to one side with faint stretch marks. He liked the imperfections. It helped a lot.

"Tien, this isn't a good idea."

"Of course it good idea. All my idea good idea. Tomorrow, you don't want me no more, you forget me and we forget this night ever happen, but right now I take charge and do all kind of stuff for you." She pressed herself close against him and writhed a little and he moaned.

In the morning he found himself alone in the bed, very achy, and bright sunlight sliced across the room to make a big trapezoid on the far wall. He got out of the bed gingerly, his head still throbbing, and, finding nothing else to wear, wrapped himself in one of the blue silk sheets. The living room was so bright and blue he had to look away for a moment, a rich blue carpet and powder blue velvet sofa and chairs. The tables and cabinets were all glass and stainless steel that reflected even more blue, and one wall was a three-dimensional sculpture made of mirrors at angles that gave so many crazy reflections that your eyes couldn't focus. He did look long enough at one section of mirror to see a wasted-looking man wrapped in a blue sheet with a big shiner under his right eye.

Beyond the sofa was a full wall of glass that looked out over a patio to a lightly rippling yacht channel. Across the channel there was a row of overlarge nouveau riche houses, each with a big boat tied up in front. Tien Joubert was sitting on the patio in a blue bathrobe, nursing tea and a laptop computer, and she hadn't seen him yet. Just past her was a silly looking little boat with a fringed canvas top like something that plied the false jungle at Disneyland.

She noticed him and grinned and clapped her hands. She beckoned to him just as an old woman appeared on the patio out of nowhere. He wrapped another fold of sheet around himself decorously and went out the sliding door into a sudden hum of traffic and a light breeze. He couldn't see where the traffic noise came from. The bull-dog sat impassively at her feet, snoring.

"Good morning, Jack Liffey. Sit down. Auntie Pham will get you tea or coffee."

"Coffee."

"You don't look so good, you know?"

The old woman moved away with tiny steps.

"You should see it from inside."

"You very sweet in bed last night but you fall asleep in middle. You owe me now."

"I really would like my own clothes back." He tucked the sheet and sat, feeling every vinyl strap of the lawn chair under him.

"Ah, you my prisoner here long as I keep clothes."

"I wouldn't take kindly to that."

"Fantastic! Sorry, I got to finish, few second." She pecked at the computer, and he noticed it was wired to a cell phone that sat on the cast iron ice cream table. She grinned and signed off. "I just double money on gloves, you know, surgery gloves. They open plant in Singapore and then sell to big American medical company. I just make twenty-three thousand dollars."

The coffee came and he was surprised at how shaky his hand was when he picked up the cup to sip at it. There was also a plate of croissants, and little pots of butter and strawberry jam.

"Thanks," he said to Auntie Pham but she left without acknowledging him.

"All that money fall from sky, I can buy you fine clothes now easy."

"I can't accept it, Tien. I'm kind of attached to my old pants."

"You going to redupiate me this morning?" she asked. Her eyes looked hurt all of a sudden.

"Pardon me?"

"Oh, that wrong word. You know, like pushing away."

He thought about it a moment.

"Repudiate?"

"Yeah, think so," she said mournfully. He set his big clumsy-looking hand on hers. At another time, they might have had a big laugh about the malapropism, but not then.

"You're a sweet woman, and I think you're a lot more vulnerable inside than you act. But I have to call the woman I live with and tell her I'm still alive."

"I use wrong word a lot." He noticed she had a way of just ignoring the turns of the conversation where she didn't want to follow. "I much smarter in Vietnamese, even French. You not ever have trouble in foreign language?"

He settled back in the chair and sipped at the coffee, overwhelmed by a morning caffeine rush, a kind of thrill and lethargy at once, that he couldn't remember experiencing since he'd quit smoking. "I don't speak any other languages." It must have been the lethargy that set him talking. Or, as she had insisted, maybe he felt he owed her something. "But I have a peculiar insight into the way language breaks down."

A yacht came slowly up the channel with a whole deck of bikini-clad women and one pot-bellied mariner in a Greek cap, and he worried for a moment about the sheet he was wearing, but he guessed it would probably look like a bathrobe, and who cared what the idle yachting rich thought, anyway?

"Ten years ago, my father was diagnosed with a brain tumor."

"Oh, I so sorry."

"It was slow developing. They cut out a hemisphere right away and got a lot of it, and the rest took almost two years to kill him. On the way down, it hit his language center. His voice was okay with the half of his brain he had left, and he could recall simple verbs with little trouble, and he got the linking words, too, but nouns drove him crazy. He would talk along for a while and then come to a dead stop in frustration. He'd rage and go through the letters of the alphabet until he got what he thought was the right initial letter, he could usually do that, and then he'd throw out random additions to the letter, hunting for the word. Something as simple as *table*, he'd get to T and then flounder around, *turnip*, *taco*, *telephone*, until he got it or you got it for him."

She was touching his hand now, soft as a flower petal.

"Watching him, I always imagined that the mind had some kind of somatic recall of verbs. You could shuffle your feet and the word *walk* would come back to you, but nouns were stored in all these arbitrary little cubbyholes facing you, like at the post office, without much sense of order. It was the key to the order of the boxes that he'd lost and he had to scan them in some kind of imposed order."

He shrugged, remembering the terrible struggles his father had gone through, and also the way his looks had changed toward the end, with the chemotherapy taking his hair, and the bloat of inactivity, and his second wife, not Jack Liffey's mother, overfeeding him. Cooking was the only thing she could do for him, and his face came to look far too small, a tiny set of features painted into the center of a big white hard-boiled egg.

"And then I noticed that there was a pattern to the words he had the worst trouble with. *Wife* and *son* and *sister*. And then *hour*, *day*, *week*, *year*—all the words for time. They were the things that hurt. The family that he was leaving, and time—knowing he didn't have time. Language betrayed him little by little. The cancer was a real bastard, hitting him when he was down."

He ran down. He was scaring himself with thoughts of death, and he could feel a line of sweat across his forehead.

"That too much grief. It just break your heart there so much hurt in the world." She gave his hand a platonic little squeeze. "I don't want make it worse. You don't have to do nothing you don't want. You come back if you want or you stay away. We friend."

He nodded and felt the cool wind probing up the skirts of his sheet, stiffening his penis against his will. It just kept happening. At this rate, he'd have to walk back into the house bent double. It had been difficult to relate to the slippery, fast-talking, intense nugget of ego-energy she had put forward, but her sudden generosity and a peek at her vulnerability did a lot for his sense of affection.

"I do you favor today. If you feel okay, I take you to Industrial League. I know them. You ask them about Phuong Minh. Then I take you back to your car."

"Thanks, Tien. I need to make a phone call now."

She detached the cellular from the computer and handed it to him. It turned out she hadn't discarded his clothes after all. Auntie Pham had washed and ironed them and mended the tear at the pocket, and they were so tidy now he would have trouble convincing anybody he'd been mugged in them. Tien Joubert went into the house to let him call in privacy.

First, putting off the hard one, he called MediaPros and delayed his visit a day, which didn't upset them at all, then Marlena, who was nearly hysterical.

"I know, Mar, I'm sorry. I was beaten unconscious last night by a half dozen thugs. I'm okay now except for a big black eye and a lot of bruises. A Vietnamese family here took me in and patched me up. I'll be home soon."

Vietnamese *family*, he thought. Another sidestep on the long downward ethical course of his life.

eight

A Hamster Named Stuart

It was a black Mercedes 560SL, pretty much what he would have guessed, and she didn't drive it very well. She was erratic, slow for a block, then speeding up for a while as some tune in her head changed, decelerating abruptly, and every now and then drifting a foot into the next lane as her mind went to something else. He thought of asking if she'd ever considered hiring a chauffeur, but it wasn't a chauffeur sort of car.

Suddenly she pulled over in a red zone, a tow-away zone, and pushed the shifter all the way up into park and looked at him as if she was worried one of them was about to die. "I don't want you to get wrong idea. You look at me and maybe think all Viet Nam people crazy and pushy like me. I not same as them mostly. I told you I want to be big and strong and loud because it's the squeaky door that gets grease. You got to say what you want in the world. Most Viet Nam people not like that. Americans always want you to represent your people, like everybody got to be a little chip off the big blockade."

Indeed, he thought. A police car doodled past them. He was a little uneasy about the tow-away zone but he let her run.

"The really most important thing my people love is delicacy and very quiet, very strong respect. Buddhism say—the second big Truth of Buddhism say this thing—the big cause of problem in life is passion, you got to push passion away. You got to repudiate it." She smiled in satisfaction at getting the word right this time.

"But me, I get a taste for passion. Maybe in France I get this thing, and I say, No, the big problem in life is stay quiet and delicate and let yourself be floor mat. Passion is okay, make a squeak, make lots of squeak. You see what I say, I'm different?"

"Yes, I see. You're a remarkable woman."

She touched his knee lightly. "I want you come back to me, Jack Liff. Will you come back?"

His ears burned and his forehead buzzed. "I don't know, Tien. Do you just want a big hairy American? That shouldn't be so hard."

"You something special. I been with American guy and they got a bad attitude. They don't respect you. You different."

"I don't know if I can come back the way you mean, Tien. Can we just let it sit for now?"

She smiled. "Okay, man. I see you one torment guy."

"You're going to get a ticket stopped here."

"Who cares? It just money."

She stopped on a red curb again in front of the nondescript high rise and jumped out. The building was not far from the Fashion Island Mall on the cliffs overlooking Newport, just another upended Kleenex box, but it would have super views of the town below and the sparkling blue-green ocean, with a wind stirring little whitecaps.

He pointed at the curb and she shrugged and said, "I not stay. I just introduce you and go shop. Fashion Island got good Neiman-Marcus."

In the elevator, she pushed the button for the next to top floor.

"Are you a member of the Industrial League?" he asked.

"You kidding, huh? You in Fortune 500, they ask you be member. You run Joe's Laundry and Dry Cleaning, you get polite note to go down street to Chamber of Commerce. I on advisory board from Little Saigon—that about like advisory board from kindergarten. It mean nothing, but I never say no, member of anything. It good to make friends."

The office was on the side of the building that would have the view. She rapped once on a wood-and-frosted glass door that must have been rescued from some Victorian building. Gold-bordered black letters on the glass said only ILOC, like a discreet private club, which in a way it was, he supposed.

Inside there was an unattended lobby with antique furniture and big then-and-now aerial photos of the county. Off to the right he could see into an empty conference room with a rosewood table and high-back padded chairs. All the other doors but one were closed. The open office had a young man with long blond hair, who craned his neck back to see the visitors and then stood.

"Hi, Ms. Joubert. I haven't seen you in a while."

A young woman in slacks came out of the same office. She wore round wire-rims like John Lennon, which made her look studious and mannish. "Mrs. Joubert."

Tien Joubert took their hands and introduced Jack Liffey without naming either of them. "I want you take good care of this guy, he big special guy. He got important questions."

He felt himself blushing a little as she left. The blushing made his eye ache and immediately he told them he'd been mugged to get it over with. They didn't seem very surprised.

"I'm Dick Bormann, but no relation," the young man told him jauntily. "My dad did not hide out in the Argentine jungles after World War Two."

The young man had a way of standing slightly sideways and watching you at an angle, as if preparing to bolt.

"Neither did Martin," Jack Liffey said. "I'm sure he had a nice suite in a hotel. Perón helped relocate thousands of Nazis."

"You're a historian, too."

"Just an amateur."

"I'm Debbie Miller. We're grad students, working here part time. The director is out this week. He spends most of his time in

Washington and Sacramento." She plucked at short dark hair, and tapped a foot nervously.

"You two work with Phuong Minh?"

"Sure," Dick Bormann said. "Come see."

The blond young man sidled away to lead Jack Liffey into the conference room, which was even bigger than he'd guessed, while the young woman hung back and then banged around in the office outside as if hiding the drinks from her parents. The outside wall of the conference room was a good thirty feet long, all glass, and had a staggering view of the ocean. Several container ships were crossing the horizon stacked with their colored shipping boxes, and he could just make out the southern end of Catalina in the mists.

"You can see Catalina over the nearby mall called Fashion Island where Mrs. Joubert always goes, and that's a great shot of the Pacific, isn't it?"

Jack Liffey almost said, I thought it was Lake Michigan, but let it go. He was beckoned to the side of the room, where there was a posed photo in a redwood forest, a half dozen young people kneeling in front and another half dozen older people in back. "This was our staff at a retreat last year. Phuong's there."

She was right in the middle, with a wan decorous smile, holding a large ceremonial gavel in both arms.

"This isn't Bohemian Grove, is it?" he asked as Debbie Miller came in to join them.

"The very place. The private playground of the ruling class, where the Rockefellers play ping-pong with the Kissingers and then tell them which country to invade." He chuckled and spread his arms wide. "You've stumbled into it, Mr. Liffey. Isn't it amazing? This is the private meeting room of the inner sanctum of the ruling class, at least the local fraction of it that deigns to visit go-go Orange County, and right this minute it's all run by *us*, two grad students."

A 737 came over, still fairly low and rising steeply, from John Wayne Airport behind the building.

"Not *run* exactly," the young woman corrected primly. "The

board meets here four times a year and the director carries out their wishes. All we do is their research and odd jobs."

"Did Phuong work with you?"

"The past tense? Has something happened to her?"

"Her father's worried. She hasn't been home for a while. When did you last see her?"

"Oh, gosh . . . maybe ten days. I was beginning to wonder. Would you like some coffee?"

"Sure."

They got him a mug of mediocre coffee and took him back to their own office where they sat at desks that had been positioned in the four corners of the room. They swiveled their chairs around to face the middle, like a bunch of sophomores in the library discussing Kierkegaard, he thought, if kids still did that. There was a strange smell in the room that he couldn't identify. Barnyard came to mind.

"What did Phuong do here?"

"The same thing we do really," Debbie Miller said. "We've been working on nothing but the airport issue for months. The Industrial League feels very strongly," she added in a pompous singsong voice, as she held up a slick tri-fold with a faraway airport on the cover, "that it is imperative for the future of international trade and the expansion of the job base to develop El Toro as a regional airport."

"And you don't?"

"There's arguments on both sides," Dick Bormann said. "In fact, Phuong was informally our 'deep-six' editor. She was in charge of the inconvenient facts that we were supposed to find some way to answer or hide."

The young man stood and reached across, past Jack Liffey, to what must have been Phuong's desk and picked off the top a little metal file box with flowers on it and opened it up. His eyebrows went up as he read the first card. " 'A house loses approximately 1.33 percent of its value for every decibel of additional airplane noise.' Try *that* on your homeowner out there, or this: 'The value of a house increases approximately 3.4 percent for every quarter mile it is farther from the flight path.' "

He plucked out another card. " 'Seventy-nine percent of the businesses in south county oppose the airport.' Needless to say," he added, "these aren't companies traded on the big board. This is Tammy's Needlepoint Supplies and George's Surfboard Wax."

He became aware of a very faint scrabbling sound, like rats in the wainscoting that the two researchers were doing their best to ignore.

"Do you think Phuong could have made any enemies doing this research?"

"Only if the people affected actually mind losing their life savings. Seriously—people are pretty pissed off, but not at us. Heavens, we're just lackeys."

"We did get threats, Dick." Debbie Miller volunteered. "You just don't take them seriously. I took the very first one on the phone. Some gruff guy said he was in the Mission Viejo Homeowners Association and he'd blow us to kingdom come, one by one, if we didn't drop the stupid airport idea. Obviously he wasn't an official representative."

Dick Bormann chuckled. "I just can't believe a goofball is that dangerous."

"We got more from the same guy; we've all had them. Phuong had one, too, and it shook her up. He guessed she was Asian, maybe she gave her name, and he used some racial epithet."

"Have you ever had picketers? Slashed tires?"

"Naw," the young man said. "Not many people even know we exist. If there's a real focus for all the hatred, it's Ron Kitsos. He's the guy who owns Air Forty-Niner, you know, the Happy Gold Bird. He's fanatical about wanting the airport. He'd love to make El Toro a regional hub."

"Who's publicly opposed?"

"A lot of people. Debbie?"

She made a few faces. It seemed to help her think. "Probably the best known is Sam C. Treat. He used to be a pilot for Forty-Niner and before that he used to fly for the Marines out of El Toro. He loves to go to public meetings and tick off the big three no-nos against the airport."

"Which are?"

"I can never remember. Dick probably can."

His eyes swung back to Dick Bormann, who put the filing box back gingerly, as if he couldn't stand to have it near him a minute longer. "Well, first you've got to understand that planes can't take off to the west because that would put them in direct conflict with the landing approach to the existing airport, so all the plans are to have them take off only toward the east. Treat loves to point out that you can make a military pilot do anything, take off blindfolded or standing on his head in the cockpit, but civil pilots just will not take risks, it's a moral obligation. And he says the east takeoff at El Toro violates three basic safety rules of aviation. One, the runway is *up*hill. Pretty steep, I think, as those things go. Two, it's *with* the prevailing wind instead of into it. Three, it's more or less right into a mountain range. An F/A-18C with full afterburner can pull a hard bank to avoid the mountain, that's one thing, but imagine a 747 scraping its underbelly on the live oaks every time it takes off."

"You sound like an opponent."

The two of them looked at each other and something private was unsaid. "Everybody's got a point. John Wayne Airport has only 500 acres and one runway. It'll be up to its capacity in five years. I'm glad it's not going to be my decision."

"What is that smell?" he asked finally, when he was satisfied that it wasn't coming from one of them.

The young woman grinned. "I'll show you."

In a moment she came back in with a large wire cage that held two hamsters, like fat golden mice. "We're not supposed to have them here, but you won't snitch on us, will you?"

"Heaven forbid."

She set the cage down on the unused desk, where it seemed to belong.

"That one's Basil. And this is Stuart." She giggled.

"Stuart Ross is the league's director," Dick Bormann explained.

"If I had an animal named for my last boss, it would have to be a snake," Jack Liffey said. "I guess there has to be one hamster wheel at the heart of every big enterprise."

He tried to get more information out of them about Phuong, but neither of them seemed to know much about her at all, except that she was Vietnamese and very polite and very smart. It was like wearing a big mustache to rob a bank. Nobody ever noticed anything but the mustache.

He was waiting for the elevator in the hall when Debbie Miller slipped out to talk to him.

"Dick doesn't like to make trouble for people, but you'd better see this."

She handed him a feature article cut out of a newspaper. There was an inch of yellowed tape on the top as if it had been stuck up on a wall. A photo of a stocky man in a wheelchair was shaking his fist at the sky.

M.V. Residents
Found Anti-Airport
Citizen Panel

"I think it's the guy who calls. He's probably harmless."
"Thanks. I'll be discreet."

He settled onto a big ugly concrete stanchion by the curb, the kind of thing government buildings had started putting out to keep suicide trucks loaded with fertilizer and diesel oil from crashing into lobbies. There was probably some branch fed office in the building. The article told of the founding of an emergency committee of homeowners from south county cities like Lake Forest, Mission Viejo, El Toro, and Irvine to stop the airport. They were quoting the wheelchair-bound Marvin B. Resnick because he was quotable and colorful, not necessarily because he had any official position in the group.

"If they won't listen to our grievances, we ought to get us some SAMS and blast the first airliner to lift off that runway right out of the sky!"

Nice, Marvin, he thought. That kind of talk ought to get you a long way in an upscale suburban neighborhood organization.

The moment she picked him up he'd noticed she was even more bubbly than he remembered, and as she parked next to his forlorn old Concord at the Little Saigon mall, she plucked at his sleeve.

"Wait. Before you go 'way, tell me one thing 'bout me you like."

"Is this a trick?"

She shook her head, but something was cooking, he could tell.

"I like almost everything about you. The only thing I don't like is a square inch just below the elbow. I don't like that."

She frowned and looked at her elbow, then decided he was kidding. "You joking. Say 'everything' is same as say nothing. You got to say one thing, two thing."

"Okay, I like your energy . . . your candor, and your happiness. That's three things. And you're very beautiful."

She beamed. "You got right answer." And she handed him a small white cardboard box like an award. He had a vision of her going down on one knee and springing a diamond engagement ring on him. He hesitated, but took the box and opened it to find an expensive-looking gold tie clasp with a pale jade stone. He hadn't worn a tie since the layoffs, and he hadn't worn a tieclasp on a tie since junior dances in high school. He didn't know they still made them.

"It's beautiful, Tien. Very. Is it jade?" He met her eyes and they were gorgeous, the dark surrounded by pure white. The affection in them was quite flattering and he felt her presence buoying him up.

"Number one. Real Asia jade, not the dark jadeite you get lots here."

"I shouldn't accept this, but I know it would be insulting not to. Please don't get me anything else, though."

" 'Anything else' mean I see you again?"

He smiled. She was quick. "I have to go home now. I'll come back tomorrow to look for Phuong some more. Could we meet for lunch?"

"You bet. You call."

After she'd baroomed off happily in the Mercedes, he found the note on his windshield, the scrawled message aimed inward once again: *Go home, fuck you, dead dead dead.* Spelled right this time, but the punctuation needed work.

He carried the big plastic bag into his room and set it on a corner of the red desk and then pushed aside all the French books to make a clear area. First he took out the blister-wrap card with the track on it. He tore open the plastic bubble and took out one length of railway track, with its little brown ties attached, and threw the rest away. Then he broke into the big orange box labeled Rivarossi. The chatty clerk had kept trying to tell him about the Italian company, reputedly Mafia owned, that it was not nearly as good as the German and Swiss ones, but Billy Gudger just wanted to get his find out of Hobby City and get it home.

He set the vintage railroad boxcar on the track and sat back to study it. It was an HO scale model, about the size of a desk stapler and mostly yellow. *P.T. Barnum Circus,* it said across the top, and the side had a mustachioed face surrounded by a lot of elaborate tracery, plus animals and circus scenes. The clerk was right. The model boxcar wasn't all that well built and the decoration was just printed onto a card that was glued to the plastic, but it didn't matter at all. It would do fine.

He would just have to find a way to get his mother to stumble on it so he could study her reactions.

A ring which seemed set with a dull, darke stone a little swelling out, like what we call (tho' untruly) a toadstone.
　　　　　　　　　　　　　　　—John Evelyn, *Diary* (1645)

* * *

At that moment, a line of Orange County Sheriff's auxiliaries and deputy cadets still in training, plus a few volunteers from the Eagle Scouts and the nearest Neighborhood Watch Association in the Tustin Hills, were pacing slowly across the grassy hillside five yards apart looking for clues in the Sagebrush Killer investigation. They had all been warned to wear sturdy boots against snakebite, and they weren't far at all from where the two victims of the Sagebrush Killer had been found, in fact only one gully away. They'd been at it for several hours and mostly weren't taking it very seriously. After all, there were a lot of other cases to clear and no one had any idea that there would be a third body so close by.

nine

To Be Good You've Got to Succeed

"**H**ey, Jack! Man, you look *bad*."

Marlena's nephew Rogelio was sitting in the living room with his feet up, gesturing with a Budweiser. Two young Latinos Jack Liffey had never met sat opposite with their own beers, and they were curious about his shiner, too. The TV was going but ignored, a Mexican soccer game.

"This is Paco and that's Solomon. This is Jack, Marlena's boyfriend."

"Hey."

"*Ce mal, esse?*"

"What happened to you, man?"

"About six guys happened to me all at once. A lot of the parts you can't see hurt, too."

"No shit, man. You need some help?" One of them was already stirring, as if to roll up his sleeves and fight.

"It'll be taken care of. Thanks. Mar in?" A beer would be good, he thought. It would also help him bond with the boys, but he'd sworn off and he meant to stay off.

"She's doing laundry, I think."

"I'd better touch home base."

"Take it easy, man."

Marlena was in the little cramped laundry room, folding underwear out of a wicker basket on top of the dryer. She gave a squeal
when she saw his eye and crushed him against her, bubbling and cooing. "Jackie, Jackie, you look so *damaged*!"

"Don't squeeze too tight. I'm sore a lot of other places, too."

"Oh, *Jackie*."

Actually he was enjoying the respite from her corrosive jealousy.
And he was trying not to enjoy the irony that the respite came just
as she should have been cranking it up. He hoped none of Tien's perfume had stayed on him.

"You see a doctor?"

"It's not necessary. Just bruises and this eye. If they'd had
another few minutes to work on me, it might have been worse."

After he explained it all four or five times and she had calmed
down, he helped her finish the underwear and then the sheets, taking the corners and walking toward her with a kiss at each big fold.

"You're not going back there, are you?"

"This won't happen again. Don't worry."

"I don't want you in no danger, *querido*. You're too precious to
me just like you are. All this stuff is precious." She was pressing softly through four layers of sheet against his penis and testicles. "Is it
all okay?"

"A kiss will make everything better."

She smiled. "I'll kiss you everywhere you feel bad, and everywhere
you feel good, too."

"Then I won't have to make up my mind which is which."

While she made dinner, he opened a ginger ale and sat with the
boys watching the soccer. As much as he hated sports, it didn't matter very much that he didn't even know where Pachuca and Iguala
were and he couldn't follow the frenetic commentary. The game was
just a long tormented ballet in which men ran around on grass, leaped
straight into the air and jumped in front of each other without ever
accomplishing much of anything. A pretty good metaphor for life,

after all, he thought, though in general he felt life didn't really need a metaphor.

"So why don't they just pick the ball up and throw it?" he asked disingenuously. "It'd be a lot easier."

Rogelio knew he liked to tease.

"Esse!"

"Man, it's not supposed to be *easy*. That's the whole point."

"Then tie their legs together. Make it harder. Wouldn't that be more interesting?"

"How come in American football they don't just carry guns and shoot each other, eh?"

"Hey, Paco, they *did* last weekend at the Coliseum."

"Oh, man, I forgot."

They all laughed and Paco made a pantomime of shooting one finger of each hand at the players on TV. "Oh, man, full combat soccer. That would be so rad."

"Rogelio, how's your computer course?" Jack Liffey knew he had enrolled in a computer repair class he'd found on the back of a matchbook.

"It was too hard," he complained. "And they wanted a lot of money off me right away to buy stuff."

"I was afraid of that. You could try the JC up the hill."

"Maybe." It was a pretty vague maybe and Jack Liffey wondered if he could think of a way to draw the young man into something that would interest him and give him a future. He liked Rogelio's cheerfulness, his readiness to assist anybody who needed help, his ability to apply himself when the spirit moved him, and a kind of bedrock decency in him that it would be very hard to overrate.

Jack Liffey looked through the archway at Marlena in her frilly apron, bending forward to peer into a big pot. He liked the way the dark skirt stretched taut across her bottom, and he was overwhelmed all of a sudden with a wave of tenderness that felt so strangely like loss that he had to get up right then and hug her to make sure she was really there.

* * *

They found quite a few things they could do in bed in between his bruises without him wincing too badly, and then he was so exhausted he thought he'd sleep forever, but he woke at half past three, wide-eyed and jangled. There had been a dream of some sort, in a strange city with a lot of urgent obligations he had to see to and he kept forgetting where he'd parked the car. He watched her sleep for a long time, as if he'd never seen her before, then he spooned against her and ran his hand under the nightshirt to cup one of her large breasts. She made a few satisfied breathing sounds and wriggled once against him. That wasn't much help sending him back to sleep.

After a while he got up and sat in the kitchen. The yard was still dark out the window set into the back door, and doves were cooing and gurgling somewhere. He stood at the window and watched a pickup truck with the lights out accelerate down the alley, up to no good. Rogelio had left an old automobile tire mounted on a wheel right in the center of the yard, and he wondered once again about that peculiar trait. When something no longer had an immediate use for Rogelio, it went out of existence. Jack Liffey found screwdrivers in the sink, empty beer bottles in the bookcase and, once, a half-eaten coconut inside the washing machine that Rogelio had just cleared out. He wondered if it was just a hyperactive sense of focus that moved on to its next object too quickly. Jack Liffey got up abruptly and rescued the note that he'd tossed in the trash under the sink: *Go home, fuck you, dead dead dead.*

If you saw a note like that in a movie, he thought, it would just be words on paper and you'd forget about it, or maybe you'd think the grammar a little quaint and sad and *then* you'd forget about it—but that easy equanimity would be there because the note hadn't invaded your personal space. It was remarkable how all your illusions of security could be swept away by a simple token of someone else's ill will. The ridiculous note with its childish-looking capital letters and bad punctuation constituted a gross violation of his space in the world. It was like stumbling on a burglary that left you gaping blankly in awe at the wall where the TV and stereo once had been. He hadn't realized how the note was going to prey on him. He was naked in a universe where a shitstorm could come down any minute.

He realized he hadn't checked the answering machine in his condo-office, and he called it up and keyed in his code. There was only one message. "We don't forget so easy. Maybe we come get you where you live." It was an Asian voice and he was glad the answering machine was in a guarded condo complex, four miles away.

Hello there, Death, he thought, prickling with sweat. He wondered if there was anything at all to be done in those moments when the foreboding and gloom fell through unexpectedly, just plopped down into your consciousness to haunt you with the one simple idea that you couldn't shake: things come to an end. There is no after. You don't get to find out who becomes the forty-fourth President. Perhaps, he thought, what you did was just look square at the foreboding and curse it and say, I'm going on, man, the hell with you.

Fuck you, Death, dead dead dead.

He came very close to invading the liquor cabinet, but he started reading the labels on cups of dried soup and boxes of instant mashed potatoes instead, and finally he grinned, pretending he was at ease and confident, in order to send the foreboding on its way. He wasn't at ease, but it was the best he could do.

"Come on over!" the man in the wheelchair bellowed from the far side of a small koi pond.

Jack Liffey had found the address in the phone book, about as elementary a detective technique as you could get. It was a tasteful cedar-sided ranch house located on a meandering street called Vista Del Montana in a whole tract of tastefully meandering streets with tasteful Spanish names. But this one was different out back. Redwood planked walkways led through a mannered wildness of papyrus and reeds and elephant ears to give the look of a jungle. Even a stream, and a little Asian-looking hump bridge.

"Watch out for the tigers! Come on around, man!"

Jack Liffey passed a short banana palm as the man in the wheelchair did a wheelie and propelled himself rapidly toward the little bridge. He was wearing a threadbare khaki fatigue jacket with RESNIK on the name-label, and he had a scraggly beard and unruly hair that made him look like the police mugshot of a sex-offender. "Whee!" he cried, going over. "*Airborne* Ranger, Green Beret, this is the way we start our day!"

A few minutes earlier, Jack Liffey had offered his hand and introduced himself as a detective looking into scandals associated with the El Toro airport.

"No shit, Jack. It's about time. Where'd you get that eye?"

"Mugging."

"Too bad, too bad. Should'a called down an air strike."

He'd led straight out back and, by flinging his big wheels in opposite directions, he'd spun once around on a high patio that was like the observation deck of a game park. "How do you like my jungle?"

"Looks like you put a lot of time into it."

"I got *nothing* but time, man. Police up those grounds private!" he bellowed and spun back. There was no private in evidence.

The tour completed, the man seemed to settle a bit into a funk, but then emerge unpredictably just as rambunctious as before. "You look about the right age, Jack. You over in the big Nam?"

"Not really. I was a technician, stuck off in a trailer in Thailand."

"But you know what it was *about*. You got with the *program*. You had *enthusiasm* for the mission. You were one of us despised few."

"I don't know about the despised."

The quiet Asian woman who had met him at the door brought out a tray of iced tea. Resnik seemed to go into a calm mode with her presence. He introduced her as his wife An, speaking with real tenderness, and some private look of forbearance passed between them before she set the tray on a bench and drifted away. "My other little souvenir of Nam," he said softly. "I mean that with no disrespect whatsoever. The first souvenir is three ounces of metal imbedded about *here*." He wrenched around to indicate his back. "Air Cav grunt, just minding my own business sitting on the deck of the chopper. A mortar, if you can believe it, came right through the door of the Huey and—*sayonara* spine. It's a freak I lived. Everybody else bought it and the ship nosed in. I bet I'm the only person in the history of warfare ever mortared in flight."

"I'll bet you are."

"But all injuries follow the logic of human probabilities," he insisted. "Somewhere, 100 fucking monkeys are writing up my citation on 100 fucking typewriters right now. They'll get around to me right after they write *Hamlet*."

Jack Liffey sat on a teak bench and sipped at an iced tea, hoping the man might settle down again. He wondered if Resnik had missed his mood stabilizer for the morning.

"What do you require from me, Jacko?" He took his own iced tea off the tray and slipped it into a cup holder that snapped up from the arm of his chair.

"What do you know of the Industrial League?"

"Scumbags!" he shouted. He flung up his arms. "Doing the dirty work for the rich assholes who want to wreck the value of my home and send me packing."

"Have you had any contact with them?"

Now he started to get supicious. "Who you working for, sport?"

Jack Liffey told him the truth, that he was looking for a man's daughter, Phuong Minh, who was missing.

"That's not exactly a scandal relating to the airport, is it, *Jack*?"

"It is if she's been hurt. You've been giving them a hard time, haven't you?"

"Roger that. If I had access to some C-4, I might just air them right out. I telephone a couple times a week, let them know they ought to get real and pull out of this one. I didn't kidnap some poor girl though. Here, you secure that drinks tray, and I'll show you what this little firefight is about for me."

He spun once more and wheeled toward the house and Jack Liffey had to follow. A sharp turn inside the wide glass door led into a bright kitchen that was unlike any kitchen he'd ever seen. The counter tops were all black granite and set at mid-thigh, and most of them you could run a wheelchair right under to chop up vegetables. The sink and rangetop were low, too, and there were two shorty fridges side-by-side. It was like a world made for elves, the only thing more than three feet off the floor a band of photos of tropical scenery that ran around the wall to keep the top half of the room from looking too empty.

"You don't think this cost a pretty penny?"

"I'm sure it did."

He gave a broad beckoning wave, a squad leader bringing his troops up, and led along a hall and into a very large room that had probably once been two bedrooms. Near the door was a rack that held a strange-looking pump shotgun with a long flexible tube that ran out of the stock into some kind of stanchion, like a small gasoline pump. The man hit a switch and the far wall lit up faintly. Jack Liffey could see it was a projection screen. As the apparatus gathered steam, a rural lake came into eerie existence on the wall. The room lights went down gradually and the scene took on reality. The lake was surrounded by willows and poplars, ruffled by a faint breeze. There was even the sound of the breeze, and a distant honking of geese, from hidden speakers somewhere.

Marvin B. Resnik shouldered the shotgun and backhanded some control on the stanchion. Before long a goose flew low out of the edge of the picture and Resnik tracked ahead of it and fired. There was a blast, about half what a real shotgun would have produced out in the open, but somehow the long gun actually recoiled. A small bright burst seemed to stun the goose and it fell out of the sky. There was no splash, however, just the eerie sound of a splash as the plummeting goose vanished as it touched the wind ripples on the lake that went on and on.

"Gotta stay *loose*." He pumped the shotgun. "Get your *goose*."

Another bird came out of the opposite wall. Marvin fired and brought this one down, too. The illusory lake was starting to get frightening. It was like a siren call from another world, a beckoning. *Just saunter forward into this beautiful land, my friend, and Marvin B. Resnik promises not to blow you away.*

"There's another scenario on this doohickus called 'Smoke the Perp!' "

He hit some control, and Jack Liffey started a little as the entire wall flickered and became an urban street scene in the dusk with an alley leading away between four-story buildings with their windows blown out and rusting fire escapes. Trash cans, heaps of broken boxes, and a moan of wind with a distant fuss of sirens and traffic. A man with a pistol popped up in one of the windows and Marvin Resnik fired. There was the same small bright burst where the man had stood, and the sound of a body thudding to the floor.

"Goin' *down*!"

Resnik pumped the shotgun. A sniper with a rifle appeared on the roof and Resnik blew him back off the parapet. Then a gunman jumped up from behind the trash cans in the alley and Resnik pumped and fired twice, three times, in a frenzy.

"*Get* some, motherfucker!"

He was breathing heavy and then he rested the butt of the shotgun on the floor and leaned on it to get control of himself. "Want to give it a try?"

"No thanks. It's quite an illusion."

"Gets the juices goin', don't it? There's also a low-level chopper attack comin' at ya over a forest, Russian Mi-24s, HIND-Ds, but it lacks something in realism, taking out a big hunter-killer chopper with a shotgun."

He racked the shotgun and spun the chair around. "Whoa!"

His wife looked into the room. "Do you require anything, Marvin?"

Resnik just shook his head, and she slipped away. "I got three quarters of a million dollars tied up in this house, *Jack*. And a secret conspiracy of rich fucks that live in Newport and Nelly Gail Ranch up on the hill think they're going to put me and a lot of other folks at the end of an intercontinental runway for 747s. When I bought here I was assured El Toro would remain a Marine base for the duration and all we'd get would be a few dozen small jets a day, and most of those pull afterburner and turn north over the hills the minute they're off the ground."

Jack Liffey could sympathize, but he couldn't work up that much concern for a guy with three quarters of a million dollars to sink into a house like Disneyland. When they'd put the Century Freeway, the 105, through the working class areas of Hawthorne, Inglewood and Watts, they'd given poor old couples so little money that a few years later they couldn't buy a doghouse with their fair market value.

"I'm not going to let them make me fall back and regroup, no fucking way, but I'm not as crazy as I look."

He started slowly out of the room.

"I think I know the girl you're looking for. At least, I think I talked to her on the phone." He smiled. "I put a scare into her but it's just a game."

"They said you used a racial epithet."

He turned back and scowled. "Take a good look at my wife, *Jack*. Do you think I'd do that?"

"It's hard to break the habit sometimes. Those words just rolled off the tongue in the Army."

He shook his head. "Not with me, no *sir*. Those words even think of coming out of my brain, they stick on the back of my tongue and make me choke. I had heavy training from a mother whose maiden name was Lovejoy and who was proud of having some famous Abolitionists way back in the family in Illinois." He changed gears.

"Down the hall is a room full of computers, but you've seen computers. The point is, I'm dug in here and I ain't about to let the choppers haul me off the roof."

He rotated and backed expertly into a living room that had handrails all over the place.

"How far would you be willing to go to stop the airport?"

"I read this philosopher once, he said, 'Not everything that succeeds is right. But to be right you've got to succeed.' I mean to stop that airport."

He backed his wheelchair up near a tall bookcase full of paperbacks and rocked it back and forth restlessly.

"Have you ever met Phuong Minh in person?"

"I am a freelance copywriter for a number of advertising companies in Newport and Irvine. I work back there on a computer, and I teleconference by computer, and I send stuff in by modem, and money is transferred to my bank electronically. I haven't left this house and this yard in two and a half years. The only way I am going out of this place is in a pine box. Now you get out of my house, *asshole.*"

t e n

The Toadstone

First thing the next morning he phoned Art Castro at his office. Castro worked for one of the really big detective agencies, and he had a grand rosewood-and-marble office in the historic Bradbury Building with a view out over downtown L.A. They owed each other a half dozen favors, and he wasn't sure who was ahead.

"Could I talk to Art?"

"Could I tell Mr. Castro who's calling?"

Jack Liffey seemed to have a permanent problem with receptionists. "I doubt it," he said.

Eventually she put him through, but there had been some sort of prologue because Art came on suspiciously.

"This isn't Bob Browning, is it?"

"Naw, he's off with Elizabeth Barrett, writing poetry."

"Jack, for *Chrissake*. How come you won't never announce yourself? I got to be careful, I got a pissed-off husband after me."

"I bet it's not the first time."

"It's not something I done. It's what I found out. Anyway, you got to be more polite to young women."

"It seems to be an abiding problem. Anyway, I've got a small favor."

"Why else would you call?"

He let that go. They'd met in the 1970s during a brief flirtation they'd both had with Viet Nam Veterans Against the War. Art tended to act hard and cynical but he still cared about a lot of things, and Jack Liffey knew he was working with the veterans group that was campaigning to get the U.S. to sign on to the landmine convention.

"You've got vet friends down in Orange County, I'll bet."

"Orange County. Man, you got to watch yourself down there. That's wall-to-wall angry white guys."

"Uh-huh. There's a particular angry white guy down there named Marvin Resnik. He's eccentric enough that he's probably pretty well known. He's a paraplegic from Nam and he claims he hasn't been out of his house in two and a half years. Anybody you could ask if that's a crock?"

"I can always ask. You still chasing down AWOL kids?"

"That's me."

"There's no money in it, man."

"I'm beginning to figure that out."

"You should come on in and join the big league. I could introduce you to Manny here."

"I really love your outfit, Art. Union busting, going after the poor on behalf of the landed rich, investigating some beat-up wife who finally fell in love with a nice quiet guy at work. I think I prefer the peewee league. I'll give you a call in a day or two."

"Sure. Don't spend all your retainer in one place."

"Then if you turn the big knob, it'll fast forward," the production assistant said with an icy awkwardness.

"Thanks."

"I thought you were coming yesterday." There was a note of grievance as Jack Liffey sat down in front of the rolling cart that had a big complicated video player on a shelf and the monitor on top.

"I called. I was busy being mugged. Sorry, did you set something up special yesterday?"

"I was out sick."

Then what are you complaining about? Jack Liffey met his eyes for a moment. There was something a little off in them, but that was probably just his imagination after sitting up a lot of the night staring at a death threat. But there was something a little off in his clothing, for sure, a bright checked shirt and unfashionable tight polyester trousers that looked like they had come from Pic 'n Save.

"Do you remember Phuong?" he asked the production assistant.

"No."

"She signed the release for you."

"Everybody signs a release." He walked away without another word, and Jack Liffey figured his social skills were going to keep him from advancing very far in the company, unless maybe his dad owned it, which would explain a lot.

He pressed Start and nudged the big shuttle knob to speed up past a talking head-and-shoulders of a doctor, then he cranked a little more to fast forward over several shots of a black teen-ager who was drumming as if his life depended on it. Then shots of a Latino playing the guitar. Some of the shots got flashy, tilted off-kilter, or drifting back and forth. Suddenly there was a shot from behind the guitar player and he hit Pause. You could see a crowd of people against a garage wall, or more likely a stage set made up to look like a garage wall. A young Vietnamese woman was right in the middle, smiling with real enjoyment. Either she could act, or she really was getting a kick out of watching the band.

The director was wrong, he thought. Phuong could easily have played young enough to be a high school student. There were several people around her, clapping and bobbing their heads, and he let the tape run again, but she didn't seem to relate to anyone in the crowd at all. Tom Xuan must have gone home already.

The end of the tape was a series of isolated shots of faces in the crowd. When Phuong's closeup came, she called out something but she wasn't miked so when he backed the tape up and brought up the sound, he found the music covered everything.

Jack Liffey looked up to see the production assistant in the doorway of the cubicle, watching him intently.

"Need the office?"

"No, no."

He seemed to want to say something, and some intuition told Jack Liffey to encourage him.

"Your name's Billy, right?"

"Uh-huh."

"What was your last name?"

"Gudger. It's not real. It was something longer and mom shortened it."

"Real is whatever you want it to be."

The boy smiled, with a kind of shy sarcasm peeking out. "That only goes so far. I was given a real body that turned out much shorter than my aspirations."

Jack Liffey flashed a big grin to put him at ease, though it didn't seem to work. "I meant in names, but I get you. I wanted to be brilliant, and I drew a pedestrian kind of mind that just can't handle abstractions. I need things concrete."

"That's really too bad."

Most people would have volunteered one of their own weaknesses in trade, a nice unimportant one, but this was one strange young man.

The PA in the hall honked. "Attention MediaPros employees, the catering truck has arrived."

"Where does the truck come?" he asked the young man.

"Down the hall 'till you reach the far end of the building and right. You'll see."

"Can I get you a doughnut? Coffee?"

He shook his head hard, as if Jack Liffey had offered him something really distasteful.

Jack Liffey stood up. "I left too quick this morning to eat."

Billy Gudger didn't say anything, but he trailed Jack Liffey down the corridor, a few paces back, like a puppy not quite sure of being tolerated. Jack Liffey slowed up, wondering if the young man knew something about Phuong and was having trouble coming out with it, or if he was just flat desperate to talk to another human being. He did seem the sort of kid that most people would go to some lengths to avoid.

"You planning a future in media? Directing?"

"No. It's just a job." He walked in silence a moment and then blurted, as if a little surprised himself that he was so forthcoming, "My talents lie on other gradients."

I hope they aren't all as steep uphill as this one, Jack Liffey thought. "What would that be?"

"I'm teaching myself philosophy, calculus, and languages. I'm into Sanskrit right now. And some other things. Not to want to improve yourself is an unspeakable sin."

Jack Liffey thought about that a moment. "*Shantih*. That's the only Sanskrit I know, and that's only because of Eliot's *The Waste Land*. Peace, isn't it?"

"It's grander than that. Peace beyond human understanding."

"No wonder I couldn't understand it. How's your Greek?"

"That's next year. It is important to be firmly rooted in the old before undertaking the new."

"I can buy that," Jack Liffey said as he pushed out a glass door into a parking area in back where the lunch truck, side panels up, was swarmed by a couple dozen people. "And I can buy a nice Danish, too. Sure I can't get you anything?"

"No thank you." This time there was no horror in the refusal. The young man took one look at all the people crowding the truck, closed up visibly like a sea anemone, and skedaddled without another word. Jack Liffey watched his checkered shirt disappear past a roll-up door into the gloom of a warehouse. There was no end to the varieties of human pain, he thought.

An hour later he needed to see Billy Gudger again. He'd been scanning the last tape and suddenly he'd come bolt upright, slowing the tape to normal speed. It was toward the end of another crowd scene, and he'd rewound and cranked up the sound. Right after somebody off shot called "Cut," and then, "Okay, new Setup," a tall young man sidled through the crowd to speak to Phuong. He was tidy and blond and well-groomed, like a former Doublemint Twin, the sort of young man who looked like he'd end up one day running a Lexus dealership. The tape went black after they'd exchanged only a few words. She didn't seem to be unhappy about talking to him.

Jack Liffey had run it several more times, but couldn't make out anything they said. He finally found Billy Gudger in the mailroom, copying his way through a stack of papers with yellow Post-its hanging out like limp tongues.

"Billy, can I show you something?"

"Uh, yes?"

"If it's inconvenient. . . . "

"It will not be inconvenient."

It was as if he'd learned the language from books and never actually had much opportunity to speak it, Jack Liffey thought. The young man followed him back along the corridor and just as he turned into the room where the playback monitor burred, he heard Billy Gudger ask softly, "Do you know what a toadstone is, Mr. Liffey?"

"Call me Jack. No, I don't." He expected a follow-up, but nothing came. The machine had cycled down out of Pause on its own, and he had to fire it up again and wind the tape to before the cut. "What's a toadstone?"

"Actually it can be two things. Geologists use the expression to mean a dark inclusion or a layer of basalt that is trapped in limestone."

Jack Liffey had reached where he wanted to start the tape, but he waited a moment for the boy's other shoe to drop. It didn't seem to be coming on its own. "That's *one*."

"It also means a kind of little stone you find that's made up of fossilized fish teeth and palate bones. Superstitious people have treasured them since the middle ages as jewels and good luck charms. It was once widely believed, even by the scientific community, that they formed in the head or body of a toad. An old Romany superstition suggests that toadstones may form in the heads of some extraordinarily lucky people, too."

"Do you have one?"

The young man's face darkened so fast that Jack Liffey realized he must have misunderstood. He chuckled. "I don't mean in your head."

Billy Gudger seemed relieved and smiled uncomfortably. "No, I wish I had ownership of one. I've never even seen one."

"Do you feel lucky?"

The same conflict seemed to arise in him. It was clear the young man had some dragon guarding his portals of speech. But Jack Liffey was running out of patience for dragon work.

"I'm very lucky," he said finally.

"I'll let you pick my next lottery ticket. In the meantime, look here." He ran the tape forward slowly and paused it just as the Doublemint Twin approached Phuong and opened his mouth to speak. He tapped the screen. "Who's that?"

A palpable wave of apprehension swept over the young man again and his eyes shifted away abruptly. "I don't know."

"You've got the releases. Can you find out?"

He hurried away without a word. Jack Liffey decided it was a good time to call Tien Joubert and arrange lunch. He expected a song-and-dance out of her receptionist, but she came on the line herself. She must have given him her direct line.

"Oh, Jack Liffey, oh oh! I been trying reach you, but no way. You must come now, hurry. Poor Phuong dead. She very dead. Oh, it's too terrible!"

A chill swept through him. "You'll be at your office?"

"Yes yes, here. Don't go see Phuong father now. He very upset. Come here, see me. I know all what's up."

"I'll be right there."

Dead, he thought again. After all his forebodings about the Angel of Death visiting himself, the Dark Animus had been hard at work elsewhere. He wondered when and where and how, and he hoped Tien would know.

On his way out he found Billy Gudger sitting abstractedly in a very tidy cubicle.

"I've got an emergency and I've got to go. Can you give me the name?"

He was reluctant, but he wrote on a slip of paper. *Mark Glassford*, and an address in Garden Grove.

"Thanks."

It was very disquieting, Billy Gudger thought, this strange new conflict in his feelings. A part of him had attached itself almost immediately to Jack Liffey that morning, the way the man's deep blue eyes searched him out and waited peacefully for him to speak, *wanting* him to speak, wanting to hear what he had to say and responding to it, too, with what seemed patience and concern and real interest. And a part of him, an equal part, feared the curiosity he saw in Jack Liffey and the malice that always waited beyond curiosity.

And, of course, Jack Liffey had come to MediaPros about that laughing Oriental girl and that meant trouble. Billy Gudger had tried time and again during the morning to hold back and ignore the man's presence, but he couldn't. Something in him had been desperate to drag him into Jack Liffey's presence, to make him talk, to share ideas, even to listen to what the other thought about things.

He sat at his blue desk but could not read. And then, miraculously, there was a knock on the door. He didn't know how he knew, but he knew it was Jack Liffey out there, and when he opened the door, sure enough it was, big as life.

"Hi, Billy, how are you doin'?"

"Pretty good. Do you want to come in?"

"Sure, thanks." And Jack Liffey came in, carrying a six-pack of Cokes.

"Have a seat on that other desk chair. The one with the arms is pretty comfortable."

"Thanks. You're very considerate. Have a Coke."

They both opened cans of Coke. It felt very cold. Jack Liffey tipped his head way back and drank with gusto then burped once with his mouth covered decorously and excused himself. "So, what've you been reading?"

He glanced quickly at the desk. "Do you know Hall's *The Invention of Romance?*"

"Huh-uh."

"It's amazing. It seems a lot of what we think of as romance was invented in the middle ages, based on a big religious heresy."

"Really?"

"These people called the Albigensians in Southern France sealed themselves into caves and starved away in longing for the perfect and unattainable life of Christ. It was really strange, and it seems to come out of some kind of Mediterranean belief in a duality of body and spirit, and a rejection of the body."

"I've never heard that."

"The Pope declared their beliefs a heresy, but they carried on anyway, and then the troubadours sang songs about them and little by little over the years the story got shifted away from religion toward earthly love, and the troubadours changed the heroes so they were pining away for their perfect unattainable lovers and never touching them. Isn't that weird?"

"It sure is. Maybe we can trace all our lipstick commercials and romantic novels back to this medieval heresy."

"That's what's so strange, isn't it?"

"You read an awful lot, don't you, Billy?"

"I try to. It's what I'm good at."

And then, Jack Liffey wasn't there any more, just a projection of Billy's will to believe. He stared at the small irregular black stone on his desk. It was a nothing, really, found beside a dirt road in the Tustin Hills, just a simulacrum of an idea. He wasn't even sure any more if he believed in the toadstone. The part of him that could believe in it seemed to have evaporated some time ago along with that first death that he had actually witnessed. In a way it had seemed a relief. The loss of that belief had taken a burden off him.

But now, after talking to Jack Liffey that morning at MediaPros, he no longer wanted not to believe. Perhaps belief was wriggling back to life inside him.

There was an image of the virgin. At the feet was a toad-stone, indicating her victory over all evil and uncleanness.
—Murray's *Handbook to English Counties* (1870)

eleven

The Real State of the World

As he pulled into the lot next to the mall, his eye went by chance away from the mall to a half dozen young Vietnamese men in black who stood with crossed arms guarding a storefront in a strip mall nearby, like Secret Service men waiting for the president to buy his wife some perfume. But this wasn't a perfume shop, it was the Mekong Star Night Club, with big neon stars on the wall, discreetly back in the dogleg of the strip-mall. The black-clad young men bore a strong resemblance to the *Quan Sats* who had beat him up. He did a u-turn and their eyes followed his car as he drifted past and parked not far from them.

The leader with the pink eye wasn't there, but two others sauntered in his direction. He headed for Tien's office and then about-faced as if he'd forgot something at his car and caught them peering into his window. They didn't know quite how to react as he came back. He got in the face of the nearest.

"Can I help you? I know it doesn't look like much, but it's a mean customer. You should see what happened to the other car."

"You not supposed be here."

"Are you fucking with me, small man?"

The second one stayed rooted in place but spoke harshly in

110

Vietnamese, probably some curse or threat. Jack Liffey's temper was right on the knife edge where it climbed whenever he ran into this kind of petty menacing.

"Ooo-tay," Jack Liffey said. "Other-may ukers-fay an-cay lay-pay is-thay ame-gay, asshole. Catch that last word, did we?"

They turned and walked back toward their friends, and he found his hands wanting to strangle something. "Have a nice day, kids."

The mall seemed strangely empty of shoppers as he crossed the entrance to get to Tien's place. He'd expected a bit of hubbub at her office, too, but it was pretty quiet, the receptionist looking askance at his black eye for a moment as if contemplating some awkward fashion choice, and then sending him straight in.

"People shook up, stay home a lot," Tien Joubert explained. Her eyes were red and wadded balls of Kleenex waited in ranks on her desk; she'd been crying. It seemed a bit out of character. She was wearing an elegant short skirt and a silk blouse with gold and green paramecia on it. "Many people frighten down deep now. Phuong really nice kid, but people see be *nice* no protection here. That the hard part of life in another country. You don't know what to be scared of. You don't know how to stay in good side of gods."

"Those gang boys were out there guarding the night club."

She nodded. "That they place. Owner pay for protection and time like this, he like to see it."

"How did Phuong die?"

"She found in hills, like dead guys last week. Most Vietnam people here, this first time they even think of hills. Maybe the kids who ride around in their cars been in hills, but for most older people there only this mall and TV and all the house of family."

She was distracted and she got up and looked at something in a small inlaid box on a shelf behind him. She came past him on her way back and stopped and touched his shoulder and then kissed his cheek very lightly, like a passing thought of a kiss. "I miss you. I scared and need comfort, too, Jack Liffey."

A thrill went all the way through him and he grasped her arm reflexively and then made himself let go.

"You still not so sure," she guessed.

"I'm still not so sure. How was Phuong killed?"

Tien sat down demurely and adjusted her skirt. "They say she was shot with a gun and not molest. All her clothes was okay."

She shook her head and a tear trickled down her cheek. She could shift moods faster than he could keep up. "What kind of place eat up children like this? You think it wouldn't be so hard for us, don't you, huh? We all been in wartime and we see many friend and family die in war, but maybe that what make it so bad. We come ten thousand mile. We finally think we okay here and no more surprise dying, all finish, and we relax and learn new business and raise our family and learn to become American, and, boom, it all come back with no warn. This new American life more danger than we think, and now we know it never never never gonna be okay. We kidding ourself. War is real state of world, not peace. She was *such* good kid, gonna *be* somebody."

A scrape of real grief had entered her voice, and he couldn't help himself. He went around the desk and she jumped up and he held her, pressing her small body hard against him. Her head only came to his chest, and he felt her shudder and sob against him. Her small arms went around him and hugged hard and she seemed to fit perfectly against him. He tried to imagine what the Vietnamese community had been through the last two or three decades, and he couldn't get his mind around it. There should be a limit to the flexibility the world demanded of people.

"Can we eat now?" he suggested, when she was just starting to turn the hug into something else. "I think it would be a good idea to get out of here and do something."

"Okay, you. You go on and off like radio."

"So do you, Tien. Only you change stations a lot, too."

She tilted her head to think about it. "You right. I FM, AM, long wave, TV, *boom*. That how I keep going, keep head out of water, keep up business, help friends. Keep on move. *Pho '92* a good restaurant."

"Have they got *bun bo xao*?"

"Course. Let me fix my face."

It was a dish of sauteed beef and noodles and it was the one Vietnamese dish he knew that had little or none of the *nuoc mam* fermented fish paste that was definitely an acquired taste. She turned away from him at the desk to pat something onto her cheeks in a little hand mirror.

"Is Mr. Minh too distraught to talk today?"

"You bet."

"Maybe I'll leave him a note. Sympathy." He found himself talking telegraphically, like an unwitting caricature of her speech pattern, and he forced himself to stop it. It was probably a reflection of how commanding her presence was. Whatever else she meant to him, he liked being around her energy and her total focus, probably the way Loco perked up whenever his master came into the room, and if Jack Liffey had a tail he figured he'd probably be wagging it now, too. "I have to tell him I didn't get very far, I'm afraid, but I'll give Lt. Vo what I know before I quit."

She whirled around in the chair. "You not quit."

"It's a police matter now, Tien. It's not a lost kid any more. The cops don't want amateurs getting in the way in a murder investigation. It's not just an ordinary murder investigation either. It looks like a serial killer."

"No no no no no. You got to help. These cop, a lost thing they will never find. You know the saying? You got to keep looking for bad guy that did this."

"I'm afraid Orange County is going to be in the big leagues of the media circus for a while. Tom Brokaw is going to be standing in front of whatever landmarks you've got, Disneyland maybe, on the national news and dozens of L.A. TV reporters and lookie-loos from Riverside will be trampling over the place where they found the bodies and guys just out of the funny farm will be confessing they did it because God told them to and flying saucers are going to make a special appearance overhead and down in the Latino community people are going to be finding the face of the killer in the scorch patterns on tortillas. The cops would hate me for jumping into all that, because they know my face already."

She shook her head, and he could see nothing was going to budge her. "You not want money? I got money. You quit Mr. Minh, I hire you twice as much. This free country to look and ask question."

They argued off and on all the way through lunch, interrupted by servers and comments about pretty dresses that Tien noticed suddenly on other women and songs she recognized on the P.A., until she wore him down and he finally agreed to spend another day or two running down the one lead he still had, Mark Glassford. The money didn't hurt, either. With it, he could get all the way out of arrears on his child support and see Maeve all he wanted.

As he was walking her back to her office, she said, "You my employee now. I want report this evening."

His whole body tingled with the thought. "I'll call it in."

"Phone at home broke, you come," she said quickly, and he laughed for a long time.

The first ominous sign was the fact that Lt. Vo didn't call him into his office, but into what Jack Liffey recognized immediately as a felony interview room. A bare wood table, a videotape camera on a cheap tripod, pointed right at him and humming, and beside Vo was the second ominous sign, a hefty man with a round face and a buzz cut who looked like a Marine drill sergeant. This man wore a rumpled gray suit with a soup stain on it. Vo introduced him as Commander Something-or-other Margin, the head of the sheriff department's Sagebrush Shooter team.

"We prefer to call it the Serial Killer Team," he said icily. "Tell us about your black eye, Liffey."

"That's one of the things I came about." He described the ambush in the parking lot and the leader of the gang, the man with the pink eye and one long tuft of cheek hair. Margin turned and glared at Lt. Vo, as if he were part of the gang.

"Don't tell me you've got a lot of thugs here who look like *that*," Margin insisted.

"That's Thang Le. He sometimes calls himself Uncle Ho."

"Uncle Ho?"

"He has no politics at all. It's just guaranteed to enrage every elder in the community. His gang is called *Quan Sat*, short for body count. They're into extortion and home invasions for jewelry and cash stuffed under the mattresses but I can't prove it. No one will testify."

"Could they have killed this girl?" Margin demanded. "Or could they be doing a copycat to conceal some other business."

"I doubt it, either way." Frank Vo looked at Jack Liffey. "But it sounds like *Quan Sat* think you suspect them."

"How do you prove a negative? I told them I didn't." Actually, it sounded like Margin suspected Frank Vo, but there was no point pissing either of them off by pointing it out.

"What do you know, Liffey?"

He told them everything he knew about the *Quan Sats* and about the Industrial League and their mystery caller, offering his threats relating to the airport, and about visiting Tien Joubert, and he repeated his encounter with the younger kids with the checks cut into their hair. He told them, in fact, everything he knew about Orange County except MediaPros. It didn't seem fair to turn Margin and the Serial Killer Team loose on Mark Glassford just because the young man had offered Phuong a kind word on the videotape. And poor skittish Billy Gudger. If Margin as much as glared at him, he'd go into permanent earth orbit. He would talk to Glassford and if the young man was the least bit suspicious, he'd tell it straight to Lt. Vo. Margin, on the other hand, could kiss his ass, the way he was turning out.

The questioning went on and on to no purpose, raking over the same ground. He knew better than to ask if he was a suspect. Everybody was a suspect to cops like Margin, and up to a point it was understandable. Almost everybody the man talked to, day in and day out, lied to him, probably even his own family. You just had to lie to a hard-ass like him.

"You're not going to be looking over our shoulder as we investigate this case, are you, Liffey?"

"What do you mean?"

He sat forward and his brows furrowed. "Are the words I used too big? Which one is difficult for you? *Shoulder? Investigate?* Are—you—still—on—this—case?"

"My job was trying to find the girl. She's found, no thanks to me, so that job is over. I'm not working for Mr. Minh anymore, as soon as I tell him."

It was almost the truth. He just hoped Margin didn't notice that it wasn't a direct answer to the question.

"Go home, Liffey," Margin said. He turned to Vo. "*You* tell Minh that this guy is off the case."

There was an odd pattern of quick raps at the door and it came open. Another cop in a jarhead haircut and gray suit looked in. It was as if they had cloned Margin, then slimmed him down a little and let the extra flesh sag. Margin went to the door and the two hard-asses talked in soft voices. He and Vo sat patiently, like petitioners with a hopeless case.

"I've got to go," Margin said to the airspace over their heads. "You finish up here."

When the door shut, Jack Liffey and Lt. Frank Vo looked at one another. "Nice guy," Jack Liffey said.

"Uh-huh."

"Don't say a word. I realize you have to live here."

"This interview is concluded," Vo said aloud and he spoke the date and time and his name. He stood up, turned off the camera and popped the tape cassette.

"What didn't you tell Margin?" he asked.

Jack Liffey thought about it a moment. "Mrs. Joubert rehired me and asked me to keep my hand in for a day or two. I need the money.

I'm going to talk to a young man Phuong acted with for an hour in an industrial video. This was at a place called MediaPros in Garden Grove. I have *no* reason to think it means anything at all, and I didn't want to turn Godzilla loose on the poor guy. I'll tell you all about it, whatever I find. Is that satisfactory?"

"It is my duty to warn you about interfering with police business and withholding evidence."

"I can tiptoe. Look how nice I was to Margin."

A smile stole over Frank Vo's features and then evaporated, leaving little trace of its touch-and-go landing. "I should warn you about Tien Joubert, too."

"Really? What?"

This took some thought. "She's a very strong woman. She gets what she wants by hook or by crook. If she doesn't, she eats you up."

"Is this a veiled way of telling me not to get close to her?"

"It depends what 'close' means to you."

"Not to sleep with her?"

He smiled then and shook his head. "If you do such a crazy thing, count your body parts afterward."

"It was because I recognized her," the young man said. He still looked like a Doublemint Twin, with tidy khaki trousers and a knit shirt with a little polo player on it. "And I wanted to say hi."

Jack Liffey had taken a flier that Mark Glassford would be home in his apartment on the edge of Garden Grove. It was in one of a pair of rather seedy two-story buildings with catwalks past all the doors. The buildings faced each other across a pool that was in the process of being retiled, and it was all guarded by a huge decaying tiki god out in front.

"Recognized her from what?"

"A meeting the Industrial League had at my parents' house. My dad is P.R. for Forty-Niner Airline."

That was certainly a coincidence, Jack Liffey thought. Glassford's apartment was almost barren, except for a lot of worn Danish furniture from the '50s that probably belonged to the building and some bricks and boards making up a low bookcase. There was no stereo, not even a TV.

"Can I get you some tea? I can't offer you anything stronger; I don't drink alcohol."

"Neither do I."

"Do you have trouble with it," the young man asked, "or is it religious?"

"Neither, really. Just a decision."

Mark Glassford went into a shabby kitchen, still in sight of the living room, and put a teapot on. "The meeting was at my dad's house a month or so ago," he called.

"What was the meeting about?"

"I wasn't really in on it. I gather the opponents of the El Toro airport had just formed an emergency action committee and the League had to decide how to respond." He smiled as he turned the burner on. "Informally, the opposition called its group the Malcolm X Committee. You know, *by any means necessary*."

"That sounds ominous."

"Tempers are high down there. There's a lot of rich people involved on both sides and rich people are used to getting their way. It seems to be the defining characteristic of their worldview, actually."

It sounded like the young man did not consider himself one of them, for some reason. "Do you know anything more about the committee?"

"The umbrella group is called the South County Coalition for Responsible Development. A lot of the upscale cities around El Toro contribute and send reps. I think they *officially* call their emergency group SOS, for Save Our Skies."

He came back in and sat, and they could both relax. Jack Liffey had always hated shouting from room to room. It reminded him too much of forced heartiness, a family trait he'd long struggled against.

"I may want to speak to your father about them," Jack Liffey said.

"You'd best not arrange it through me," the young man said equably. "We're a little estranged, dad and me."

"Why is that?"

"I entered a seminary. I want to be a Methodist minister. I'll bet you didn't know there are 37 divinity schools in Orange County. Anyway, my dad doesn't approve. It's not on the success track. The MBA, the big house, the boat."

"I suppose it isn't." This news didn't absolutely rule out suspicion of the young man, of course, but it sure banked it down.

He talked about his decision for a while, how for a number of years he'd experienced a growing revulsion toward the expensive toys all his friends in Newport had chased after, and how he had shed them all, little by little. "It's amazing how dumping the TV calms you down. No more clamoring news, getting at you. You can retune yourself to other rhythms, instead of all that keeping up." He smiled. "I got rid of my fancy word processor, too. Then I gave away an old typewriter I had, and then my ballpoint pens. For a while I wrote with a fountain pen. It slows your hand and makes you think about the sensuousness of the words, and then I even dropped that. I use a dip pen, hard to find these days. I like words, and you get to think word by word."

"I hear chiseling into stone can make you think serif by serif." He tried to keep it good-natured because he actually admired the boy's abstemiousness.

The boy smiled amiably.

"What were you doing acting in a video?"

"They came to school and solicited volunteers. The program was to teach high school students about the dangers of the resurgent TB bacillus, and I always volunteer for things now. Give blood, serve meals at the missions up in L.A."

The teapot started shrieking and Jack Liffey accompanied him into the kitchen. His new-found virtue apparently didn't include tidiness. The sink and counter were full of dirty dishes.

"What did you talk to Phuong about?"

"I just said hello and asked if she remembered me. I offered her a ride when we were done, but she already had one, so we talked a little about the noisy band we'd been listening to. We didn't really have anything else in common. I found out right away she's heavily into all the material things I'm turning away from."

"Do you know who her ride was?"

"She said one of the crew had offered and he lived near her. If you've been there, you've probably seen him. That rather sad, introverted boy, I think he's the production assistant."

That perked Jack Liffey up, all right. Mark Glassford poured himself a cup of hot water and put a teabag in.

"You sure you won't?" the young man asked, raising the mug, and Jack Liffey shook his head.

He held the mug in both hands as if enjoying the warmth that came through the ceramic.

"Did you see them leave together?"

"Not literally. But I noticed her walking toward his old VW. Really old, black with a cloth sunroof. It was 1962, I think." He smiled. "I remember a few things from my materialist period. Could you please tell me now what this is about?"

"Phuong was murdered, possibly even that night."

Hot tea spewed across the floor as the mug shattered. The young man put both of his hands to his eyes and leaned back against the sink, as he gave a strangled little cry. "Oh, my God."

Jack Liffey shook hot tea off his shoe, but kept his eyes on the young man, who seemed to be repeating some silent prayer. Finally he opened his eyes. "I'm sorry, sir. It's like time stops when you hear something like that. And then I was looking inward at myself and trying to figure out what I was feeling about it. I've become very self-conscious since entering religious studies. Do you think that sort of narcissism is wicked?"

"No."

"I was surprised when you told me, especially since I'd just been talking about her so lightly, but I'm not pleased that I don't feel more pain. I hardly knew her, I guess."

"No one can weep for every death. That's megalomania. Let's make some more tea for both of us and sit down for a minute." He wanted to go over the whole afternoon of the video shoot with the young man.

A police siren was passing somewhere nearby and he found his lips forming the sounds weeoo-weeoo-weeoo as if all the noises in the world had to emanate through him. He tapped one foot and his lips formed bang-bang with the tapping. It was an interesting sensation, and a very powerful one. He looked at one of his mother's steak knives sitting on the counter and thought, *Move. Rotate like a compass needle.* It budged a little and that was enough to maintain the feeling of power.

"What are you *doing* out there?" The complaint came shrilly out of the living room, but without pause for an answer, the TV sound came up. *Jeopardy*, that tinkly music that was like yanking his spine out of his back and flaying it. He would turn that off soon enough.

He had not been able to think up a way to get her to stumble on the circus boxcar in some casual way, so he had gone in the other direction entirely. He was going to make it a surprise, a big deal. He imagined how pleased she would be to be reminded of her life with the circus and her lover.

Billy Gudger had gone to the supermarket and bought boxes of animal crackers, the ones with the animal cage on the front of the box, and he had set them out on the glass cake tray surrounding the railroad coach, as if they had been offloaded and were in the process of being set up. The scale was a little wrong but that didn't matter, because they only added atmosphere to the real centerpiece. He had taken an old plastic toy soldier and cut off the rifle and replaced it in the figure's hands with a tiny brush and palette he had made out of a toothpick and cardboard, and he had heated and moved the arms so the man appeared to be an artist holding out his tools. Then he had daubed the figure with nail polish to turn the fatigues into a colorful vest. The painter stood before the circus boxcar, eyeing his handiwork, and resting on a small easel made of toothpicks was a card that said *Will Detrick, Famed Circus Wagon Painter.*

He patted the cracker boxes a little closer together so the big chrome cake cover would fit over the entire diorama.

"What's a subordinate clause?" he heard and then, in the host's braying voice, "That's correct!" and an eruption of applause.

When he carried the cake tray in he stopped to elbow the TV set off with the push knob. The abrupt end to the music was a delight.

"Hey! *Damn* you, Billy, I could have got that one. What are you up to? This isn't my birthday."

He just kept to his superior smile and set the cake tray on the clutter of women's magazines on the flimsy coffee table. Her huge bulk was sprawled on the sofa under a knit afghan and he knew she wouldn't be able to reach the cake tray to take the top off herself without a major rousing so he would stay in control. He could see her curiosity had been stirred, but she wouldn't admit it.

"They were doing grammar and I know about that, so you don't have to act all smarty pants." Despite her words, her eyes were fixed on the cake tray. The floor lamp glared on the chrome cover. "You can't even button your shirt without getting the buttons wrong. Look at the top button."

But he wouldn't be distracted. The anticipation was wonderful. Her awe and delight would be something to behold.

"Okay, come on. If it's something to eat I want it. Right this minute!"

He smiled and pulled back the sliding latches that held the chrome cover in place.

"Ta-*daa*," he said, lifting.

"You do still partake of the telephone?" Jack Liffey asked.

Mark Glassford smiled and nodded. "For now."

"Could I make a call?"

"Sure. It's on the wall in the kitchen."

It was an old wall phone, the first generation of pushbutton phones with no extra buttons or answering machine or flashing lights or food processors.

Tien Joubert answered by repeating her phone number, a nice prudent practice for a woman living alone.

"Your home phone does work after all," he said. "I want to make my report."

"No," she barked. "You come here, report, or I no pay you. Come right now!"

And she hung up to leave him no option.

twelve

The Anxious Type

She had a folding workout bench with powder blue barbells up on the rack tucked into the corner of the all-blue living room. And just to complete the surreal scene, a massive cabin cruiser was passing slowly down the yacht channel outside, lit up like a casino on the move. "You wait and sit. I got to finish exercise. You can give report now if you want."

Tien Joubert was wearing a skimpy stretchy top in some fleshy color that didn't leave a lot to the imagination.

"Wouldn't that interfere with the entertainment that's been laid on?" he said, but she ignored the inconvenient comment as she leaned back and ducked under for her bench presses. There probably wasn't more than ten pounds of weight on the bar, two very small plastic-coated disks, so she had little trouble manipulating the weights all by herself as she lifted off and began the presses.

"Got to exercise with weight now, they say, protect the bones for us old women."

"You'll never age," he said. "This is a waste of time. You'll have the body of a twenty-five-year-old until the earth's orbit decays and the sun uses up its fuel."

"Flattery get you everywhere. Five-six-seven."

Jack Liffey waited, thinking over what he should do about Billy Gudger. He would need to talk to that strange young man once more before telling Frank Vo about him. Perhaps there was some innocent explanation, perhaps he had actually dropped her off somewhere that night, somewhere he could prove. Jack Liffey could just picture the Orange County SWAT vans squealing up to Billy's house from all directions and men in flak jackets and riot helmets hurling out of the armored blue vans to pound across his lawn, the one in the lead carrying that big black battering ram. He didn't want to see the kid spooked right up over the high side by those dragons he had guarding the frontiers of his touchy sensibility. If he found himself the least suspicious about the kid's answers, he'd go straight to Lt. Vo. And it could certainly wait a day. Phuong wasn't going to be any more dead.

"You got report, Jack Liffey?"

"I'll trade you. I'll give you my report if you tell me something about your life in Viet Nam."

"That long time ago."

"But it's an important part of you."

She was huffing a little. The bench presses may have been laid on for his benefit, but she was really doing them. She stopped and toweled off with a powder blue towel. "All sad story exactly same. I very innocent and very weak. Big strong bad guys come kill everything, take everything. I very hurt and sad but stay innocent. I run away and start over. End of story. Moral: don't be weak next time."

"I'll bet there's some details that make your story different."

"You mean, like, before bad guys come, I and my friend Ly play tennis every day at Cirque Sportif in Saigon. Then we put back on silk *ao dai* and go drink tea on verandah of Continental Palace Hotel and walk through flower market on Nguyen Hue on way home? That stuff some detail, but not instructive at all. Or peasant boys from National Liberation Front ride truck into Saigon, smash in my door and steal my beautiful picture of the dragon who marry the fairy spirit and begin the Vietnamese people way back in the before time? That not instructive either. Come with me."

She walked down the hall and he had little choice if he wanted to keep talking to her. He saw what Vo meant about Tien getting her way. Before he realized that he'd just followed her into a large bathroom, she had stripped off the exercise leotard and turned to make sure he got a good look as she stepped gracefully into a large stand-up Japanese-style bathtub that was steaming away.

"You can join or sit there, it okay."

He sat on a little bench with scrolled ends that reminded him somehow of Napoleon.

"Ooooh. Feel good *all over*."

"So what sort of detail would be instructive?" he asked.

Her face took on a funny expression. "I leaving Saigon on Huey chopper and I put ten kilo heroin in suitcase and I take heroin to Paris and build whole commercial life on money I make. *That* instructive. It not true, but it instructive."

He wasn't so sure it was untrue, from the quick and confident way it had come to mind. It would explain a lot.

"I wouldn't really blame you," he offered. "It was a rough time. And you were on your own."

"You bet. You want get in? Hot water super-duper on the soft parts of you."

"No thanks."

"You report now."

He told her about visiting the divinity student, and how what the young man had told him meant he had to make another visit to Billy Gudger to find out if he'd given Phuong a ride home, but she didn't really seem all that interested. She told him she had talked to Minh Trac that afternoon and she had money from him for the work Jack Liffey had already completed, plus the first day's wages from her.

She got out of the tub and stood there naked and dripping on the tiles. Her body was remarkably well toned for a woman who was probably in her late 40s, and there was something fascinating about a woman who had no shame at all about her body. He wondered if it was Buddhism.

"Now we make love very nice," she said.

"I don't think so."

"You like me better if I wiggle my eye at you, say, 'Ooh, Meeester Leeefeeee, you soooo strong?' "

He laughed, and she sat right next to him on the antique bench. Before he knew it, she was fiddling with the top button of his shirt and he tried to stop her, but not very hard.

"I was warned about you," he said.

"Who said?"

"Lt. Vo said you always get what you want."

"He absolutely goddam right."

When he dropped off the freeway at National Boulevard in Culver City, he saw a fire flaring up in the darkness ahead. He slowed as he approached, and he could hear sirens in the distance but none of the fire trucks were there yet and it didn't look like they were going to be able do much good anyway. A small bungalow was already engulfed and a score of people stood around hurling things into the fire from piles of possessions that appeared to have been moved out of the house earlier. He saw a ladder-back chair silhouetted clearly as it sailed into the blaze, carton after carton of assorted goods, an armload of shirts on hangars. One hefty woman charged the fire with a floor lamp like a lance and hurled it in through a window that was too bright to look at.

A tricycle sailed high but missed and bounced back off the front wall, and to the side he noticed a young man expertly shagging paperback books into the conflagration with a baseball bat. It was remarkable, he thought, how he'd lost much of his curiosity about a scene like this. Only a few years earlier *the reason* for all this odd behavior would have piqued his interest. But was it reason, he thought, as explanation that interested him, or reason as motive, or reason as cause, or just reason as an ordered, sane way of thinking about the world? None of it tugged at him any longer. Safety was what counted, and he drove on.

He had repeatedly showered Tien's smell off him, but Marlena still fussed and complained and accused, and for the first time since they had begun living together, she was absolutely right, but he had to fight her and resist and demur just exactly as he always had, despite the guilt and dejection that soured his self-opinion, or she would know for sure. A drink would have been wonderful, he thought, as she followed him from room to room, tugging at his clothes and patting him down as if a foreign pair of panties might fall out of one of his pockets.

"Mar, please. You can't chain me up in the house. I'm out hunting missing kids."

"But I'm *afraid* and you don't *care* that I'm afraid," she wailed.

"What can I *do* about your fears? Tell me."

Then she was weeping and before long she was better again, poking in the fridge to find some food for them to eat and making him feel even guiltier. There had always been an adjustment period every time their paths diverged and then ran back together, but it had been getting longer. And the downward spiral of his own ethics wasn't helping.

While she was cooking, he called Art Castro at home. "Hello there, Arturo. How's the family?"

"They're up in Fresno at my mother-in-law's for a week. She's got some niece doing her *quinceañera*, you know, the 15-year-old coming-out thing."

"Uh-huh. I think I must have missed mine."

"Boys got a different thing. Don't you Irish do anything?"

"I don't think anybody outside South Boston keeps any of that Old Country stuff alive. Except potatoes. My old man had to have potatoes in some form at every meal."

"Funny, isn't it? Potatoes is a new world plant but you could live the rest of your life in Mexico and not see one."

"I couldn't. I have too much trouble with the language."

"Yeah, you got to see to that, man. You just got to check the demographics to see you're living in the far north part of Mexico. They're reclaiming the place little by little with their feet."

"Good luck to them. We seem to have screwed it up for them pretty good. Did you find out anything about Marvin Resnik?"

"A blowhard of the first water. But he's harmless, and yeah, he never leaves that house. But never. They had a mudslide and flood in the big *el niño* storm season couple years ago and when the fire department cleared people out, he held them off with a shotgun and they finally made him sign a waiver to stay put. Hope that's what you wanted to hear."

"I was just eliminating him as a suspect, as the cops say."

"Suspect? Man, you sound like a real detective."

"I scare myself sometimes. Thanks, Art."

The old man with a big paunch framed by fluorescent orange suspenders stopped his push-mower and mopped his brow next door. Probably hurrying to get his grass taken care of before the rain struck. Dark clouds were creeping their way, and a whiff of moisture was on the southerly wind. Jack Liffey stepped up to the picket fence alongside the driveway. "Excuse me, could you tell me if Billy Gudger lives here?"

"If that shop doesn't fix my power mower soon, I'm going to nuke them. He lives in that place in back. You a bill collector?"

"Would you expect that with Billy?"

"It's none of my beeswax, mister."

He went back to mowing and Jack Liffey found the cottage at the end of the driveway. It had probably once been a detached garage but had been rebuilt into a stand-alone apartment. At MediaPros they'd told him Billy Gudger had called in sick again, and he finally wheedled the home address out of the gangly writer. The old black VW that Mark Glassford had described was parked at the curb out front, in the shadow of a tall neon Palm Reader sign that almost overhung the street.

He knocked at the cottage door and waited. The place was so

small you could tell any occupant would either come in ten seconds or not at all. A little brass plaque right under the peephole said, *This room not to be occupied by more then 110 persons. Fullerton F.D.* Somebody's idea of a joke, but it didn't seem the kind of humor that would emanate from the Billy Gudger he remembered. The curtain was open a crack and after a minute, he peered in. It was hard to tell for certain in the murk, but the single room was so small that anybody in there would have to be hiding in a corner of the bathroom where the door was open, or under the single bed.

Back in front he rang the bell on the big house. He could hear the ringing inside, a sort of hapless hollow plea that echoed through the house as if it would never be honored. There were no answering movements. One window beside the door had gauze curtains. Shielding his eyes, he could see a big old console television that was turned off, and what looked like a cake tray sitting on top of it. The tray was empty.

Under the big red hand out front, it said, *Palmistry, Bibliomancy, Tarot. Genuine Rom wisdom. Se habla Espagnol.* It didn't say anything about invisibility or out-of-body travel, but it was possible Sonya Gudger had her own car and they had both gone off somewhere in it. He looked for the gardener, but he had abandoned his mower and gone inside. Jack Liffey went back and knocked once more, and then decided to kill some time and come back later.

His breathing finally began to slow down. Billy Gudger stood with his back to the front door, frightened all of a sudden by the weight of the pistol in his hand. It was heavier than it should have been, as if each time he used it, it grew in mass by sucking in the souls that it set loose. He could imagine the swap occurring—the bullet zinging out and the soul compacting down and swooshing back to hurl itself down the barrel and then snug into the vacated space in the clip. It was just physics. Equal and opposite reaction. Conservation of momentum.

He had watched Jack Liffey walk up the driveway, talk briefly to

Ed Jamgochian, then knock at his own door in back. The man had even bent to read the brass Sanskrit plaque. But when he saw Jack Liffey bend again to peer in the window, his hair had stood on end and a piece of ice settled against his spine. If he did the same at the service porch of the big house, there would be trouble. Billy Gudger had got her as far as the service porch last night, but then he had no idea what was next. There was no way he could get her great bulk into his car by himself.

He kept wanting to go find his mother and ask her advice on what to do next, but of course that wasn't possible any more. Something had happened to her. His mind had trouble fixing on what it was. He looked at the old brocade sofa and saw the reddish brown stain on it and realized he would have to do something about that, too. There was way too much to do in this room and he'd been immobilized most of the night by having to deal with other rooms, clearing out of the fridge all of the food that could spoil and moving clothes out of the bedroom.

The car started up out front and he risked peeking at the window to see the old white AMC Concord drive off.

> *As for that styled a toadstone: this is properly a tooth of the fish called Lupus Marinus, as hath been made evident to the Royal Society.*
> —John Wilkins, *An Essay Toward a Real Character, and a Philosophical Language* (1668)

Live oaks and big-leaf sycamores hung overhead and a deep channel with a trickle of a stream in it bordered first the right and then the left side of the narrow road. Old frame houses and rock cabins crouched in the canyon just off the road, offering one or two places to park in little coves carved out of the hillside. It reminded him a lot of Topanga Canyon on the other side of L.A. where the aging hippies went to play country gentry. Perhaps this was where the Orange Curtain sheltered its own aging hippies.

Dark clouds gathered and it looked like they were in for a sprinkle. People up here would probably be closer to things like that, he guessed, probably even apprehensive about a cloudburst that could turn Silverado Creek into a raging torrent. He imagined they lost a cabin or two to flood every decade or so, not to mention fire. It was the risk you took playing hayseed, and he was sure most of them felt it was worth it. He had the car window open, and even over the engine noise he could hear the birds and he could smell the woodsy air.

The address Mike had given him was a rock cottage up about thirty steep steps from the road. There was a long screened porch and a chimney that was issuing smoke. He had to park a quarter mile farther on at a turnout and walk back. The one alcove near the cabin, pressed back into a stone retaining wall, had been fully occupied by a 1958 Buick that was fantastically rusted but looked like it might still run.

He was puffing a bit by the time he reached the top of the stone steps and he rapped on an old wood screen door.

"You a goddamn reporter?" crackled out of the interior in a dry snarl.

"No."

"Who the hell sent you?"

"Mike Lewis suggested I come see you." Maybe this wasn't such a good time-waster, after all.

There were a couple of indecipherable scrapes and a few other noises in the gloom, and then the screen came open and a tall wizened old man glared at him. He was as pale and wrinkled as a white prune and he held an unlighted cigarette that was so wrinkled itself that it looked like he'd been holding onto it all day.

"You'd better climb on in."

"My name is Jack Liffey."

The old man didn't offer his hand. "I guess you know I'm Philip Marlowe."

"That's what Mike said. I didn't know you really existed."

"Mike was the first one with the gumption to figure it out. I guess he was doing some article on the roots of pulp writing and he found my ad in a phone book from the '40s and thought the name was probably a coincidence. But he came to find me. Come on this way."

The old man shuffled very slowly, leading him out onto the airy screen porch where they settled side by side in decaying stuffed chairs. They looked out through the gnarled branches of a huge live oak at the opposite wall of the canyon 50 yards away, sumac and sagebrush and dry yellow grass. Shadows were scudding across the hillside to dot-dash the vegetation with light.

"I don't get it," Jack Liffey said.

The old man nodded. "Ray and me had a deal. I'd tell him about my cases and he'd write 'em up, but he got most of it pretty far wrong. I don't mind too much, though. I know he had to fix things up to make up good stories."

"So there really was a General Sternwood, say?"

He scowled. "The name was really Doheny, I got the job through a friend of Ray's who knew the oil Dohenys. The name Sternwood is a little too literary for a rich old fart, don't you think?"

"That's one of my favorite books. What do you think of Bogart's portrayal?"

He shrugged. "It's all romanticized, of course. Who wouldn't be flattered to have Bogart play him? But what burns my ass is Ray making me say things that are anti-colored and anti-Semite in the books. I was never those things. I *like* Jews. That was something that little British pansy picked up in his rotten private school in Dulwich." He waved the unlighted cigarette around and pronounced it Dull-witch, maybe on purpose.

"Chandler wasn't gay, and it's DULL-ich."

"You look close at the books. *His* Marlowe doesn't like women a lot and he gushes way too much at a bare he-man chest or some such."

"I never noticed."

"*I* did. I kept complaining to that little fop, but he wouldn't stop it. He had these big horn-rims, Ray, and always wore white gloves and a bow tie and carried a silver-top cane. Jesus. Always drunk as a skunk by noon, too. Reminds me, it's early but can I get you a drink?"

"I'm not in a drinking period of my life."

"Interesting. What do you do?"

Rain was finally beginning to come down outside, spatting on the screen and adding a twist of sage scent to the air.

"I find missing children."

"Shit. You mean, you're a *detective*."

"Only in the loosest sense of the word. I don't think I'm tough enough to bring off the real thing."

Philip Marlowe laughed scornfully, and Jack Liffey noticed he was regularly checking his wristwatch.

"Are you expecting someone?"

"Aw, the hell with it." He grabbed up a cheap butane lighter and lit his cigarette. He settled back and luxuriated in the first deep puff. "I get one every two hours. Doctor says they'll kill me, but at 93, I say, let 'em try. There aren't many other pleasures left to me. I'm like old Doheny sitting out in his greenhouse with his orchids."

"Worrying about his wicked daughters."

He grinned and closed his eyes. "Oh, they *were* wicked all right. I fucked both of them."

Jack Liffey was shocked, despite himself. "And after the war, did you marry and move out to Palm Springs like that last thing Chandler was working on, *Poodle Springs*?"

"It didn't take. She was rich and I always hated the rich like poison. Ray got that right."

The rain roared for a moment, startling them both. Drops were actually leaping up off the broad sill of the screen windows and the noise on the thin roof was deafening. He smoked his cigarette about as far down as you could and seemed genuinely bereft when it finally ran out.

"I always loved the rain. It's so powerful and important in

Southern California when we finally do get it, like snow at Christmas. And it isn't that pissant mist that barely gets you wet, like up north. Luckily I'm high above the creek."

"How do you get up and down those steps?" Jack Liffey asked him.

"The lady who does my kitchen brings the groceries twice a week. I haven't been out in 18 months, not even to the doctor."

The second guy he'd met in Orange County who never left his house. He wondered if it was something in the air. "So you're just retired here."

"Yup. My ex let me have this house in her will when she died, and Social Security does the rest."

"It must be a bore after your life."

"Most of my life was a bore."

"You didn't like being a detective?"

He shrugged. "What did I know different? Like saying I wish I had different parents. I only know my whole life was a fight against dying of yawning. The Big Yawn, there's a title for Ray." He cranked his torso around to look at Jack Liffey, as if acknowledging his presence for the first time. "You get cold sweats about dying, don't you?"

Jack Liffey nodded. "You, too?"

"Nope, but I can spot one a mile away. And don't you go getting smug about lack of imagination neither. In my experience there's two completely different types of guys. There's the anxious types, like you, and long about age 50, if they aren't stupid, they start breaking into a sweat when the thought of going *pffft* one day comes into their head. Right?"

Far away there was a grumble of thunder, like one of the gods horning in on the discussion.

"That about sums it up. And the other type?"

"We're the depressives. Man, some days any life at all looks way too long. I'm 93 and I can't wait for the Big Sleep. The Dirt Nap. The Underground Vacation."

"You said two types of guys. Does it hold for women, too?"

"I never understood women. Ray was pretty true about that. Liked 'em, but never understood 'em."

"I've gotta get back on the job. Any advice you can give me from your experience as a detective?"

He yawned. "I'd tell you where to get a good single-malt cheap, but you're not a drinking man."

"Nope."

"Then I'll tell you what I miss from the fifties. It's not practical advice, like how to find a skip-trace or keeping a gun on your ankle, but it's what I've been thinking about recently, with all this sense of *economy* and husbanding and prudence we got up to our ears today. I miss the sense of waste we were so full of back then."

"Waste?"

"Tail fins and ten miles per gallon and throwing stuff away and endless possibilities and no need to worry about spoiling something because there's more of it right around the corner. You can't have a feeling of real abundance in your life without a glory of waste. I think what did me in was getting used to that feeling and getting to need it."

thirteen

Losing a Friend

For two hours he'd sat there on the chenille bedspread that he'd thrown over the soiled sofa, completely oblivious to the thundering downpour that came and went like a series of long freight trains past the house. His mind was churning out an elaborate and foolproof way to rearrange the furniture, move the old Chinese screen in from the corner, plus subtly adjusting the curtains so he could creep his way around the house without being seen from any of the unfortunate curtain openings that had been left all over the place. It was a comfort getting deep into all the things you could control to make a secure world around you, like the way he had built a fort out of sofa cushions when he was little, over and over to perfect it. He knew he couldn't change the curtains much without revealing he was inside, and then, all of a sudden, he realized he couldn't move the furniture much either. It was all wasted scheming. He'd missed a crucial point by rushing immediately into The Plan, as he did so often. The man had almost certainly peered in the front window and presumably knew the lay of the room.

And once Billy Gudger realized that, he knew he couldn't risk leaving all the frozen foods on the floor of the service porch, either, right across from the big white freezer chest. The man hadn't looked in the back window, but he might next time and the stacks of thaw-ing peas and rump roasts and TV dinners just didn't belong on the floor. Billy Gudger had yanked them all out of the chest late at night to make room for *it*. Now he went and stuffed the sodden cartons and cello packets into two big kitchen trash bags, and dragged them into the shower stall in the bathroom and shut them in.

Getting *it* into the chest had been a major job. Using all his strength, he had just been able to drag it into the service porch on a throw rug, but then the problems had begun. Half way up, the great weight had defeated him, and he'd had to hurry outside, the chilly drizzle surprising him, to get the jack out of his VW and work out a complex apparatus of ropes and leverage to lift it over the lip of the freezer into the cavity that was sending out waves of cool mist. So there he'd been, for a good half hour, with the thing stranded in space half way into the chest, trussed up by ropes and half its weight propped on a chair, in plain sight for anyone who came to the back door and peered in the gauze curtain. The potential for disaster had grown so great he could hardly bear it, and he had no idea why but he had developed a throbbing erection that only went away after the lid of the freezer was safely slammed down.

His planning wasn't a complete waste. He saw that there was one safe and commanding place he could wait, out of sight of all the win-dows and curtain peepers, right next to the six-foot long stub wall between the kitchen and dining room. He brought a kitchen chair to the spot, and then a comfortable pillow and a glass of water. He made two sandwiches and set them on a carton that he took from under the sink and nudged right against the wall. Then he put his pistol on the box and an extra clip of the brass-nosed cartridges, the top one winking seductively at him where it protruded from the clip. Finally he had a brainstorm and went into the chest in the palm-reading room and dug out the old plastic periscope.

She had kept a lot of toys in there to entertain the children of clients, a firetruck, Parcheesi game, wooden building blocks, a ratty teddy bear with one button eye missing, even an old deck of Tarot cards secured by a fat rubber band. He looked around the palm-reading room with the periscope, sighing because this room would have been the perfect hideaway, cut off from the house by the hanging tapestry with sun, moon and stars on it, if only she hadn't left the window curtain wide open to the outside world. He came back to his sanctum and set the periscope on the floor beside the stub wall so the top part just peeked toward the back door. He could lie on his stomach, right against the wall, and see anyone at the back without being seen.

By my Bufonites or Toad-stone I intend not that shining polish'd stone, but a certain reddish liver colour'd real stone.
—Robert Plot, *The Natural History of Oxfordshire* (1677)

He settled in to wait, munching on one of the Velveeta sandwiches. One finger idly tapped the nose of the brass 9mm cartridge. He knew the man would come back.

The old wipers shrieked a bit at each slow push but they did manage to squeegee the drizzle aside. He thought about Philip Marlowe's cranky musings about waste and abundance as he drove down out of Silverado Canyon. He doubted that much of the profligacy had gone out of the culture since the '50s, maybe just all that naive glorying in it. The waste had become embedded in so much that was even worse, the narcissism of 5,000-square-foot houses for childless couples and the swagger of big top-heavy four-wheel-drive assault vehicles that never left city streets. Of course, he thought, it was easy to resent big expensive vehicles when all you could afford was a beat-up old AMC Concord.

He emerged from the canyon into a suburban tract, then a business street of fast food, real estate offices, and nail salons with cute names that might have been in any urban outskirts in America. No one walked by on his hands, and no one waved a plastic sword at the traffic. He found he missed the casual insanity of L.A., the chance that at any moment you might see two men in a zebra-suit clip-clopping along for no apparent reason. At one point in his life all that phantasmagoria had unnerved him a little, but now, it was as if his psyche had nothing much left to lose.

When he got back to the big neon palm sign, the bungalow behind it looked unchanged, and the black VW still waited at the curb, its cloth top glistening with wet. The rain was no more than a sprinkle now, just keeping things damp and leaving the streets hissy. He looked toward the front door as he walked up the driveway. There was still the little wrinkle he'd kicked up in the thin welcome mat. It was a trick he used to use at his condo during a particularly paranoid time to see if anyone had dropped by to jimmy the door while he was away. Nobody had come in or out the front door of the bungalow.

He tried the little cottage out back again, but there was no answer, and then he clomped up the four steps to the wooden stoop at the back door. White paint peeled away from the door in little tongues and eyebrows. He knocked, waited, knocked again and then shielded his eyes and peered into a gloomy utility porch with a freezer chest on one side and a vintage washer and drier on the other, separated by what looked like worn green linoleum that mimicked terrazzo. There was a small kitchen just beyond, even deeper in the murk. He thought he heard something, but then he had an inspiration.

"Billy, it's Jack Liffey. If you're in, I'd love to have a talk with you."

He let his voice die away and listened. There were those who said you could sense a presence in a house if you listened hard enough, but that was just the sort of hogwash the palm reader in there would have peddled. He felt the boy was inside, hiding out, but it was just an intuition, not a real sensation of any kind.

"I was fascinated by what you said about the toadstone. Could we talk about it? Let's be friends."

His voice sounded thin and ineffectual, bounding back from the window. Listening hard for a response, he found there were plenty of noises issuing, and they had a strange presence, the way they do in crisp wet air, and there was a sensation of an impending event, too, as if something startling was about to happen. A cricket chirruped in the yard. Somewhere not far away a dog was barking, single yelps over and over like a finger pressing on a bruise, and, farther away, traffic grumbled. At the back of the lot, just beyond a grapestake fence, a stand of tall bamboo creaked in the breeze.

"Billy, I want to ask you about an expression I read. It's a word I don't understand."

Past the small kitchen he could see the suggestion of a dining room. There was an ornate glass centerpiece sitting on lace on the table. A print of a shaggy Highland bull was on the wall beyond the table, just barely visible. He heard another creak that might have come from someone in the house, or might just have been one of those sounds wood-frame houses emitted as the temperature changed and damp soaked through.

"I'll come back. You just wait for me."

He walked back to the car. So much for intuition. He would come back just after dark. If the boy was inside, Jack Liffey doubted he could sit there all night in the dark.

In the meantime there was business to take care of: *Go home, fuck you, dead dead dead* was preying on his mind.

He lay with one cheek against the wood floor, his eye only an inch from the periscope where he had watched that man lean up to the window and peer inside. His hand compulsively clutched and released the pistol where it lay beside him on the floor, like some reflex action going on mindlessly after death. Tears from one eye coursed across the bridge of his nose and dropped onto the wood, and from the other fell straight to the dusty unwaxed wood whenever he blinked.

He wondered what it would have been like having a man like that as an uncle, or neighbor or friend. He dared not even think, *father*.

Someone to talk to, someone to show him the ropes on all those common things that defeated him so easily, and someone to listen whenever he found a startling new item of information to convey, a recurring number sequence that generated only primes, or the common vowels across the Northern European languages, or a startling correlation between business cycles and sunspots.

Impossible now. If only she hadn't bellowed with laughter so unexpectedly and so cruelly when he'd unveiled the circus wagon, and then lunged forward to smash it flat with her palm.

Tien Joubert wasn't in her office.

"At warehouse," the receptionist told him curtly, as if she were paid to keep the word count down. She had a little less makeup on this afternoon and she handed him an outsized business card. The reason for the size was immediately apparent. It had to accommodate the name *Tien Joubert Nguyen* and then *Sleepy Lotus Import/Export* and *Business Facilitation* and several lines in Vietnamese, plus a small smiling photograph of her, a logo with an intertwined N and J, followed by three addresses, an Internet website, an e-mail address, and five phone numbers. Strangely, for a woman's business card, even her home number and address were shown. Perhaps she was so proud of the Huntington Harbour address she couldn't help proclaiming it, or maybe it was traditional in Vietnamese business.

"Thanks loads."

The warehouse was on one of the side streets back of Bolsa, improbably called Harrowgate Lane, which reminded him that the town of Westminster had originally had a British theme about it. The sad little half-timbered civic center that he'd driven past the day before had harbored in the center of its courtyard what looked like the top third of a lopped-off Big Ben. Probably the only spot on earth where an imitation Viet Nam elbowed up to an imitation London.

The Mercedes was crosswise in three parking slots under an engraved wooden plaque that said *Sleepy Lotus*, and inside a small warehouse Tien was gesticulating to two Latinos in dusty work pants. He climbed the steps at the side of the loading dock and was surprised to hear her issuing instructions in serviceable Spanish. Her face blossomed with delight when she spotted him.

"My glorious lover come back!" she exulted, as if the workers weren't there. She put her arms around him and tilted her head back to demand a kiss.

Apparently she sensed his embarrassment. "Not time in whole wide world for so much modesty. They my employees *and* my friends. Oscar. Leonardo. This Jack Liffey, my special friend. *Mi amigo especial.*"

They greeted him, trying diplomatically not to make too big a thing of it. "You stay a minute." She pulled away to talk to the workers. Her Spanish had the weirdest accent he'd ever heard, but the words sounded right, and the workers seemed to be following her.

"*Descargue los cajones grandes primeros.*"

"*Sí, Doña Tiena.*"

Along one wall of the warehouse there was a rank of brand-new pink and baby blue chest-tall vending machines that he might have guessed were for cigarettes except for the colors. The Vietnamese and Chinese lettering was no help. When she finished with the workers, he asked what they were. She dug in a carton with a grin and showed him a little pink doll in a plastic bubble the size of a tennis ball. "Every Viet Nam restaurant in country have toy machine," she said. "Viet Nam people good to kids."

"So are Latinos," he said.

She looked puzzled for a moment. "Oh, you mean Mex'cans. Why you say Latino? They don' speak Latin."

"Ask Dan Quayle," he said.

"Huh?"

"Never mind. I need your help, since you're *my* boss, too. I need to speak to Thang Le, the guy who calls himself Uncle Ho. Do you know who I mean?"

She frowned. "Course I know Le. He first class cow*boy*. And only guy I know, when you give him good fried shrimp and yam, noodle and pork, he turn up nose and ask for cheeseburger and fry. His spirit still lost-in-transit over Pacific. He junkie of all bad stuff in world. Why you want?"

"He thinks I'm after him and his gang about Phuong. I want to tell him I'm not, in some way that will get through to him. I don't want to wake up some morning with a guy in a black jumpsuit holding an assault rifle in my face."

"Why don't you just forget him? He nothing."

"I don't want to die, Tien. Not prematurely anyway. I'm funny that way."

"You want me kill him for you?"

"*No!* For heaven's sake. I just want him to leave me alone."

"Okay, I know only thing he understand."

"No violence."

"Oh, no. I don' mean that. You come with me now."

She popped the door on the Mercedes for him and backed away from the wall very fast even before he settled. She accelerated across a speed bump that tossed him up off the seat, leaving him flailing for a handhold, and then squealed to a stop at the back of the industrial complex of little warehouses, where she hit a remote stuck to her visor causing an automatic roll-up door to trundle noisily up its guideway. Then she drove straight in.

This one was not much bigger than a one-car garage and absolutely empty except for a small heap of swept-up shipping labels and plastic strappings in the back corner. The light dimmed and a black shadow descended the walls as the door clattered down until the room was pitch dark. She cracked her door to turn on the interior light and turned the key to stop the bonging.

"Oh-oh," he said.

"I know you not stay with me down in county tonight," she said as she started unbuttoning her gold silk blouse. "We got time."

"I usually like a little music and sweet talk first."

"Me, too," she said. She flicked the radio on to classical KUSC. "Start sweet talk now, you big hunk of my man."

She torqued around to hang the blouse from a little hook over the shelf that passed for a rear seat. She wore a red and frilly, nearly see-through brassiere.

"You never do it in car? The seat go down some."

"Not since I was a teenager."

"I done it in some damn strange place sometime. Back of Church in Rouen with plenty old ladies praying up a storm. My body really want you, Jack."

"My body's sending me signals, too."

"Time to answer signal." She had the bra off and her body glowed like porcelain in the dome light as she started to wriggle out of the skirt. "Green is go."

He started on his own shirt uncertainly, with a dozen varieties of guilt padding around the car like wolves. The seats didn't quite come down far enough and toward the end, his foot hit the key and the horrible bonging started up to punctuate a critical moment so they both burst out laughing. When they drove out later and passed her other warehouse, a little slower, Oscar and Leonardo stood on the loading dock, grinning and applauding. He hadn't blushed like that in years.

fourteen

Murder is the Ultimate Argument

It took her about two hours to set it all up. There was a whirl of telephone calls and return calls, beepers paged, messages left and answered, favors called in, people popping into her office and hurrying away, much of it conducted in a rapid Vietnamese full of what sounded like threats and pleadings. It turned out that what it was that Thang Le understood was the Paris Peace Accords and everything that surrounded them, and that was what Tien Joubert was trying to duplicate.

As befitted the spirit of those tortuous Paris talks, the shape of the table was once again a major issue. She wanted a face-to-face with Jack Liffey and herself on one side and Thang Le and his chief lieutenant on the other, but what she got eventually was a square table with the addition on the east of Father Dang, a priest the *Quan Sats* trusted, and on the west Lt. Frank Vo to vouch for the police department's disinterest in Thang as a suspect in Phuong's killing. Apparently it took a lot of favor-calling for Tien Joubert to get Lt. Vo to make an appearance, but he agreed finally, probably out of curiosity as much as anything.

She had done most of the calling and prenegotiating from her inner office, emerging periodically to talk to people who passed through or just to pace restlessly from door to window, while Jack Liffey, feeling distinctly ridiculous and a bit guilty, had helped the receptionist rearrange the furniture in the big front room of the office. It was as if he'd gone to the family doctor to ask to have a boil lanced and abruptly found himself in the whirl of lead-up to open-heart surgery.

The receptionist's name turned out to be Loan Pham and she was a lot nicer once she discerned Tien's attitude to Jack Liffey.

"Can we move table closer here, Mr. Jack, please?"

"Sure. Just Jack. Which is your family name, Loan or Pham?"

"Pham. I turned it around in school; it's easier for everybody."

The desks and work tables were now arranged in a big rectangle, wider on two legs, and Loan had scattered tea cups and paper pads tidily around. Tien's lawyer, a natty little man with a display handkerchief in the pocket of his shiny suit, had dropped off a draft agreement of the peace treaty and left, shaking his head. Loan made photocopies and distributed them around the tables. They had everything but little flags and name plates. Finally, Loan charged up a big teamaker like a Russian samovar and armed herself with a flash camera to play both hostess and press.

By the time the priest showed up, Jack Liffey had got used to feeling like a droll pain in the ass, and he figured they all had their own agendas running, anyway, or it would never have come off.

"Johnny Dang," the priest said, and offered his hand. Jack Liffey had to assume it was his name.

"I guess we've got the same name," Jack Liffey said after he'd introduced himself. "Jack is a diminutive of John, too."

The priest bowed and smiled. "Mine was Gianni—G-I-A-N-N-I—when I trained in Rome. They had even more trouble than you people with ____." He said a word that Jack Liffey didn't catch in a high-pitched three-tone whine.

"I won't even ask you to spell that. So the *Quan Sats* trust you."

"I minister to all the gang boys without prejudice, following the spiritual example of Father Greg Boyle in East Los Angeles."

"Father G-Dog," Jack Liffey acknowledged. He was famous as the priest who believed in unconditional love, even for gang-bangers, and who never wrote anyone off. The cops hated him because he wouldn't rat out kids who came to him, and the Church had transferred him far away for a few years, as if embarrassed to find a real Christian in their ranks, but finally let him return to East Los. If the Church ever actually recognized saints, he would probably get his halo, but of course, Jack Liffey thought, like the secular society, they really only honored conformity, and only when it came in elephant doses.

Father Dang made a telephone call, apparently to confirm to Thang Le that there were no tiger cages waiting for him at the office.

"This is quite an event," the priest observed in a kindly way, after the call.

"I'm surprised myself. I just wanted to get the lads off my back."

Loan Pham brought them some Chinese tea and Jack Liffey sipped at the tepid, insipid drink that he didn't much like.

A few minutes later Lt. Frank Vo came suspiciously into the room and looked over the tables. "This is preposterous," he said.

"Most of life is," Jack Liffey said, "with a narrow enough point of view."

The policeman stopped very near Jack Liffey, and spoke softly, "Are you still looking into Phuong's death?"

"I have one more person to talk to. I haven't been able to get to him yet, but I will tonight."

Frank Vo watched him, as if having second thoughts about cutting him some slack. "Margin and the Serial Killer Team are not happy with either of us."

"What have you done to deserve their hostility?"

He put his fingers into the corners of his eyes and tugged outward to emphasize his Asian features. "They keep saying there is no yellow or white or black, only blue, but I don't think they believe I am quite blue enough."

"Are you?"

"If it means ignoring who I am, no. They don't ignore it. You would be surprised the number of times the word *dink* or something like it is scrawled on my locker."

Jack Liffey winced. "This can be a funny country," he said. "Some people are pretty good about that and some aren't. I can't apologize for the kind of guys who choose to be cops."

Frank Vo shrugged. "As a people, the Vietnamese are sometimes very warm and sometimes very indirect and cool."

Jack Liffey thought of Tien Joubert, and he could picture it. She was both.

"I think that is preferable to being sometimes racist and sometimes not."

Tien Joubert came out of her inner office and interrupted something else that Lt. Vo was about to say. "They come just now," she announced. Lt. Vo retreated to the place at the table Loan Pham pointed out to him, as Tien went to wait by the door to greet the gangsters.

In a moment she backed a foot and the glass door was nearly flung open. Two angry-looking Vietnamese men banged in and glanced around. They wore all black and took up stations by the door and crossed their arms grimly, the Secret Service stance again. In a moment one of them whistled, and Thang Le sauntered contemptuously in, followed by a younger man with big horn-rim glasses. Jack Liffey recognized Thang Le easily. It was hard to miss a guy with one pink eye and a long whisker dangling from his cheek.

Thang Le locked his eyes on the remains of the shiner he'd given Jack Liffey and smiled. "Nice eye," he said.

"Nice eye yourself, pinkie," Jack Liffey said. The smile glazed over into a glare.

"Gentlemen," Tien Joubert remonstrated. "This no way to start to end big war. We must all shake hand and sit at peace table."

After a bit of a stare-down, they shook hands formallly and everybody sat. Tien Joubert rapped on the table in front of herself. She seemed to be in command. She went around the table and named everyone present, one by one, and then launched into a magisterial preamble. "All this crazy war thing—it always come from stupid tit and tat stuff you little boys get somewhere. You all like fighting cock pushed into same cage. Some little thing happen and you do tit and then I do tit, you hurt my feeling and I hurt your feeling, and then you tit my family and then I tat your family and then whole world drawing guns like crazy."

Elegantly put, Jack Liffey thought. There was a pause while the boy in the horn-rims translated for Thang Le. He didn't know whether the translation was necessary, or it was just to honor a kind of demand for parity, or to preserve face in some way. Loan Pham circled the table quietly pouring tea, and Father Dang added his own preamble in Vietnamese.

Tien turned to Jack Liffey, the only person in the room who couldn't speak Vietnamese. "Priest say some religious stuffs about God always blessing makers of peace."

Dang smiled at the characterization but didn't amplify it.

"In this business now," she went on to Thang Le, "you already tit my friend Jack Liffey and he not tat you. He ahead. He got right to get friends and come some fine night give you all, *Quan Sats*, dark eyes for tat, but he not want to. He want peace." She slapped both palms softly together and then on the tabletop as if resting her case, and Horn-rims translated.

Then Thang Le began a diatribe that went on for some time, words bitten and chewed and snapped out, punctuated by scowls aimed at Jack Liffey. Finally he broke off, seemingly in mid word, to wait for the translation from Horn-rims. "Thang Le says the feud began much earlier than that. He knows exactly who this man is. He is one of the soldiers who went to our country and now think they know all about us because they shot us and dropped bombs on us. They cannot come into our community here and ride roughshod over us and accuse us of heinous crimes and then wait until we strike one tiny blow in return and pretend that the whole war starts just at the minute of that blow."

Tien Joubert tried to speak, but Jack Liffey cut her off. "I'd like to speak for myself since I am the invading military force here."

For the next few exchanges they refought the Viet Nam War, with Jack Liffey insisting he had been a draftee and not, in any case, a combat soldier, and as far as he knew at the time, he had gone there at the request of a legitimate government, and even if he had a lot of second thoughts about it now, he was no longer fighting that war. America and South Viet Nam had lost and it was over. Thang Le said how much he resented a country so rich and insulated from the pain it had caused that it could lose a war and fly away and leave behind the people who had fought and worked alongside it and then act as if nothing had happened. Or perhaps he said something a bit cruder and less elegant, which is what his manner and tone suggested, and Horn-rims spiffed it up in translation. As Thang Le spoke, the single whisker bobbed and waved from side to side and it was hard not to stare at it.

"This not about no Viet Nam War," Tien Joubert cut in. "You don't give no flying damn about that war. You just baby then."

The priest spoke for a moment and seemed to be taking the part of the *Quan Sats*. After he spoke, they all turned and looked at the policeman, and sure enough the issue of the war had vanished.

"No, I don't think you gentlemen did, and neither does he," Vo replied, insisting on speaking in English. "Phuong was killed with a 9mm handgun. We think it was a cheap Star semi-automatic import. I don't for a moment suppose you gentlemen would carry a second-rate weapon like that, any more than you would drive a rusty Yugo. If I went outside now and busted into the trunk of your rice rocket, I would find an AK or a Steyr or an Ingram and if you absolutely had to have a handgun, maybe an expensive Glock or Walther. I know that."

"So we are clear with you?" Horn-rims asked.

"For Phuong, yes. However, there is the matter of the Nhat residence that was invaded last month and the family tied up. A 32-inch Mitsubishi television is missing, and a rack-mounted Nakamichi stereo, 100 *luong* of gold, some jade jewelry and some cash from a floor safe."

"You've already questioned us about that and you know we were at a party on Minnie Street in Santa Ana."

"Don't make me laugh. You don't party with poor Hmong."

"They are our friends."

Now the debate seemed to spin out of control for a while, with Tien Joubert, Thang Le and his translator, and the priest all pointing and gesturing and putting in their two cents, overlapping and even speaking at the same time. Even though the discussion was all in Vietnamese, Jack Liffey could sense that he had shrunk to a minor issue and there were a lot of old ghosts rearing up. Perhaps that was good news, and he could be the derisory item that was settled easily while the tough ones were put off for later.

"We must all choose a path," the priest said suddenly in English, "so that there will be harmony."

Thang Le spoke sharply, only a few words, and so did the policeman. They seemed almost the same words.

"Can a tiger find harmony with a goat?" Horn-rims said. "It was our way once, but in this country, no one honors harmony. Wishing for harmony is a sign of weakness here, and we have learned that some things are much stronger."

"What things?"

"Americans only respect what they fear. They never respected the black man until he started carrying guns and burning."

"I respect you all and I fear you," Jack Liffey said evenly. It was about as far as he was willing to go. He could feel himself getting annoyed at being the odd man out. "I have nothing against you. I just want peace with you."

Thang Le grinned sarcastically and spoke.

"He says the respect only lasts as long as the fear. That is the way with round-eye cowards."

"The shape of my eyes doesn't matter. You haven't begun to see my rage and what it can do, *fuckhead*," Jack Liffey said. "Translate that for the little freak." He'd been okay until about the middle of the sentence and then his temper had just blown out all at once, like a very old tire hitting a pothole. This had happened to him before, a sudden, almost self-destructive need to challenge whatever was threatening him.

"Your rage does not interest us in the least."

Jack Liffey found himself breathing heavily and Tien's hand was on his shoulder. "All stop it now! Priest right, we got to find path of harmony here."

Thang Le said something else angry that Horn-rims didn't even bother translating. Jack Liffey found his hands working compulsively as if he wanted to strangle someone, and he knew he was really riding the sharp edge.

Thang Le carried on some more without any sign of relenting, and then the door came open and Phuong Minh's father strode in. Thang Le caught sight of him and wound down. The man's eyes were red and he wore an out-of-date disheveled dark suit and black tie that made him look like a small reissue of Dracula.

"Isn't my daughter dishonored enough?"

He said something in Vietnamese, maybe a repeat of the same thing, and Jack Liffey felt his anger draining away. Their ridiculous sideshow had pulled the poor man away from his mourning, and for Jack Liffey the sense of utter absurdity flowed back in like a fluid finding its level.

Thang Le spoke for a moment, but there had been a sea-change in his tone of voice. He was quiet and respectful to Phuong's father. Minh Trac turned to Jack Liffey.

"Your work is over in Little Saigon, Mr. Liffey. Nothing can bring my daughter back and I want you to stop using her name and stop whatever is happening here. I want her spirit to be able to go from among us and rest."

Jack Liffey nodded contritely. "All right."

Minh Trac strode up to the table and looked at the papers lying there and scowled. "A peace treaty," he said scornfully. "Okay then. You all sign this paper and go home."

Thang Le seemed to be agreeable. Minh Trac handed the paper to Jack Liffey and he signed immediately. When the paper was passed across the peculiar peace table, Thang Le handed it sight unseen to Horn-rims, who signed it with a fountain pen flourished out of his breast pocket. That seemed to be as far as they were willing to go.

"He signs, too," Jack Liffey said, indicating the immobile Thang Le.

A lot of eyes focused on Jack Liffey. Tien Joubert leaned close to him and whispered very softly into his ear, "He not read and write, Jack. Don' make him lose face."

Jack Liffey stared at the illiterate young hoodlum for a moment, and then nodded to him. "Fine."

They shook hands coolly and Minh Trac banged out the door and left. The *Quan Sats* soon followed, in the same protocol order they'd entered.

They all sat in silence a moment, as if a tornado had just passed over, and then Tien Joubert whispered to her receptionist about something.

"Will they keep their word?" Jack Liffey asked Vo.

He nodded. "For some reason, they believe in treaties. It's the world they know. There is honor in thieves, you know."

"Until they discover murder," Jack Liffey said. "Murder is the ultimate argument for people with no conscience. In the nastier corners of the world, sooner or later they discover murder can make you right, whether you are or not, and you never have to worry about things like your own failings." Death again, he thought. The old bugaboo.

The priest stirred. "I don't know if you know them well enough to say that."

"Psychopaths are the same everywhere, but I'm satisfied if you are."

"We did good," Tien Joubert said, and she encircled his upper arm with her two hands. "Everybody happy. We go dinner and celebrate."

The house was growing shadowy with dusk, and he adjusted a box of cereal on the counter to shield the low flame under the saucepan of soup, so the blue light couldn't be seen from the window in the kitchen door. Just in case. Billy Gudger had been sitting for hours figuring things out and his plans grew more and more elaborate, as his plans always tended to do. Things almost never worked out the way he intended, but usually took themselves off in loopy directions. Still, he felt compelled to lay out his plans. It was all you could do.

While the soup boiled he went to the freezer and checked inside for the zillionth time. What he had put there was still there, an intractable impasse. Even when he poked it hard with a finger, it didn't move. *Now you've gone too far*, a voice told him. It wasn't a real voice. He didn't hear voices, he knew that much. It was just another portion of his mind talking to himself. Everybody did that. He was just like everybody. *Quod erat demonstrandum.*

Jack Liffey came again, slipping in the door without knocking, sat again with a smile and asked what he'd been doing for the day. His voice was friendly, with that cheerful confidence that Billy loved so much. But this time the picture wouldn't stay stable, and it took off along its own trajectory. First Jack was kneeling, whining and begging for mercy and saying he would never never suspect Billy of anything bad. But then, suddenly, he was crying out in pain as somebody held his arms behind his back and twisted. Billy watched, trying to hold Jack Liffey in focus. Next thing he knew, he was gone, just like that.

But Billy was sure that he would come back, peering in all the windows again. That much was for absolute sure. And only the most elaborate of plans could save Billy from the man who might once have been his friend.

"I hope you didn't use up all your favors setting up the Westminster Peace Accords," he said. He leaned back against the gray granite counter in her kitchen as she fiddled with an egg whisk. She looked like she knew what she was doing with it and he wondered if she'd ever been a cook in France.

"With our people, favors not like that. Not just so much money in bank, write it down in book, you draw that much out some time and it gone. No, no. I do something for Mr. Minh and he do something for me and maybe I do *two* thing more. And I need favor for Mr. Nguyen, so Mr. Minh do something for Mr. Nguyen, and then Mr. Nguyen do something for me. It like a big camouflage netting. You know camouflage netting?"

He nodded. They'd had it stretched over the small motor pool at their radar base, the nylon web covered by a random scatter of cloth peanut shapes in greens and browns to hide the jeeps and 6-bys from the air. There had been a lot of jokes about the V.C. flying their bamboo reconnaissance satellites over low.

"Your own family always in middle of net but lots of people at edges, too, and everybody covered."

"Eloquent," he said. Like her description of tit for tat, he thought. Straightforward, simple, and shrewd.

"Huh?"

"Nothing. Thank you. I seem to be under the big net now, thanks to you, and I still feel I owe Minh Trac some work, but he asked me to stop."

She broke off whisking the eggs for the omelette. "Oh, you not stop *now*. No. You work for me, and I say work."

"He said he wanted her spirit to rest."

"How Phuong spirit going to rest if her murderer out there walking 'round?"

She put down the whisk and came over and pressed herself against him, and he had to close his eyes.

"You not the kind of man who walk away with job half done?"

He heard her giggle.

"I only half done, too. You got to cook me some more."

"You're very persuasive, Tien."

"You bet." She drew his head down and they kissed and it was a close thing whether they were going to get dinner or not. Tien decided for them by pulling back.

"Tao Quan watching. We save for afters. Here, you tear up salad." She handed him a big romaine and a wood bowl.

"What's Tao Quan?" he asked as she began chopping a small oval onion.

"The three kitchen gods. Every kitchen got them. Every year, right before Tet they go up to heaven and make report on what they seen."

"Heaven wouldn't approve of us smooching in the kitchen?"

"I don't know, but Tet not too far away. Why take chance? You like shallot?"

"I don't think I've ever had one."

She waved a hand. "Just like onion, but better." She set the chopped shallot aside and he was just taking over the cutting board when she hurried over. She caught his hand as he was about to slice the romaine.

"No, no, no," she said. "Metal must not never touch lettuce. You must tear up with hand. No one tell you that?"

"No one told me that," he said. Her hand was on his hand, and then her leg was against his leg and they didn't get dinner after all, not for almost two hours.

fifteen

The Sense of Evil

He watched the beat-up Concord pull to the curb in front, the streetlight glinting off the only chrome left on the passenger side of the car, a single skewed door handle. The car looked like it had rolled, or at least toppled and then slid, the whole right side flattened out and scraped raw. The engine noise stopped and he saw Jack Liffey get out and walk around the front of his car. The man checked the VW, then glanced at the front door of the house, but chose to walk up the driveway, passing out of sight around the side of the house. Billy Gudger stayed well out of the line of sight from the side windows.

He saw himself rushing out the front door and running away down the block, his legs churning as hard as he could make them. Then he saw himself curling up into a fetal position beside the stub wall where he had watched from before, and then he saw himself standing defiantly right in the archway so someone at the back door could make him out. Things felt estranged from him, and a kind of unreality held everything in a glow that vibrated in his peripheral vision in perfect time to a throbbing he felt in his forehead. Everything was prepared, so it just had to unfold this way. He backed to the stub wall, raised the pistol with an almost uncontrollable tremor and lingered as he heard feet clomp unnecessarily loudly up the wooden stoop out back.

> *The toadstone is found in the head of a certain kind of toads.*
> —John Churchill, *Collection of Voyages and Travels* (1704)

The night had a strange look, a kind of orangeness that was fading out of the lumpy brown clouds but remaining on the air, an eerie Southern California winter phenomenon that he'd heard called, for some reason, a radioactive sky. A big sedan inched along the street behind him like a gang car searching for somebody to drive by, and somewhere to the north there was a dull thump-thump thump-thump like a drop hammer in some ghostly steel plant.

Billy Gudger's VW hadn't been disturbed and the house curtains were all in the same places they had been. He could see there were no lights in the separate cottage behind so he went straight to the back door of the main house. There were no lights inside here either, but he had an inkling Billy was in there, the same hunch as before. As he came up the steps, letting his feet hit hard enough so that he wouldn't startle anyone, he saw with a chill that the door was a half inch from being tight against the jamb. No door had a tongue that loose so it had to be ajar, but he rapped with his knuckle anyway.

"Billy, it's Jack Liffey. I'd love to talk to you."

He rapped again, hard enough to test the latch, and the door made a tick and gave a few inches.

"Billy, I know you're home."

He swung the door open and stepped in, trying to make as much natural noise as he could. There was an odd smell on the air of the service porch, the kind of musty old-lady, old-cigarette, and strong-cleanser smell you got in cheap motels in the Southwest. In the kitchen, there was a box of cereal on the counter beside the stove, and he couldn't remember whether it had been there before or not. He wished he was just a bit more observant, a rather important trait for a detective, he thought sardonically.

"I've been thinking about the toadstone," Jack Liffey called evenly. "It's quite remarkable, a whole chunk of the past of our culture that seems to have dropped out of Western Civilization without a trace. It's as if we'd all woke up one day and we'd forgotten about maypoles or hopscotch."

The house thrummed all of a sudden, probably a water heater coming on or—no, it was the freezer chest behind him cranking up its compressor. He could feel it in the floor.

"You seem to have found out a lot about toadstones. I'd like to know where I can look them up."

He drifted cautiously across the kitchen, not quite sure why he was talking on and on. It was a little like whistling past a graveyard. There was an unholy mess of unwashed dishes in the sink, and a little plaque over the faucets, *The Kitchen Elves Will Do the Dishes*, reminded him of Tien's tale of the three kitchen gods. He hoped some gods or elves were watching over him now.

Ahead he could see the big glass centerpiece on the dining room table. He decided he would go as far as the dining room and then retreat if Billy didn't make himself known. He'd pass on his vague suspicions to Vo and go home, and the poor kid would just have to endure the Sheriff's SWAT team crashing through the front door.

"Billy, is something wrong?"

He came slowly around the short wall beside the stove that separated the kitchen from the dining area, and nearly jumped out of his skin.

"Stop it! Stop it, you!" Billy Gudger screeched.

Jack Liffey went completely still, though his heart raced and thundered. Billy Gudger crouched beside the wall, aiming a pistol at him with both hands. He clutched the pistol with a fierce and awkward grip, neither the classic Weaver hold that pressed the knuckles of one fist against the palm of the other, nor the sissy-grip that they taught policewomen, with the butt resting on one upturned palm. The young man had one hand wrapped around the grip and the other clasping the receiver of the automatic so that if he actually fired it that way he'd get a damn good abrasion as the receiver flew back. Of course, if he fired the way he was aiming just then, Jack Liffey wouldn't be around afterward to give him pointers on pistol technique. All of this Jack Liffey noted in a few microseconds, and then he spoke evenly and without much emotion.

"Who taught you to hold a pistol like that? You'll hurt yourself. Here, let me show you how to do it."

He reached out casually with one hand. It was a near thing. The boy's face took on a deer-in-the-headlights look for an instant, and he might actually have been at the point of handing the pistol over, but he recoiled against the wall instead, as if slapped, knocking over a floor lamp behind him, startling them both with the *whump* and the breaking bulbs. Jack Liffey didn't like the way the pistol was trembling.

"Don't touch me! I'm *mean*!"

Jack Liffey opened his palms in a friendly way. "No, you're not. I won't touch you."

"I bet you think I'm harmless!"

Absurdly, he thought of Philip Marlowe dividing the world into the anxious and the depressed. People were always dividing humanity along some simplistic axis. "Billy, I'd prefer not to think of people in terms of harmless or harmful. I'd like to think of you as bright and sad and interesting. I want to ask you about the toadstone."

"Forget that! That's *over*."

"It can't be over if you've got one in your head," he said, his intuition working overtime.

The young man looked so stricken that he knew he'd struck paydirt. "That's none of your business. Here, I'll show you how dangerous I am. Turn around!"

"Clockwise or counterclockwise?"

The young man's eyes dilated and he seemed to steam and throb for a moment, like a cartoon character letting off an excess of internal pressure. "Can I give you some *advice*, Mr. Liffey?"

"I don't think I'm in a position to decline."

"Don't you ever laugh at me."

Jack Liffey nodded, as sincerely as he could, and he turned around to face away. "Okay."

"I really *really* hate it."

"We all do, I think. I'm sorry. Irony is a pretty bad habit. It's really just a way of stating something while you pretend you don't actually inhabit the thought. It doesn't leave the other person a legitimate way to respond."

"That's it *exactly*." The young man backed past him very slowly into the kitchen, then all the way to the door and shut it. "I want you to come out here slowly. Come to the freezer and look inside."

Uh-oh, he thought. All the hair on his body was prickling. He had a horrible premonition of what he might see inside the freezer. It couldn't be Phuong, of course, but if the young man really was a serial killer, the possibilities were endless. His mind couldn't help itself and he pictured a freezer full of hacked-off limbs, severed heads in Saran. . . .

"Are you sure this is a good idea?" Jack Liffey asked. "Perhaps we should just talk."

"Come here!"

He walked slowly to the waist-high freezer chest. It was an old Amana, scratched and dinged and still chugging away. A snap latch held the top down, and when he released it the top popped up a few inches, as if something within was trying to get out. Pandora's Box for sure, he thought, but this situation didn't really need a classical antecedent. He lifted the lid and felt the breath of winter, and it took a moment to work out what he was looking at. It was a shoulder, back, and rump, an obese woman who had been folded over to fit. She had her knees tucked, but her torso was so large it nearly filled the chest and her head had been pressed down unnaturally and forced in. There was fresh-looking blood on her dress, a lot of it, but he saw no wounds so he guessed she'd been shot from the front and then had lain bleeding on her back for a while. The skin of her neck was pale and pasty.

Sylvia Gudger? Or was the name Sophie? It had been on the sign out in front, and once again his powers of observation came into question. He'd better crank them up now, he thought with a deep foreboding. It was possible his survival was going to depend on his ability to read the tormented soul of this strange young man. Was this the mother, stepmother, aunt, older sister? He decided it was probably not a very good idea to ask.

"You still think I'm harmless?"

"No. Not at all." Should he say he was impressed? He just let it sit.

"I can be powerful. *Shantih, shantih, shantih.*"

"Did she laugh at you?" he guessed.

"Maybe. It happened sometimes."

"What happened sometimes?"

"You know."

"No, I don't," Jack Liffey insisted.

"*This.* People laugh and end up like this."

"It doesn't just happen, Billy."

"Yes it does."

Jack Liffey closed up the freezer chest and latched it. It wasn't easy to do, physically or emotionally. That had been a human being. When you got too far from childhood, he thought, for no particular reason, life got dangerous. "Do you want me to help you?"

He heard a snort of exaggerated derision. "By calling the police?"

"If I wanted to call the police, they'd be here now, lots of them." He turned around and watched the young man carefully. His guard came up and so did the pistol. "I came by myself because I didn't want a bunch of SWAT cops shooting out your windows and hurting you."

"You're just trying to trick me."

"I didn't know . . . *this* had happened, I won't lie to you, but I knew you needed a friend. Didn't I say that through the door?" He tried another surmise. "You needed someone like an uncle or a father to talk to."

"Don't give me a lot of Freudian father stuff. I don't believe in all that."

"Actually, I think Freud thought boys had a natural rivalry with their fathers. I don't believe that, either."

"Fathers are just bullshit. You can make yourself into anything you want, and you don't need some damn other one to help you."

"Maybe you're stronger than me. I hurt for a long time after my father died. I felt alone. I didn't even see him much the last few years, but I think I needed to know he was there, and he was still somebody I could go to. Somebody who knew a lot of things I didn't know, who'd seen things and places and people I'd never see. He was a decent man from another era than mine. I wish I'd started talking to him more and listening to him."

The young man seemed on the verge of tears. Somewhere Jack Liffey had read an article of advice to young women worried about being abducted which favored establishing as many human ties as possible with the abductor. It seemed a sensible idea.

"My father was a lifelong pacifist. During the war he got himself a job in the Merchant Marine so he could contribute to fighting Hitler but wouldn't have to carry a gun. I want to tell you about a time when I was about nine years old."

There didn't seem to be any objection.

"We were walking along the tidepools at White Point in San Pedro. I don't know if you know it." The young man shook his head. "Back then it was pretty isolated, down at the bottom of a cliff with only a dirt road that descended pretty steeply to a spot where a few cars could park beside the rocky beach. We took the old Mercury down there and we were walking along the rocks, peering into the tidepools at sea anemones and hermit crabs and mussels. I think I was looking for pretty shells to stick in my pockets, though we might have been collecting big flat rocks. My dad used them to build walls around our house.

"All of a sudden we noticed a seagull flapping on the shingle of pebbles just above the tidepools. It had probably flown into the cliff and broken its wing. The poor bird flapped around in a circle and made a sad little cry over and over when it saw us. It was almost as if it was begging us for help. My father took my shoulders and turned me away. 'Don't look,' he said. But of course I did. I peeked and saw him walk over to the bird and go through a little pantomime of indecision for himself, and then he reached down and wrung the bird's neck. Now, my dad never fished or hunted, never raised a hand to me. I don't think he ever harmed another creature, except that one time, as far as I know. He saw a duty he had to do and he did it, no matter what it cost him in hurt."

Jack Liffey wished that the father-son anecdote that had come to mind hadn't been about killing, but it was too late now. The boy surreptitiously took a tear out of the corner of his eye with a fingertip, or maybe he was just poking at his face. Jack Liffey didn't want to seem to be looking too close.

"That story doesn't say everything there is to say about my dad, but it says something about the bedrock of his character. It's good to have examples like that to let you know when you're straying off the right path."

The young man stuck out his jaw as if he was going to tough out some ordeal. "If a thing doesn't exist for you, you can't miss it."

"Oh, I think you probably can. Especially if you have a good imagination. Let's sit down and talk."

The compressor switched off and they both stared at the freezer chest in the sudden quiet. Like a summons to a more dangerous fate.

"It's too late for talk. You understand that, don't you?"

"People can always talk, as long as it's not done out of cruelty and they're trying to understand one another. There's no harm in it. Come on, we can go in and sit and relax. Tell me what you're reading; tell me the long-range goals of your studies."

He could see that the young man was going through some internal struggle, and as long as he could keep stoking that debate, there was a chance he could find himself a chink to exploit. But Jack Liffey was also deeply, coldly frightened, and he wondered if a lunge for the pistol right then might not be the best idea. Any TV detective worth his salt could have done it. But the boy hovered just a little too far away to make success plausible. It wasn't as if he was dealing with a neophyte in pulling the trigger.

"Go very slowly into the house, but don't try to get an inch closer to me."

"Sure."

Jack Liffey started to back up, and the young man followed slowly into the dining room, where he gestured for Jack Liffey to go into the living room. A shabby sofa with a ribbed bedspread tossed over it faced a TV on a metal rolling cart.

"Sit."

He did and Billy Gudger turned on the TV and dialed around to a music program and cranked the sound up loud, a crooner on a darkened stage complaining about some unspecified hurt. Then the young man took a pair of handcuffs out of his pocket and tossed them to Jack Liffey.

"Put one side on your ankle."

They were good Peerless cuffs, cop issue, but just about anyone could go to a law enforcement supply store and buy them. He had a pair himself that he'd never used, still sitting in their box in his desk. He set these aside. "I won't put these on me, Billy. If I did that, I'd be completely helpless and it would destroy the equality between us. We couldn't talk the same way. You'd think of me differently."

"Instructions specify what you've got to do! Do it now!" All of a sudden, the young man sputtered and rushed, as if speeding on some drug. He waved his free arm and clutched at imaginary objects in the air. "You got to do what I say, got to got to, you got to! I won't feel safe to talk if you can jump up at me anytime, you got to see that! You just want to trick me and go and make a fool of me!'

He raved on for quite some time, babbling about trust and trickery and people who laughed at other people they thought were indecisive, and Jack Liffey watched the pistol wave around, the young man's eyes flitting from place to place in the room, never meeting his own. The sudden irrationality was startling and terrifying, but he decided it was not a good idea to back down once he'd made a reasoned stand.

"Billy, you can't expect me to participate in my own captivity. If you feel you need to handcuff me, you're going to have to put them on me yourself. You have the power."

Billy Gudger seemed to run down and pant for a moment, staring at Jack Liffey's feet. The TV talked about Chevrolet trucks. Like a rock. "Don't disrespect me."

"I don't, Billy, but I need respect, too."

That seemed to startle him and he glanced up directly into Jack Liffey's eyes. Something seemed to be whirling around right behind the young man's eyes, changing the frame of mind they imparted from moment to moment.

"Lie on your stomach. Right there."

Jack Liffey nodded and slid forward on the sofa cushion, then went to his knees on the floor. He let himself down on the carpet that smelled of smoke and cat and fried fish. He wondered where the cat was, if it had been one of the first victims. The young man approached him cautiously and pressed the barrel of the pistol against the back of Jack Liffey's neck.

Jack Liffey's shoulders and arms went tense, and he couldn't help clamping his eyes shut as if that might ward off a shot. His body went cold from head to toe as the barrel of the pistol dug a little and he hoped he hadn't made a terrible mistake. Then he felt the cuff go on his right ankle. The other half of the handcuffs clanged on something metal.

"Put your hands together back here, I mean it."

Jack Liffey brought his hands up behind his back and felt the gun barrel withdraw, and a second pair of handcuffs snapped into place around his wrists. He tried to remember if any of the serial killings had had ligature marks around the wrists, but he hadn't paid much attention.

Some whitebread soul singer on TV was moaning about being loved and left, and Billy put a hand under his armpit and helped him back onto the couch. It was uncomfortable with his arms behind his back but he wriggled into a position that wasn't too bad. So much for refusing to submit to the handcuffs.

Billy erected the fallen lamp and kicked the glass to one side. He slid over a big leather ottoman that was expelling a wad of stuffing through a torn seam and sat facing Jack Liffey, but he still carried the pistol, which he waved about when he gestured. The young man was a little too animated for Jack Liffey's taste, as if he was heading off on some manic jag now. He wondered if it was a result of getting a taste of power over someone. That probably wouldn't be a good sign.

"Mr. Liffey," he said with a portentous frown, "do you always tell the truth?"

"I don't think anybody tells the truth in all situations."

"What do you mean?"

"Well. . . . Nobody pulls a badly hurt five-year-old girl out of a car wreck and tells her that her mother just died. There are degrees of inconvenience in every situation. Personal and otherwise, and you balance them the best you can."

"Or you go chicken. Like facing somebody determined who's got a gun?"

Jack Liffey shrugged. "It's different for everybody. Some people don't fear death. I do." He thought of Philip Marlowe's conceit about the depressed who feared boredom more than death. Billy Gudger looked more like the anxious type. Or, more likely, the kid spun on another axis altogether, his sensibility wooshing off along some tangent into left field.

"Maybe some people fear embarrassment or humiliation even more than death."

The young man's eyes clouded, as if Jack Liffey had hit a nerve. "What do you think makes somebody go bad?" he blurted. "I want you to tell me the truth."

"You're talking about the idea of evil, aren't you? I think that's a big sloppy word that's almost meaningless. It falsifies the world." He wondered if this was the safest approach to take. The young man was obviously troubled by the idea of evil, probably felt he'd crossed the line himself. It was likely that Billy Gudger had spun off into some freemasonry of his own imagination, and it might be safer just to acknowledge whatever fuzzy metaphysical nonsense he came up with. Jack Liffey realized that he'd been sucked into a terrible realm where every thought and every assertion might just have dire consequences, and the intensity of it all was already exhausting him.

"You don't believe in evil?"

"I don't know," he said, trying for an attitude that he could nudge off in a new direction if necessary. "Usually, when you look close at what people mean by the word, it turns into something like short-sightedness, or selfishness or ignorance of the consequences. Even a misunderstanding. Going to Viet Nam wasn't a very good idea for America, but the way it happened was far too complicated just to call it evil."

"What about something just one person does? Sometimes, it's really simple." Billy Gudger leaned toward him like a professor who already knew the answer.

"Do you mean things that boil up out of the unconscious?"

"Hurting a child, for example."

"I think it's a pathology, something is broken and hurt down in the psyche. It's not theology. But what is it you want to tell me? You're trembling with it."

The young man pressed his hands together on the pistol, and brought it down on his knee to steady it, as if his tremor had given away a secret.

"*You* just think there's no such thing as evil because you live in a world where nothing *really* bad has ever happened to you. You were protected from it. You've never *done* something and had to look at yourself different. It's easy to go on for years and years just acting the way you know is normal and then one day something you do turns out to be contrary. You didn't make any decision, not really. You sort of sneezed. You just did something you never did before and it gives you a . . . feeling inside, like something's really new."

His jaw was fiercely set. "And you do it again, and maybe again, and you get used to it. You're not different, but you see yourself in a new way. There's this snap in your head, and you say, 'Hey, I'm *bad*. I'm not good after all.' "

"Some people call that guilt."

Billy Gudger shook his head. "You can actually enjoy it. It sets you free."

sixteen

The Theory of the Oscillating Substrata

Billy Gudger must have punched the TV to an oldies channel because Jack Liffey heard, and then saw, a young Richard Widmark emit his gruesome hyena cackle. Hee-hee-hee. Widmark was Tommy Udo in his first movie, *Kiss of Death,* and before long, in one of the most famous acts of pure cruelty on film, he was going to push an old lady in a wheelchair down the staircase and voice that terrible psychopath's giggle again. He had read somewhere that two generations of street hoodlums in the roughest townships of South Africa had modeled themselves on Tommy Udo. This was not something he wanted to watch while he was handcuffed and helpless.

"Sit forward!" Billy Gudger snapped and then yanked Jack Liffey's wallet out of his back pocket. He went through it, looking closely at all the business cards and tattered old notes with phone numbers and things to buy at the store. Jack Liffey had set this punitive expedition off himself, experimenting a little with the technique of offering friendship and encouragement and then suddenly withholding it, which hadn't turned out to be a very good idea. Billy had fumed for a minute, like a spurned lover, and then he'd got a bit frantic, probably egged on by the noise level. The TV was on loud enough to cover any shouts for help, and racket like that could make anyone edgy.

Something in his newfound sense of power seemed to crank up the deep-seated mania the young man carried around inside him. He started tearing up the cards from the wallet with overlarge gestures, like a self-conscious act of sacrilege.

"I thought we were friends, Billy."

The young man stopped and puffed for a moment like a fighter between rounds. "Don't bullshit."

"I'm not. I want to talk with you. Can you explain what you were saying about alternation."

"You really want to know?"

"Of course. It sounded interesting."

"Okay, don't *fuck* with me." The profanity had an odd character in his mouth, almost as if the word were so foreign to him he had to use it in italics.

Billy Gudger threw the wallet ostentatiously against the wall, stuffed his pistol down into his trousers, and abruptly went out to the kitchen. Jack Liffey heard the back door open and considered letting out a hearty shout, but decided it probably wouldn't help much over the bombast of 1940s movie music. He settled for scooting forward on the sofa to try to work out what his ankle was cuffed to. The chenille bedspread on the sofa draped onto the floor, making a little tent at the three-link chain of the handcuff at his ankle. He yanked his foot a few times, and the cuff clanged metallically, seeming to be attached to something pretty solid. He guessed from the lumpiness under him that he was cuffed to the bedframe of a pull-out sleeper.

Then he tipped himself forward until he went off onto the floor. He wanted to see how much mobility he had with his arms cuffed behind him and one leg pinioned. It was no easy matter getting back onto the sofa. He wriggled and repositioned himself and he finally got an elbow up to give himself leverage. In the last heave with arms and legs together, he wrenched some muscle in his hip that hurt like a bastard. He wasn't sure what good any of that did him, but accumulating information seemed to be the only recourse he had at the moment.

* * *

Billy Gudger sprinted up the driveway to his cottage and fumbled a bit with the key as he opened up. He wondered if there were any way at all to rescue this situation from all the bad karma that had developed. He knew he wanted to have Mr. Liffey on his side, and, except for a moment here and there of perverse obstinacy, the man seemed genuinely to like him. As long as he was in complete control, he could afford to give it a little longer period of test. Even if something bad had to happen in the end, he could say he'd done his best to work things out. You couldn't do more than that. If only Mr. Liffey did his best, too, maybe together they could find a way to come out into the clear.

He dug frantically in the papers he kept in five color-coded cardboard banker's boxes, and finally he found the latest version of the big treatise. It was his *pièce de résistance*, rewritten dozens of times until he had got it nearly bang on. He knew there were a few things about it that still didn't seem quite right, and maybe Mr. Liffey could help him on those.

He stopped at his door and looked back. All of a sudden, the cottage where he had lived for so long had come to seem utterly alien, the home of someone else who was not him at all. He looked at the obsessively color-coded desks, the reading schedule on the wall, the mussed bed. It was a place unquiet and out of kilter. The room was suddenly a secret festering place, not a sanctuary. And there was a sense, not a vision exactly, nor a fully formed hallucination, but an insinuation of some sixth or seventh sense that from far in the back corner of the room something dark was coming toward him. He felt a chill all the way down to his toes.

Something had changed, torn loose inside him, and he felt he was not in complete control of himself any more. The darkness seemed to get closer before he made himself turn away. It was very unsettling.

It felt odd sitting manacled in that decrepit living room with no one else present. It was like being made part of an exhibit of some past civilization, pinioned amidst all the abandoned pots and grinding stones of a defunct race. The ancient TV on its wheeled cart, so old it still had a rotary channel dial, the flight of brass ducks stuck to the wall, the fringed floor lamp, a hook rug and leather ottoman, and the huge blond wood phonograph cabinet with doilies on it. In the dining room there was the big cut glass stemmed fruit bowl, an array of napkins in little round napkin rings, a print of a little girl with huge eyes and the egregious Highland bull. It was American working class, circa 1957. To his left there was a heavy plum-colored tapestry on rings walling off a big alcove of the house, probably where she had done her tea-leaf reading. He decided he had better discreetly find out what the young man's relationship to the woman in the freezer had been, and what had led him to snap.

On the TV he saw a dark staircase and looked away. There was a rush of footsteps at the back of the house and then the kitchen door slammed and he realized it had been standing open all this time. Billy Gudger skidded into the room breathlessly and looked around as if he half expected police crouching in the corners. When he was satisfied, he pushed the ottoman back into the middle and sat down facing Jack Liffey, holding what looked like a screenplay, about 100 sheets of paper bound at the edge with big brass brads.

"You sure you want to participate?" he said.

I always want dangerous fruitbats to read their deepest thoughts to me, Jack Liffey thought. He nodded, but wondered if this was going to be like sharing a cabin in Montana with the Unabomber.

" 'The Theory of the Oscillating Substrata,' " Billy Gudger read, then looked up. "I think it needs a catchier title, and we can make that the subtitle. I'm not good with titles."

"Maybe I can help when I've heard it."

"I hope so." He took a deep breath and set in dramatically. " 'The greatest philosophers have always begun with the study of absolutes and ideas and what is real and how ideas relate to what is real, and they have generally and often learned that they have to move their

bright searchlight of concentration to the primary task of phenome-
nology, or what we can generally assume we can know, before you
can decide how real what you know is to be.' "

Inwardly Jack Liffey groaned. It was going to be even worse than
he'd thought. He had never had much tolerance for listening to prose
read aloud, but when it was not only abstract prose but a weird logical and grammatical mishmash, it was going to be just about impossible for him to follow. And follow it he would have to.

" 'It came to me one afternoon shifting gears in my car that
processes always tend to go one way, but then they return and go
back over the same ground, but in a different form, or a different level
in some way. It's only a very absurdly simple example, but there's first
gear up at the top, then second down at the bottom, but to go
higher or faster, you have to go to the top again for third gear.' "

After a bit more of this, Jack Liffey had to bite his lip to suppress
the mirth that had bloomed suddenly. The tension of his captivity
must have made him woozy. Yes, there was an idea in there somewhere, he thought, but it was an idea that was punch-drunk with all
the customary failings of the self-taught, all the wrong-headedness of
isolation. Which was a perfect argument for going to college, he
thought, and exposing yourself to the whole gamut of ideas available
from the past. It was so easy to direct a lonely study along some
avenue that caught your fancy and to miss all the other avenues that
made up the map, the slow accretion of the civilization. One idea
explained everything: it was the conceit of the crank, the solitary
prophet who refused to relate his one or two insights to the body of
what others had discovered.

"There are distinct intrinsic patterns to the world and our activi-
ties satisfy those patterns, first in simple ways and then in more well-
developed ways. It's like a marble running down the little zigzag
ramps of one of those clock-timers."

There was a lot more like that. The general idea seemed to be that
the world worked itself out in a series of hiking trail switchbacks.
These paths—paths to what? he wondered—climbed the cliff—

what cliff?—in a repeated zigzag. If you looked at the big picture from above, it might seem you were following the same path back and forth, but in fact each dogleg was at a slightly higher place or taking a higher form. It was all so vague that it made Jack Liffey's teeth ache. Alas, there were hints that before calling it a day, the young man was going to apply his grandiose theory of the oscillating substrata to every aspect of mind, will, history, science, and political science.

"In an oak tree, for example, the Idea of a Big Strong Oak is carried by the DNA and then the gene and then the chromosome, and then the acorn, the twig, the stem, and then the big solid trunk of the tree. Each level yearns upward to repeat the essential idea of a big solid Oak Tree in a new form."

And then Jack Liffey lost it for a while, his mind going numb with exhaustion. His eye went to the twitch in the young man's right hand, the pistol abandoned on the floor, the way the headlights of a passing car threw a little light on the big tapestry on his left, the sharp cheekbones and nose of Richard Widmark as he leered. None of this seemed worth much as a Houdini-esque aid to escape.

"You're drifting."

"I'm thinking about what you're saying. It's extraordinary. Have you read Hegel?"

"A little," the young man said darkly. Perhaps he felt it was demeaning to be compared to other philosophers.

"I think you anticipate him in some ways."

He glared but didn't speak. Somebody on TV screamed not far behind the boy's head, and he winced and reached behind to lower the volume. "Don't get any ideas. I can put the sound up in a lickety-split."

"No problem."

"Why am I like Hegel?"

"He wrote about forces that moved to higher levels, too." And as Jack Liffey was speaking, improvising desperately in fact, he realized all of a sudden where Billy Gudger's madness lay. Hegel spoke about opposing forces colliding out in the world and giving rise to something new. Billy Gudger's philosophy, if you could call it that, was only about the working out of some freewheeling inner logic. There were no outside forces impinging on his actors. It wasn't megalomania exactly, it was just that the young man—out of his colossal loneliness—could not really imagine social interaction, and if you couldn't see interaction, you couldn't really envision transformation. Everything was stuck with its own inner nature. Billy Gudger's oak trees would never bend to the east on a windswept Monterey shoreline or wither from an iron-poor soil. It wasn't something he wanted to point out to the young man, however. "I think you might have a more interesting way of looking at it than Hegel. He was a long time ago."

A chill traveled from the top of his head down to his toes. Jack Liffey found he was really quite frightened all of a sudden, as if the danger had just come home to him. If he just let things slide, he knew he would be doomed, but it was hard to see what he could do about his peril. He'd tried withholding fellowship and that had inflamed something in the young man. Perhaps he could worm his way into Billy Gudger's psyche and make himself indispensable in some way.

Jack Liffey thought of himself as something of an outsider, too, at least since he'd lost his comfortable marriage with its comfortable suburban home and comfortable middle-class aerospace job, but he knew he didn't really have a clue what it was like being trapped inside the fog of this young man's mind. He could imagine loneliness, a fragile self-respect, maybe a buzzing that came and went in one ear, odd keepsakes kept in a drawer, solitary thoughts that spun away in eerie directions on their own, but he guessed that he had no real idea of the thwarted needs that reeled around in there, banging against everything.

"I wish I could read your manuscript. Honestly, I have a hard time following groundbreaking work like this when it's read aloud."

"I'll read slow."

"It's something about seeing the words. It's just the way my mind works."

"You can read it later."

He set in reading again and Jack Liffey could see that the point of the exercise wasn't really critique, it was audience.

" 'In political science, it is possible to imagine a person who was raised to be kindly and empathetic, who is drawn as a young person to the Democratic Party that he sees as the party of sympathy for the poor. Then this person might be exposed to someone who argued that it is the health of capitalism that helps the poor, as in the famous saying that a rising tide lifts all boats, and he would become a Republican for a while. Then he meets someone who explains the work of, say, Franklin Roosevelt, and he decides that it is the Democratic Party that is going to save capitalism *malgré lui*. He might even be exposed to an even more sophisticated argument for the Republicans, and so on. It is not a question of which party is the correct embodiment of his sympathy, but how his inner sentiment works itself out in ever more refined forms, forcing his political course into what an outside observer would see as a seeming zig-zag of loyalties.' "

He looked up and Jack Liffey nodded. There was at least a sense of the social world in this example. He took a stab at his intuition. "I see your argument. It's good. Did your mother change parties at some time?"

"Why do you mention my mother! Damn you!" He hurled down the essay and it tented open on the hooked rug.

Wrong again, Jack Liffey thought. His intuition was working overtime but it wasn't getting him anywhere very useful.

"Damn it, damn it! People like you are always reducing things to the personal level, as if I couldn't think them out myself!" He was working himself into another paroxysm, flushing badly.

"No, I didn't mean that—"

"Shut up!" Billy Gudger picked up the pistol, and the barrel hovered and looped erratically in the air in front of him. "You're no good. You don't care who I am!"

"Of course I do."

"Tell me about your *moth*-er!" he said in a wrenching parody of a psychoanalyst, his face screwed up in sarcasm. "Tell me about m-m-masturbating!"

It was the first stammer Jack Liffey had heard from him. He'd blundered into his own raw nerve on that one.

"Well, fuck you and your mother theories and the horses you all rode on! Sit back!"

Gone into attack-dog mode again, he seemed now to zero in on the papers in Jack Liffey's shirt pocket. He stood up and wrenched at the pocket, tearing it and coming away with the little appointment book that Jack Liffey picked up free every year from the Hallmark shop. The young man thumbed brutally through the date book until he got to the current month. " 'Meet Tien,' " he read aloud. " 'See Tien, Tien Tien Tien.' Who's Tien, I wonder?"

His brows were furrowing, and he was making a humming from somewhere deep in his throat. Jack Liffey wondered if he even knew he was making the noise.

Then Billy Gudger shook the little booklet and several business cards fell out, which he retrieved. Jack Liffey caught a glimpse of a green one he didn't remember at all that the young man tossed over his shoulder, then one of his own cards, tossed, a coupon for bar soap that Marlena had given him on his last trip to Von's and he'd forgotten all about, then Billy Gudger wound down staring at the oversized card Jack Liffey remembered all too well. He felt a chill on his spine.

"Sleepy Lotus, Import/Export, Facilitation, Tien Nguyen Joubert." He read it aloud, pronouncing it Tine Na-goo-yen, like most English speakers. "I'll bet this is the Asian girl's mom."

It was the first time Phuong had come up in a long time. So the young man had a pretty clear idea what this was all about.

"No, she's just a businesswoman the girl once worked for."

He glanced up at Jack Liffey with a cunning leer. "Sure. That's why you been seeing her every ten minutes this week. Man, you must think I'm stupid. I bet she knows where you are right now. I bet you tell her everything."

"I know you're not stupid, Billy. Phuong's mom, like a lot of Vietnamese women over here, is so quiet and timid she rarely leaves the house. She can't even drive a car. She could never run an import business."

The young man flapped the card thoughtfully across his fingers, then studied it again. "Look here, it's even got a home address in Huntington Harbour. Do you think she could maybe *facilitate* things if she came here for a consultation?"

"I promise you, she's *not* Phuong's mother. Phuong's family name was Minh. You can read it in the newspaper or your own files from MediaPros."

"They all use different names all the time. You can't rely on foreigners. They've got different customs."

"Billy, don't make this any worse. We can find a way out of it the way it is right now." But he cranked the TV sound up again, a commercial blaring away about long-lasting deodorant, and Billy Gudger went into the next room. Jack Liffey had a terrible premonition of doom.

"Billy, talk to me! Let's work this out!"

The young man came back in with a roll of silver duct tape and taped Jack Liffey's mouth shut, running the tape several times all the way around his head. It was going to be a bastard with his hair caught in it in back, he thought. If he was still alive when it came off.

"You got blue eyes like me," the young man said and patted the top of Jack Liffey's head, then he turned the TV up another notch and left. Jack Liffey could just barely hear the VW starting in front with its distinctive air-cooled roar and clatter as a woman with a nervous manner worried publicly about the flavor of her spaghetti sauce.

seventeen

Coming Up Against the Outside World

He had never been down into the yacht-town of Huntington Harbour before and, slowing on the bridge to glance down the yacht channel, it seemed as remote to him as a European postcard, just like the pretentious British 'U' in the name. A car honked and he jumped in the seat and almost stalled the engine as he popped the clutch to drive on. Billy Gudger did not like to look behind him because he did not want to catch even accidental sight of the darkness that was following, loitering, drawing nearer.

The VW turned into the street listed on her business card. The community had strung itself out along the yacht channels so every house seemed to have a tall mast rising out of the backyard. There were three-car garages everywhere, and still there were a handful of rich cars parked in front, a Mercedes, a big 7-series BMW and one Cadillac convertible. No people were to be seen, and the garish houses didn't even have windows on the street side, as if they were only false fronts. Probably all their life force was directed out the back onto the boats.

Tien Joubert's address didn't seem to possess a sailing yacht or maybe it was out to sea because there was no mast. Billy Gudger parked and watched the house for ten minutes without seeing anything at all, but then there was no way he would unless the owner came out to mow the postage stamp-sized grass yard or the garage door swung up suddenly to let someone drive away. It was like watching a blank wall.

Did your mother change to a Democrat? After all his reading, and all the thought he had put into the essay. . . . He was annoyed that Mr. Liffey would sit and listen to his carefully framed and refined argument and then suggest it was just some excrescence that had bubbled out of family events. They always tried to do that to you— reduce what was new and thought-provoking to personal psychology. You pointed at something novel and shouted, *Look*! and they all gathered around and stared at your finger and said, *See*, that's the trouble, that strange finger! Why wouldn't they take the trouble to really look?

After a while he simmered down and examined the neighborhood again. This is the way the rich live, he explained to the Martian. Though really it's just the *new* rich, he corrected himself. The old rich from Orange County probably lived up in L.A. somewhere or back East or kept a mailing address at some old hacienda engulfed now by suburban sprawl—though, in fact, they'd moved on to spend much of the year on the French Riviera. These new rich types probably made their money running McDonald'ses or little electronics companies and they hadn't grown up with boats, but they felt they ought to have them, so they bought one and kept it tied up at the dock and once every six months they got up the nerve to take it out into the bay.

I don't know how I'm going to deal with this woman, he went on. But I'm sure you can see that I can't just leave the girl's mother out here, not if she knows about me. I've got to do something about her, too.

He imagined, as he did sometimes, that he was a wisp of vapor and he was drifting out the car window and then across the roadway. He drifted up the wide pebbled walk and then curled once around a little tearose bush and made himself thin to slide through the crack between the door and the glass panes beside the door—those are called side lights in architecture, he explained to the Martian. Too bad he couldn't see so well as a wisp. It could tell him a lot, without risking a thing.

But he wasn't a wisp, so he worked out in his mind exactly what he would say when he got to the door. Then he ran through it again and again so he wouldn't clam up at the last minute. When he was satisfied, he got out and quickly tucked the pistol into the back of his pants under his shirt, the way he saw in movies. He smelled salt air right away, and tar, and he heard a pennant flapping hard in the breeze and then a squawk of birds. He could see a thick shelf of really evil black clouds blowing in from the northwest under the gray high cloud. There would be hard rain soon. The darkness was sneaking up, wherever he looked, and it seemed the stone no longer protected him.

A toadstone ring (the fossil palatal tooth of a species of Ray) was supposed to protect new-born children and their mothers from the power of the fairies.
—Wiliam Jones, *Finger-Ring Love* (1877)

He walked as quietly as he could up to the door as if, by making no sound, he could change his mind at any moment and turn back without leaving a trace on the world. The doorbell made a strange little five-note musical tune inside the house. He waited a few moments and then pushed it again.

"Yeah, okay, I come." He heard a woman's voice, and he could see a shape moving through the rippled glass. The shape seemed very short. The door came open and a Vietnamese woman, no taller than he was, met his eyes with a directness that surprised him. He'd expected her to be timid. She was wearing a belted trenchcoat but it hung open, as if she'd just thrown it on, and underneath she seemed to be wearing a leotard.

"Hi, what you want?"

"I'm a friend of Jack Liffey's," he said.

She cheered up immediately.

"Good for you." When he didn't volunteer anything, she added, "I'm friend, too. You got something for me, huh?"

He showed her her own business card. "See, he gave me this to come find you."

"Yeah, sure."

She wasn't saying the right things back to him, and it threw his scripted conversation into turmoil. Her brows darkened when he didn't add anything. He could feel he was screwing things up, as usual, and he would get to a bad place soon if he didn't come up with something. The rest of the plan just began to evaporate out of his mind, and he could feel the darkness edging up behind.

"What you wanna say?"

"Mr. Liffey, he wants you."

"Yeah, sure."

She didn't get it. "He wants you to come see him. He has something you need to see in person."

"This about Phuong?"

"Uh-huh."

"Where he at?"

He didn't seem to follow, and then he realized she wanted him to tell her where to go. She didn't realize he was asking her to come with him. Maybe he hadn't said it right at all. He wasn't sure. His whole perception had tunneled down to a narrow focus on this pretty Vietnamese woman standing there impatiently in a trenchcoat. The periphery of his vision had gone fuzzy, and everything he did seemed to be running about ten seconds late.

"He says I need to take you to see him," he said.

"I don't think so. You tell me where I got to go."

"It's hard to explain. I'll drive you."

"If it gotta be that way, I follow. You come and wait while I get dressed."

She pulled the door open enough to invite him in and then walked away across a blue living room and down a hall. He closed the door and stood and looked around. He could take care of her right there in some way, he could feel the pistol riding so uncomfortably in his back that he wondered why everyone including this woman didn't know it was there. But he didn't feel like doing anything at all just then. He had reached a curious stasis. Darkness moaned an invitation to him, and he shut his mind to it.

The blue of the room seemed oppressive, and he could see right through and out a wall of glass to a patio and the channel beyond. The coming storm was churning up the surface of the water in the channel, and a buoy leaned away from the wind. There was a little Toonerville toy boat tied up at the patio, leaning into the channel in the wind with several bright pennants and the fringe on its top whipping away.

She came back in a businessy navy blue dress, carrying the trenchcoat.

"What your name then?"

"Billy."

"Hi, Billy. I'm Tien. But you know that, you got card."

She stuck out her hand and it startled him. He shook her hand and felt his own perspiring and clammy. She opened the door, ushering him out. "What you drive?"

He pointed to his VW and she winced.

"Beetle no good here. Air cool engine burn up in heat. You got to get you little Honda CRX. That sweet car. I know good place for trade in. You get in your car now and I come."

The door shut behind him and the sky rumbled a warning and he felt as if he hadn't even got a word in edgewise with her. But things seemed to be working out okay, anyway. He started the car and before long the garage door came up and a black Porsche Targa squealed out backwards, like a vastly matured version of his car. She waved as the door was closing and he pulled away.

The horrible TV rattled on and on, an old cowboy movie now with commercials for dish soap and department store white sales and anthologies of meaningful organ music, but he did his best to shut it out and give his full attention to consideration of Billy Gudger and how to coax the disturbed young man back to earth. He didn't want to rile him, but he couldn't just go with the flow of events or he'd end up dumped in the Tustin Hills. He assumed Billy was responsible for Phuong and the other bodies he'd been hearing about. And Billy had warned him himself: Don't laugh at me. It was chilling to think about.

Perhaps the young man had been driving Phuong home after the video shoot and made a clumsy pass at her or said something stiff and risible, as he seemed fated to do, only to have her laugh dismissively and send him around the bend. What had the woman in the freezer done to touch him off? Was it his mother? Even the word *mother* had upset him, and Jack Liffey decided he had to find some way to get the young man to talk about himself.

Suddenly the TV flickered in the corner of his vision and a flare went off at the windows, and, just as he was trying to figure out if it was a nuclear strike, thunder slammed into the flimsy house like a huge fist. In his excitable state it just about gave him a stroke, and he had to tighten his diaphragm for a moment to try to stop his runaway heart. Do not forsake me, oh my darlin', he thought, and then realized why he was thinking it, that was the song that had been playing on the TV as the lightning struck, and the tune was back full strength now after the short brownout, the sweet chestnut moaning away as black-and-white cowboy boots strode down the dusty street. *High Noon.* Just about the only movie he'd ever seen with a hero who'd been scared to death from the first frame to the last and had done his duty anyway. He'd once liked it a lot, this movie full of irony, written by a Communist, but set in a town whose masses were cowardly and wouldn't come to the aid of their sheriff, and starring a right winger who'd testified against Communists—after playing one ten years earlier in *For Whom the Bell Tolls.* And then Howard Hawks himself had later said he hated the movie because the sissy sheriff had gone around *asking* for help, which his favorite individualist icon, John Wayne, would never have done. All of which was pretty irrelevant, but Jack Liffey's mind was jetting every which way after the lightning blast—to avoid the inescapable fact of his helplessness—and he seemed to have stumbled on a motherlode of irrelevant film lore that he'd stored away.

Thunder rumbled far away, and he brought himself back to the smelly sofa in the cluttered bungalow on the edge of the Orange County hills, and to the handcuffs that chafed his wrists. His current predicament didn't seem to have much to do with the rest of his life, neither the former-condo, now-office in Culver City, nor the pleasant house he shared with Marlena in Mar Vista, nor his sweet and thoughtful daughter who was, he hoped, home with her mother doing math homework, nor his lost job, nor anything else from his wasted and squandered past. According to Billy Gudger's theories, his wretched present position had to be contained in some way in the fact of his existence. Some plan in his DNA so vast that if he had access to it all, he could deduce where each of his atoms was going to be ten years from now, his whole life spinning out of this painstaking internal blueprint. But he knew perfectly well that doctrine led to the most absurd of megalomanias, with even the butterflies in Siberia taking just the right tacks in their flight plan so as not to disturb Jack Liffey's certain course to his ordained fate 10,000 miles away.

It was all nonsense, of course. You never could know enough, even a god couldn't, and every atom banged into other atoms and went reeling. So in the end, everything in the world was arbitrary, everything was gratuitous, the deranged bungalow, the handcuffs, whether or not he found a way to outtalk a near insane young man who had all the social skills of a water buffalo. His fate was an existential crapshoot. It was terrifying, even nauseating, but there it was.

He finally decided that his best bet was to go back to the role of kindly but officious uncle, offering a guiding hand with just enough edge of criticism to give him room to maneuver. Then in a lull in the TV sound, over the steady beat of the rain, he heard the single whoop of a Porsche engine being shut down by somebody who'd been told about clearing the carburetor, and he had a terrible feeling that Billy Gudger had lured Tien Joubert into his nightmare world. He'd been in her Porsche.

He thought he heard a scuffling on the walk in front and the door came open. Immediately Jack Liffey started bouncing and hammering his feet and made as much noise as he could through the duct tape. She had good instincts of self-preservation. She fled at once, crying for help, and Billy Gudger grabbed for his gun and slammed the door as he took off after her. He must have corralled her toward the back, because there was the sound of another struggle out on the service porch and she cried out in pain. Jack Liffey cursed the racket of the rain and the television because she was certainly doing her best to attract attention.

"I not go nowhere with you!" he heard out of the kitchen. And she was so agitated that she flooded the house with Vietnamese for a few moments, and then French, as if hunting for the language that would work the trick.

"Shut up shut up shut up!"

"You the bad guy that hurt Phuong? You got to be ashame!"

Then there was the sound of a blow and something falling and she whimpered. The TV was ominously rolling the tail credits of the film, and then Billy Gudger backed into the room, dragging Tien Joubert along the floor by the collar of the trenchcoat she wore. There was a cut on her cheek and forehead, but even dazed, she was thrashing a little as he tugged her along. The young man dumped her in the middle of the floor beside the ottoman and strode across the room to press the barrel of his pistol into Jack Liffey's temple.

"Shut up or I'll goof him right now! I mean it!"

She looked over and subsided into a moan of defeat, as the rain flailed at the windows. Jack Liffey noticed that her purse had fallen onto the floor beside the ottoman and he filed the fact away for reference. A gaggle of lifeguards in red suits were running toward the camera as rock music pounded out of the TV.

"Don't disrespect me!" Billy Gudger shouted at no one in particular, rather like King Kong looking back at a building he had just punitively stomped.

He checked the bleeding of her forehead and seemed to dismiss it. It didn't look serious from where Jack Liffey sat either. Then he tied her hands behind her with the belt off the trenchcoat, picked her up easily and tossed her on the free end of the sofa. She wore a navy blue skirt that bunched awkwardly, and she looked over at Jack Liffey.

"This guy in bad way, I think."

"Shut up!"

It took awhile to find the right key on his key loop and then he unlocked the cuff that bound Jack Liffey's ankle to the metal frame of the sleeper-sofa. He yanked and fussed and Jack Liffey considered trying to give him a big kick but rejected it. The angle wasn't right to get up any steam, and now he had to worry about the young man taking out his anger on Tien, too. In a moment he found his ankle manacled again, apparently attached to hers, and apparently the links on the cuffs passed around something because his ankle was held even tighter than before.

Then Billy Gudger taped Tien's mouth shut, looping the duct tape around the back of her head, and he used some more over the belt that bound her hands, just to be sure. He sat on the ottoman and sighed and looked at the two of them for some time, hands on his knees, as if considering what to do next. It was probably a good sign that they were still alive, and they weren't out in the hills somewhere. He and Tien glanced at each other and the best he could do in greeting was to raise his eyebrows, whatever that might mean to her, and lean his shoulder against hers.

When he glanced up, Billy Gudger was standing up going through Tien's navy blue handbag. He took out a cell-phone and dropped it to the floor where he tromped on it again and again until the plastic plate that carried the dial buttons broke off and wires spilled out. Next he lifted out her keys, with a little cylinder of pepper spray attached. Too bad she hadn't had it in her hand when she stepped in the door and needed it, he thought, but you never did. His own .45 automatic was home inside a hollowed out *Oxford Companion to English Literature*.

Billy Gudger sprayed a little pepper into the air experimentally, and screwed up his nose at it. Pens and pencils, makeup and lipsticks, a Palm Pilot and a little box of Tic Tacs. He made a heap of it, upended the rest of the handbag's contents into the heap, and then kicked it all aside, studying the mess like a miner watching for gold flakes to rise out of the sifting.

Finally Billy Gudger picked up his treatise and hunted through it, flipping pages rapidly. Apparently he found what he wanted and nodded to himself. Then he took out a Swiss Army knife and locked open the main blade. Jack Liffey winced when it approached, but the boy carefully cut a slit in the tape between Jack Liffey's lips. He forced his lips as far apart as he could during the sawing and just managed to avoid the blade. He sucked, breathing in through his mouth which he could now open to a half inch pucker.

"I want you to listen to this part about the individual recapitulating the evolution of the race, and don't give me any *ad hominem* crap about my mother."

Loving but severe uncle, Jack Liffey thought. "Look Billy, if I'm going to get this situation straightened out, you've got to stop shutting down when people ask about your family." It didn't help that the duct tape only let him open his lips a half inch and made him speak in a tiny voice as if he had just sucked on a lemon. He was careful not to say "mother," though. "Asking about your family means people care about you. I don't just want to hear your philosophy. I want to know about your friends and your pets and how you felt about school and what games you liked and the places you've visited."

The young man rocked back a little, as if struck. "That's all subjective crap."

"Of course it is. We're all made up of subjective crap. Don't you want to know my subjective crap? I want to know where you went on your last vacation. I want to know your favorite movies, and what schools you went to."

He stuck out his chin. "My favorite movie was *Silence of the Lambs*."

That gave Jack Liffey a little chill, rising from the small of his back. "I don't believe you. You aren't like that at all."

"He was smarter than everybody."

"Hannibal Lecter didn't have a heart, and you do. This woman here is a very bright, strong, resourceful person. She has rescued herself from a bad situation in life more than once. You don't want to make the world worse by hurting someone like her or me. Let's find a way to save everybody here. So we can all be friends. It's not too late."

Billy Gudger sniggered. "Yes, it is. You know it is."

Jack Liffey shook his head. "No, they're going to blame this on sickness. Even if they're wrong, that's what they'll say, you know that, so the worst that can happen is you're going to end up in Vacaville. We can all visit there. You can read books. You can write. We can exchange critiques. I can look at your writing in comfort and then we can both read other writers and talk about them." He rolled on desperately. "I think you're missing some things in your philosophy, but I have to think it over in peace to figure it out. I don't mean you're wrong, but you've only got part of the truth, and you need to bounce your work off other people to refine it. A lot of people, not just me. Every philosopher has to do that. I can find people I respect to read what you've written and tell you what they think."

The young man's brows were furrowed up. "What's *missing*?" he said darkly.

Jack Liffey decided to take a flier, anything to keep Billy talking, put him off balance, get through to him. "You've read *Hamlet*, haven't you?"

"Of course."

"Hamlet delays and delays and delays, it's famous, and all that delay is because of what's inside him, just as you say. Something is working itself out in his character to make him hesitate and have second thoughts and wait too long before he acts."

The rain roared and a lightning flash caused the TV image to shrink for an instant, then the thunder crashed over them like rage. Somewhere inside, Jack Liffey wondered if he shouldn't have chosen *The Tempest* instead of *Hamlet*.

"Hamlet isn't alone on stage, Billy. He's delaying in relation to the people who come up against him, against the king who took his father's throne, against Polonius, Laertes, his own mother, Rosencrantz and Guildenstern. And all that changes *him*, too. It's the conflicts that make the story and make Hamlet what he is. I don't think your oscillating substrata *simply* develop out of an internal logic. You've got to find a way to combine your idea with all this contact with the outside world."

The young man stared bleakly at the treatise in his hands, as if it had betrayed him somehow.

"Just the way you're coming up against me now, and it's changing you. Can't you feel it? You're still you, but you've gained something new."

He clutched the bound essay to his chest protectively. "It all makes sense just the way it is."

"It doesn't hurt your ideas, Billy, it makes them bigger and richer. When they're perfected, they may be recognized as a real advance in philosophy. But I don't think they're ready yet."

He looked up suspiciously. "You're just buttering me up, trying to buy time."

"Of course I am. I want time for all of us. I want to be part of perfecting your ideas. I promise we can work this out."

Billy Gudger looked around, letting his eyes drift from object to object in the room, as if seeing them all in some new way, as if he might have to decide now to purchase or discard them. The object he decided on seemed to be the duct tape, and he tore off a strip and approached Jack Liffey.

"Billy, don't. Don't walk away from a chance to develop and perfect your ideas."

"I have to sleep on it."

He sealed up Jack Liffey's mouth again and stalked away through a door that appeared to lead to a bedroom. The TV brayed about great deals on used cars, and Jack Liffey looked at Tien Joubert, whose eyes were wide with some emotion, probably fear. They rubbed shoulders and the rain stroked and caressed the house all over, roof, windows, doors, trying to get in, like something out there with wicked intent that would keep at it until it found a way.

eighteen

A Duck's Quack Does Not Echo

She leaned slowly toward him like an antique tower deciding at last to topple and rested her head against his shoulder and he could feel her tremble, just a faint tremor like the passage of a subway train far under the street. It surprised him, she was usually so strong and self-contained. He tried to speak and was reminded of the terrible frustration of the gag, as the TV bellowed and blustered about a wet-dry vacuum that could suck a quart of beer right out of the rug. He glanced at the closed door to the bedroom, but it gave out no information. Now and again, as Tien rubbed her head rhythmically against his shoulder, there was a flash of white light reflecting back off the far wall and several seconds later, a faraway peal of thunder. Seven seconds was a mile, he remembered, the difference between the speeds of light and sound. He begged for a nice close lightning strike, no delay at all, that would take out a transformer and a few blocks of the power grid and shut off the egregious television. If it did, he tried to think of a way he could make some noise, but there didn't seem to be any way short of lifting the whole sofa off the floor by main force and hurling it through the front door. A newsbreak came on breathlessly, a flustered woman in a plastic raincoat talking about a mudslide somewhere in Silverlake that was taking out a half dozen hillside homes.

He turned his head to look into Tien's eyes, all glittery and wet with fright. The sight filled him with so much tenderness that he tried to tell her he loved her and he leaned over to rub his forehead against her. He felt her pressing the crown of her head back against him and making small mewling sounds and was astonished at himself when he started to get aroused. She moaned deeper and he let the side of his head slide down until he was rubbing his ear slowly across her breast. The jacket of her suit had come open and at first he just grazed the silk blouse and then he pressed harder so he could feel her breast in a very thin brassiere yielding under his temple, back and forth. It was surprisingly erotic when it was all you could do. He could sense if not quite feel her nipple stiffening against his cheek. He supposed it was like the fleeting glimpse of an ankle to the Victorians, just sufficient when it was all you had, and he felt her pressing back against him, almost crying with shudders of emotion. There were deep animal sounds from the back of her throat and only for an instant did he notice the jangly opening of an episode of *Starsky and Hutch*.

He tipped slowly and let his shoulders down until his head lay in her lap. It was impossibly uncomfortable the way his leg was pinioned, but he ignored the pain and let her thighs thrust up against him as he rubbed and rubbed with his chin, welcoming this strange conjunction of eros and fear. After a long while, he felt her tremble and then shudder and at last she gave a muffled cry. When he levered himself back up, he saw tears streaming down her cheeks, and somehow, as she rested her head against his shoulder again, releasing more terror with each sob, it was actually a relief to watch the everyday banality of a plumber swinging out of his truck with a friendly smile to promise rapid service, any day, any time.

Rain was pit-a-patting noisily in a downspout outside as her small head pressed against his chest and then slid down to rest her taped cheek against him. After a moment they could both feel him swelling, and his hips dug slowly against her. He wondered, if they should live through all this, if he would ever forget the incredible progression of foodstuffs that teased him then as she rubbed against his penis, over and over, the split bagel with cream cheese dewy with moisture, the egg-and-steak-and-hash browns breakfast at a chain restaurant, the steaming macaroni and cheese out of a packet, and the broken open chocolate candy bar he had never even heard of, the Groodle-bits, holding huge dusty almonds in its nougat. Seeing so much food reminded him of other appetites and how hungry he was, but not enough to distract him from the steady coercion of her cheek.

I'll never ever abandon you, he tried to say as emotion swept up through him and something tore open and light burst out of the place where he had torn open. And then they leaned against each other and she was humming a lullaby as the rain swelled and hammered and he did his best to follow along, humming, too, and death was so close and so tragic and so irrevocable that he felt something inside him changing imperceptibly, inch by inch, until he gave up all need to control the way things developed around him and only wanted to live to witness more and more.

In his mother's huge oversoft bed, he slept fitfully, but without his usual dreams, all those repeating motifs that he knew so well—the tidal flood rising slowly across some familiar town, the misplaced implement that he needed desperately, the circle of faces glaring at some mistake he couldn't have anticipated. Instead of these, he was being surrounded, approached by a simple cloud of pure darkness. His usual nightmares had always filled him with dread, but their extinction now seemed like an even more dire punishment. The darkness billowed closer, a palpable thing, squid ink on the air. And there was something inside that velvety murk, stirring, just waiting to spring at him.

He must have slept, because he woke with a jolt. It was still night and Billy Gudger stood in front of him, shaking his head darkly.

"It makes me too nervous," he explained. He held the pistol a-dangle from his hand, half forgotten.

Jack Liffey wasn't quite sure what the young man meant, but he had a bad feeling.

"It's too dangerous here."

He noticed that his foot was free of the sofa, though it was still cuffed to Tien, and he was barefoot now. He was astonished that Billy Gudger had got his shoes and socks off without waking him.

"Get her up now." He backed a few feet away while Jack Liffey nudged Tien Joubert awake. Her eyes came open with a start, and there was no recognition there for a moment, just a wild animal at bay, and then he could sense her awareness slowly filling up behind the blank black eyes like a warm liquid, and she made soft noises that could have meant anything.

"Help each other stand up."

Someone on the TV was giving advice on how to screw in a wall bracket to hold a curtain valance. The rain seemed to have stopped, because all he could hear from outside was the slow metallic drip in the downspout. By leaning forward they both managed to stand up, and Jack Liffey got a glance at an old Rainier Beer clock that said it was 3:45. He noticed that she was barefoot, too. For some reason he wasn't quite as frightened as he had been, though he had no illusions about what was happening. Jack Liffey was quite focused: their lives were in his hands now and he had to stay absolutely alert for the chance. There might never be an opening, but if there was, it would come and go quickly, and he had to take it without hesitation.

The same thought must have gone through Billy Gudger's mind for he kept his distance, and he'd taken to clutching the pistol against his chest, like a precious toy that might be snatched away by a bully.

"This way."

He took them through the kitchen, past the baleful freezer chest, and out onto the stoop. The wood was splintery and cold underfoot. The VW had been moved to the driveway, parked at the path that led from the door, and Jack Liffey could hear wind swishing in some huge dangly eucalyptus trees, an old farm windbreak at the side of the lot. The sky was dark and lumpy from horizon to horizon and there was enough moisture in the air for him to feel scattered pricklings, even drops. There was more rain coming. He was alert moment to moment, but there was no opportunity to do anything. Billy Gudger lowered the rear seat and hooked it flat and then forced them to get in and lie down on their faces in an unnatural tangle of limbs.

He heard the door slam and cranked his neck around to see the back of Billy's head, but they were cramped by the car's geometry and Tien was between him and the front seat so he could find nothing whatever that he could do with his right leg still fixed to her left and their arms manacled behind their backs. There was a screech like a finger on a blackboard, and another, and he craned up to see that the passenger-side wiper was missing and the metal arm was carving an arc into the windshield glass.

Jack Liffey held his head up as long as he could, watching as the car came out of the drive and turned left, then he let it droop and rest. Tien Joubert was trying to offer him some short message over and over near his ear, four or five words, but he couldn't make it out no matter how he tried to fit logical words to it. *Dum-ditty-dum, ditty-ditty-dum, dum-dum.* At the same time there was the screech-screech of the wiper scoring the glass, and then he could hear the rain picking up again on the roof. The young man drove badly, clutching and jamming the shift lever at the wrong shift points and sending the car into little lunges and jolts as it did its best to adjust to his shifts.

Dum-ditty-dum, ditty-ditty-dum, dum-dum.

Billy Gudger turned on the radio, an all-news station offering a cute story about an unauthorized delivery of forty-five pizzas to the Orange County central jail, and Tien Joubert gave up on her message. Soon the radio snapped off again. The car rocked to the side in what was probably a gust of wind.

"Local news is so bad," Billy Gudger offered over his shoulder, as if trying hard to entertain a date. "They should be ashamed."

He certainly seemed to have compartmented off what he was doing. Jack Liffey wished he could talk to him to try working him around, but there was nothing much he could do with grunts and moans. He scraped his mouth again and again against the rough carpet under him but the tape wouldn't budge. When he raised his head again, he thought they were heading along Chapman toward the hills and that made him a little sick to his stomach. The very hills where all the bodies had been found, including Phuong's. He had seen no traffic at all on the shiny streets, and reminded himself it was after 4 A.M. now. A corner with two overbright but deserted gas stations and then a few dark businesses petering out to the beginning of the foothills and soon the only light was their own headlights, even that hardly showing up on the wet streets that were reflecting almost all of the light forward. The wiper still screeched on and on in its insane rhythm.

"Did you know that a duck's quack doesn't echo?" Billy Gudger informed them. "No one knows why. It's strange."

Yes, it was strange, Jack Liffey thought, but he had no free mental capacity for thinking about a duck's quack. In a few minutes, he craned his neck up again and saw a lighted compound in the distance behind a chain-link fence with a lot of earthmovers and graders. They were passing over the torn-up landscape where the new toll road was coming through, and he realized that they were following exactly the route he had taken to talk to Philip Marlowe. He supposed there was something ironic in that, but thinking about irony wasn't very fruitful.

The off-side tires hit gravel and Billy Gudger yanked on the wheel to correct. "Oops," he announced after the car had settled back onto the pavement. "I'm not a very great driver, I guess."

The engine gave a little hitch now and then, but that had been a characteristic of the carburetion on his own old VW, too, and a breakdown out here was too much to hope for. Tien Joubert rested against his arm passively, seemingly given up to her fate. In a few minutes there was a real jolt and then the car carried on hammering on its springs and they'd obviously come off onto a dirt road. When Jack Liffey looked he could see nothing at all to the side of the car, so he craned his neck to the front and saw headlights picking out a curving fire trail. The hillsides off the trail were a little less dark than the sky and, for just an instant, he saw the witchy gnarled shape of a live oak.

"I'm sure glad they graded this road recently."

For quite some time, Jack Liffey could feel the car climbing and descending and winding along the rough road in noisy second gear, and he didn't let himself think about death. He knew, with their high clearance and so much weight over the drive wheels, VWs were pretty good at bad roads, and he couldn't count on getting bogged down. All he could do was stay alert to every fact he could gather in, approximately where he was, the sounds, the time—at least 4:15 now—the weather, and the psychological tenor of Billy Gudger. He kept himself hanging on the knife-edge, lit by the searchlight of his intense concentration, waiting for the most minute fault line in their fate.

"Hey, this looks pretty good."

The car came to a stop with a little gravelly skid, and Billy got out and yanked the seat forward. He backed away, holding the gun on the two of them, the whole strange tableau visible in the dome light.

"Come on out. It's only drizzling."

Jack Liffey wondered what on earth they were supposed to think this was all about—a little excursion to study plant life in the hills? But Billy Gudger probably wasn't thinking rationally just then, and it may have taken his full attention to cordon off whatever was going on in his consciousness. Jack Liffey remembered that passive tense— "something had happened" to Billy Gudger's mother. Something was almost certainly about to happen to them, too.

He delayed as long as he could, readjusting his leg to make it difficult for Tien to unfold herself, considering what he could do out there in the cold, damp, dangerous world. The headlights were still on, though the engine had stopped, and a gusty breeze was tearing past the car, driving shimmery curtains of drizzle before it. They were parked on a turnout off the dirt road, scarred by many tires and broken up by shallow pools of rainwater. It stopped abruptly at a low line of weed that seemed to indicate a dropoff into a canyon. It was hard to orient in the darkness.

Then they were both standing beside the car, his feet hurting on the sharp chilly ground, and Billy Gudger, who stood near the edge of the canyon, was watching them like a hawk twenty feet away. If there was going to be a crease in possibility, Jack Liffey knew with an abrupt chill of dread unlike anything he had ever known before, it had to be right about *now*, and he didn't see one. Lightning flashed and gave him an instantaneous vision of the surroundings. There was indeed a canyon, and a hillside on the far side of the canyon maybe a hundred yards away, but it was impossible to know how deep the canyon was, or how steep the drop-off was past the weeds, but the rolling hills weren't rocky and the far side didn't seem all that steep.

"I want you to see something," Billy Gudger said and beckoned.

Jack Liffey guided their steps away from the car, closer to the young man than Tien seemed to want, but not close enough to alarm him. He kept between them, and trended slightly toward the young man but turned his eyes to the ground as if all he was interested in was keeping his footing and avoiding sharp stones. A little turn, a misstep, as if avoiding a sharp rock. If only he could yell to her, he thought, but this inability to communicate was just another handicap they were forced to carry.

Surprise was the only thing he had. And if he didn't get a sliver of opportunity, he would have to make one. At his closest approach to the young man, Jack Liffey hesitated, timing himself, waiting until both he and Tien had their weight just coming off the feet that were bound together, then he let all his fear and rage go and hurled himself all at once at Billy Gudger to butt him sprawling back. Then he turned and threw his body at Tien Joubert so together they fell into the weeds at the edge of the little plateau and he wrenched around and kicked out so they went over the raw edge. He tried to cry out at the freefall into the dark, but he couldn't, and then they hit the slope and his shoulder and arm were scraped by a giant cheese grater. A gunshot flashed above them and another, echoing and rumbling in the hills like more thunder. They came to rest where the slope leveled off and she was up again even faster than he was and they high-stepped further downhill the best they could in utter darkness with their feet lashed together. Their salvation would be if Billy Gudger lacked a flashlight. He'd never get the headlights pointed downhill.

Two more shots were squeezed off, but there was little danger from that now. He could spray the darkness all night and have little chance of hitting them. Jack Liffey tripped on a shrub and they fell again, and he tore a lot of skin off his right knee as the tumble turned into a bewildering muddle of limbs. He felt a sudden yank on his leg and then they seemed to hit bottom. A few inches of fizzy ice-cold water ran around and over them.

He lay still and caught his breath. Over the gurgling of the rain-creek he heard a plaintive wail, "Come back! I'm not going to hurt you!"

There was a delight at the absurdity of Billy Gudger's wail, but even more at the sudden prospect of continued life, and Jack Liffey tried to laugh, which the gag turned into a choke and swallow. Tien Joubert lay stock still beside him, and he hoped she hadn't been badly hurt. As he lay, he felt the rain grow heavier and he offered his thanks to the rain gods because the sound would cover any noises they made and probably drive the young man back into his car. Slowly he became aware of his body. Something had cut one of his bare feet and it hurt a lot. His knee was cut, too, and his right arm was on fire. He waited for his eyes to adjust but there was almost no improvement in the moonless overcast, many miles from city lights. All he could eventually make out was a patch of brighter cloud to what was probably the west, the underside lit a dull orange by city lights, and against that he could see the pure black of hills, and then he turned and gradually he made out a smaller pool of light above him, the headlights of the Volkswagen reflecting off a shrub. It was a lot closer than he wanted it to be.

"Nobody comes here!" he heard. Billy Gudger's voice was shrill and desperate. "I'll get you the minute it's light!" Something hit the ground and skittered down the slope. Soon there were other impacts around him, in the dirt and the stream, and he realized the young man was hurling rocks down the ravine, some quite heavy judging from the thuds.

He nudged Tien and pressed his cheek against her face until he could feel her breathing. His clothes were torn and sopping wet now and one sleeve hung off his fiery arm like a rag, and now he started shuddering with the chill. There wasn't enough light for him to see if Tien's clothes were torn up, too, or if she was injured anywhere.

He sat up to try to get what bearings he could, then realized that a strange exercise in the geometry of the human body might just be possible, the geometry of two bodies actually, the Houdini maneuver of getting his cuffed hands around to his front. He stretched his arms to their full extent behind him and wriggled and got them at last under his buttocks, wincing with pain, and then it was a snap to worm backwards enough to get his linked hands up behind his knees. He thought it would be easy from there, but it wasn't, and after a long fight with his bare feet he was almost resigned to spending the rest of a short life as a human cannonball. Pressing against Tien for leverage, he finally got the heel of the free foot bent back enough to catch onto the links between the handcuffs. He probably wouldn't have made it with the shoe on, he knew he wasn't all that limber, but he got the first foot over the barrier and then straightened his leg with a sigh. Now he only had to deal with the leg that was cuffed to Tien.

This meant passing his linked wrists under his foot and hers at the same time, and it nearly dislocated his shoulder to accomplish it. He stopped and gasped for breath for a moment. He hadn't realized he'd been holding his breath so long during the effort. The rest of the Houdini maneuver was easy. She was so slim that he slid his linked wrists up over both her legs to her hips, and then he hugged the soggy bundle of her and pulled her over on top of him so he could slide his hands up over her pinioned arms and off over her head.

Done it! he exulted, waving his cuffed wrists over his head in elation. His wrists were still linked, and he was still manacled to her leg, but there was a lot he could do now with his hands in front.

"Mr. Liffey! You said you wanted to be my friend!" The whine curled forlornly out into the rain, too near for comfort. And like a duck's quack, he thought meanly, there seemed to be no echo.

He set Tien Joubert back gently on the edge of the streamlet. First he used his hands to find the seams in the duct tape and tear the front of his gag free of his mouth to suck in a wonderful cool breath. For the moment, he left the rest of the tape caught up in his hair and turned to freeing Tien's hands. Her hands were only bound by tape over the belt of her trenchcoat. The tape gave quickly in the wet, but the knot in the belt was soggy and it took a few moments with his chilled fingers to work it loose. He got her hands free and then her gag.

"Tien," he said softly into her ear. "Are you okay?"

He felt the thump of a really large rock striking down nearby, followed by the sounds of a tiny avalanche loosed by the rock. A few grains of sand raked his cheek and he figured it was time to push on. She was still limp against him and there was no reply. Laboriously, he tied the belt tight around her waist, the way he'd seen transport belts tied to the elderly in nursing homes. He wormed his linked arms back over her head and down over her shoulders, then by grasping the belt and rising on one knee he could pull her half up against his chest. It was lucky she didn't weigh much, probably not even 100 pounds.

He leaned into her weight and stood up, tottering a little and awaking a sharp pain in his back that made him gasp. She hung limp in his arms, and he boosted her a little against his chest, as high as he could lift her with the other set of handcuffs tearing at his ankle. Little by little he stepped forward, feeling his way with his bare feet on the stones and sucking mud of the canyon. The chilly water was maybe two inches deep but it was the only guide he had to direction, and he chose to move downstream, which would inevitably be toward civilization. He knew it would probably be the direction Billy Gudger would expect, but he had a horror of moving deeper into the desolate hills, away from even the theoretical possibility of rescue.

His foot slipped on a smooth wet rock, and he caught himself and chanced a glance upward. Apparently the VW lights had been turned off because he couldn't see a thing, not even a glow where they should have been. He hadn't heard any more rocks for a while, but the rain was picking up and would cover a lot of sound, including his own. Here and there the stones underfoot were sharp and he had to hunt gingerly with his bare foot before putting his weight down. Progress seemed glacial, and he was forced to stop regularly to rest the best he could while bearing Tien's weight.

After what seemed an interminable blind progress downhill, the footing seemed to get better, sandy and yielding a bit under foot, almost like a beach. It was such a relief that he got himself moving with too much confidence, and all of a sudden the footing disappeared, just vanished from under him and they fell through space for a second. He cried out involuntarily, regretting his haste, and then they hit in an explosion of splintering twigs. They ended up sprawled side by side on some prickly bush, his arms still locked around her. He rolled a little to look around again and noticed, as the sparkles of false light on his retinas faded away, that above him he could just see the shapes of the darker hills and brush, as if cut out of flat black metal and propped up against the perceptibly lighter charcoal of the cloud cover. Downstream nearby, against a V of sky, there was one hump that was probably a sumac the size of a small car. It would have to do, he thought.

Without attempting to get up again, he crawled and dragged her along the streambed and then the few feet up the near slope. The lowest limbs of the sumac actually touched the ground, and he squirmed and tugged and finally got the two of them in under the leaf cover, raked by the branches. He wedged them there against a substantial trunk. In a moment he would try to do something about making it more comfortable, he thought, but before the moment came, his head tilted back on its own and he fell fast asleep.

nineteen

The Kind Called *Agape*

His eyes snapped open at the jolt of adrenalin. It was as if he'd actually felt the process occur inside him, a squirt of the hormone jetting out of some aperture into the small of his back with a tiny liquid sound and instantly his heart was racing like a kid revving a drag engine. There was enough light just gathering to make out the rich green ovals of the leaves that caged him in. It was remarkable how little light you needed to see all you had to. But the main focus of his mind swiveled quickly to the why of the adrenalin. What had frightened him awake like that? And then he heard a crackle and a faint scraping sound near his feet and he boosted his head so fast he smacked it hard into a sumac limb as thick as his forearm. He was staring straight into the deep brown eyes of a coyote, its bulk showing clearly in a ragged spot of the bush. The beast spooked back a few inches, whimpered once, and took a sidestep.

"Shoo, boy," Jack Liffey said gently, and the animal reared once like the Lone Ranger's horse and shot away.

His accelerator immediately dropped a notch, and he heard Tien Joubert snoring faintly against his chest and was thankful that she was alive. His arms were still wrapped around her and held there by the handcuffs. Her jacket had been torn to a rag, and the silk blouse wasn't much better, hanging off one intact sleeve and dangling across him, leaving a blue brassiere tugging awkwardly on her breasts. Her skirt rode up under the grab belt he had tied around her and it was ripped at the side. He discovered he was no clothes mannequin either. His shirt was shredded and both knees of his pants hung open like lolling tongues. Not far away he could hear the gurgle of water, and then, just once, the forlorn warning cries of a bird.

He slid his arms off over Tien's head, then wriggled his shoulders out of the foliage so he could see up into the clouds that were torn apart to reveal lozenges of deep purple sky. The sun would be up before long. The rain had stopped. The hillside nearby was a lot steeper than his mental picture of it, dotted with sumac and grassy clumps and aloes, plus one big patch of beavertail cactus that it was fortunate they had missed in their erratic downstream progress.

Beyond the nearest ridge there was a farther hill-line that still had scraps of mist clinging to low trees. There were houses on a far ridge-line beyond that, but so far away that they were only the size of matchheads. They had to be miles. He could see the fire trail where they had been driven in, maybe thirty yards up the slope, and there were no vehicles to be seen, especially not a black VW.

Jack Liffey hauled himself back under cover and lay still for a moment, then smoothed the troubled surface of Tien's forehead.

"Tien, wake up. It's okay now."

She didn't stir, and he shook her shoulder.

"Tien, don't scare me. Please wake up."

He shook harder, until one eye came open experimentally in her porcelain face. It was a moment before he saw an intelligence gathering behind the eye. Then she groaned and sat up so quick she hit the same bough he had.

"Oww. This place no good."

"Shhh. It's plenty good for cover until we know where Billy is."

"Billy! You call him *Billy*, like your sister little boy or something!"

"He's human, but his head is so full of loneliness that it made him sick."

"You got that, one hundred percent. I'm cold." Then she nestled against him, and he put his linked arms over her head and shoulders again.

"This is the best I can do right now."

"It pretty good."

He had meant just to help warm her but they could both feel him becoming aroused. This is not the time, he thought, but his libido had a mind of its own.

After a few wriggles, she craned her neck back and kissed him passionately. "You one very sweet man," she said as she slid down and bit one of his nipples softly.

Right consequences follow right thoughts, he thought for some crazy reason. And the opposite—oh, yes, the opposite. After all, they had a right to celebrate being alive.

Her small hands were hard at work on his chinos and then she had them unzipped and his penis was in her squeezing hands. He saw her lick one of her fingers and play with him tenderly in a gentle kind of sex play he'd never seen anyone do before, and then she had pressed his chest down and she was on top of him. She used her hands to help guide him and he slid easily inside her.

"Jack, Jack, you feel so good in me. I want you there forever."

Afterward, they lay back in the glowing morning as the first sunlight broke through the leaves and dappled them with bright fuzzy ovals, like some omen of providential change written into a soapy film. The fingers of light were actually warm where they touched and caressed in the morning breeze.

"We must be nuts," he said. "Making love like ferrets."

"Yeah, sure. I got to tell you something now, Mr. Jack Liffey."

"That sounds serious." He rolled a little to watch her. She put her brassiere back on, tugged the scrap of blouse over one shoulder and rubbed her hands together to exorcise a little chill. Her eyes were fixed on his chest instead of his face.

"This not so easy."

"I won't eat you up."

"We do that, too, in a little bit," she said, misunderstanding. "I got to tell you something now. I lie. I never went to no Sorbonne for no business course. I learn business things in noodle stall and shoe stall and dresses shop in the Petit Saigon in Marseilles. I keep numbers and inventory and things in my head." She poked her forehead with a finger. "And I learn business another way earlier. Uh-huh. I learn very tough way."

She had apparently reached the sticking point. There was something that was trying hard but it was caught sideways in her throat and just wouldn't tear loose.

"Oh. Oh . . . oh."

"It's okay, Tien." He squeezed her arm.

"Back in Viet Nam. I was bar girl, Tu Do Street, Jack. I was never no general wife. I was from poor family in little village and ran away and. . . . "

She was crying, a few tears trickling along her cheek.

"I great big whore, my lovely lovely Jack. Sit in many laps, guys I don't like very much. Fuck-fuck many GIs."

"Tien, I've always known that." It wasn't strictly true, but he'd guessed. She had such a bad case of bar-girl English, and there had always been something a little too streetwise about her. "In your soul, you're a beautiful, stubborn, resourceful princess, pure as new snow."

She wailed once at that, and he had to put his hand over her mouth to shush her, and then she was sobbing and bucking against him with the anguish of memories that he would probably never be able to appreciate. It was a long time before her paroxysm of memory subsided, and he lay holding her on the rocky slope listening to wind and water and a faint buzz that was beginning to arouse his curiosity.

"You know what I was and you still want me?"

"As much as ever," he said, aware of what a hedge it was. There was a practical world beyond their sheltering bush, with another woman in it and even an ex-wife and a daughter, and if they ever managed to survive Billy Gudger, he had no idea how that could all be reconciled. "If anything gets in the way, it won't be your past."

"I love you, Mr. Jack. You too too super."

"I love you, too, Miss Tien Nguyen Joubert."

She rubbed her forehead against his jaw. "Anybody tell you your pronunciation really *really* bad."

"Only people who know."

Then she wailed once again, the emotion dropping down abruptly out of the blue, and he had to cover her mouth.

When she finally cried herself out, he realized they had better try to get to civilization.

"To tell the truth, I'm a little afraid to crawl out of this hiding place, but we can't live here forever."

"Yes, we can," she said. "I keep house for you here. We put TV over there and stove there, and I show you how to cook *pho* just right."

The feeling of safety in the place was evaporating rapidly in the daylight, and fear came down the hillside from the fire road and touched him with its cool breath.

"Billy said he'd be back with the dawn, and I don't know how far I got us before we passed out here. Probably only a couple hundred yards."

He put his head out again, almost blinded by the glare as the sun streamed down through a good-sized break in the cloud. Facing in the downstream direction, toward the world, he could see faraway dark clouds still pouring out their slanting mists, and even a fragment of a rainbow.

No more rain but fire next time, he thought. There weren't even the faint sounds of traffic, just a subtle buzz that turned out to be a high tension tower that he hadn't noticed before. He decided to make for the tower. They always had cleared dirt trails alongside them for service and it would take him away from that other, more dangerous road.

"Let's get moving."

They scrambled out of the shelter, linked legs yanking awkwardly against each other. When he unfolded his limbs to stand up, he realized just how sore he was, in almost every joint and muscle, but he hoped things would improve once they got moving. She dusted drying mud off her legs and what remained of her clothing, and for the first time she noticed the belt he had tied around her waist.

"What this thing?"

"I think they call it a gait belt. It helped me carry you."

She hugged him. "This like cowboy movie. You not ride away and leave wounded friend for Indians."

He pointed down at the handcuffs on their ankles. "Our fate is one."

"Ah."

"How are you feeling?"

"Like some dinner left from other Wednesday."

He smiled and took her hand, and they set off uphill to intersect what looked like a deer track that would take them up toward the tower. Barefoot, the climb was no picnic as sharp little granite flakes made them step carefully. As they clambered up the slope, the buzz grew stronger and gained an electrical crackle. Before they got very far, she stopped him.

"I sorry, Jack, but I *got* to find a bush and do some business."

"Sure." He pointed to a dense sugarbush. She squatted and he turned away, as far toward decent discretion as he could get, and glanced around the hills vigilantly. The rain seemed to be giving up. A contrail was visible high up in a big break in the cloud and the air had that crystaline sparkle that it did after a rain, the trees along the ridge lines sharp and distinct like models for an untainted world. They had climbed enough that he had a clear view of the fire road the VW had come in on. It was on the opposite slope, and his eye traced it uphill to what must have been the turnout where Billy Gudger had parked. They hadn't come very far at all in the night.

"Okay, guy. Happy campers now."

He took her hand again and they set off. As long as he kept his offside pace short, they managed a pretty good rhythm, like experts at the three-legged race at a company picnic. Before long they reached the graded service road, which was better underfoot, and then in a few minutes the ridge where the snap-crackling power pylon was rooted on little cement pedestals, behind a chain-link fence. Looking down the other side he saw what he hadn't taken into account. The power lines tended to advance along a straight line, heedless of the terrain, and staying on the service road would force them up and down a roller coaster of ridges. But he had no intention of retracing Billy's passage in.

"Follow the yellow brick road," he said.

He waited by the dilapidated shed with his binoculars slung around his neck and the pistol tucked into his waist. From here he had a view of the confluence of three canyons that fanned up into the hills, and unless the two of them took some absurdly roundabout path he would certainly intercept them here. A red-tailed hawk circled. Signs and wonders, he thought.

This was a very bad place, he decided, the temple of some demiurge, perhaps the very thing that was dogging him from within its billowy dark aura. He realized he had brought the car to quite the wrong place the night before without knowing it. And his anger knew no bounds against Mr. Liffey. Betraying him and then running away, purposely misunderstanding everything, depriving him of a mentor who could have helped him reach a new level.

He saw a lupine blooming purple in the early wet, and he translated in his head:

> Here are fruits, flowers, leaves, and branches.
> And here is my heart which beats only for you.

It was Paul Verlaine, part of Billy Gudger's covenant with himself to master 19th-century French literature, on the way to reading the French post-structuralists. Just one night before, Billy Gudger remembered that Jack Liffey had rejected his beating heart. In fact, his rage had been so great at the rejection, standing in the cold rain in the night, that he had almost shot himself in the leg as he thrust the pistol back into his belt. It was probably only the ministrations of the toadstone, not yet enfeebled by the demiurge, that had sent the 9mm jacketed round burning down along his thigh and harmlessly into the earth. His last friend, the small freak object in his skull, and not much of a friend at that.

Everything is wrecked, he had thought last night, fuming and stomping his foot on the muddy road. Abandoned to his own devices, he had no choice but to follow the evil that was woven into the fabric of his life, and it was an unspeakable disappointment because there had been a promise of relief, if only he had been appreciated. He had gone home and lain awake, flip-flopping from a sense of overwhelming need and humiliation, from snatches of tormenting thoughts that bubbled up out of his psyche and repeated themselves over and over in his head, to drum in their laughter and ridicule. *They're going to blame this on sickness.* He heard Jack Liffey say that phrase over and over, until he could no longer make out the tone the man had used, and his fears convinced him it had been contempt.

They're going to blame this on sickness.

Lying in his bed, no, *her* big bed in the main house, his head had filled with grief, then emptied, filled again, until he decided he had to find a way to make this much suffering mean something. He made a conscious effort to think of the kindness Jack Liffey had shown him, the offers of help and companionship, and then he found it in himself to forgive, and he wept for an hour straight. It was love he knew he then felt for Jack Liffey—not romantic love, of course, but the kind called *agape*, the more common of the two New Testament Greek words for love, the one that was sometimes crudely denoted "brotherly love" but in fact carried the immense weight of the preciousness and worthiness of the one loved. Even thinking it now, his eyes filled with tears at his own virtue in offering Jack Liffey his *agape*.

He had slept two hours before dawn, and awoke refreshed, and now he had to find Jack Liffey and express this feeling for him. It could change everything. The woman was irrelevant. He would not harm her because he knew doing so would be bad for his relationship with Jack Liffey, but he cared neither one way nor the other about her and never had.

He searched the sopping wet hillside with his binoculars. Nothing yet, but they would come. The toadstone throbbed like a small hard point of purpose at the center of his head, and for the moment, the dark cloud seemed to hold back, bustling and purring now.

They came over another ridge and he saw below that the power line road intersected a firebreak. The roads came in at an angle, and for some reason he remembered Casey Stengel's famous declaration, "Whenever you come to a fork in the road, take it." Indeed, he thought.

In the crotch of the fork, there was a ramshackle little shanty that had probably once held tools for roadwork, though in his experience you found these little huts in every out-of-the-way area in the West, from deserts to mountain ravines, and you never would figure out their purpose. He considered shouldering in through the corrugated metal door, and wondered if he'd find a tool to pry at the handcuffs, or even something he could use as a weapon. He felt terribly defenseless.

"I'm so hungry I could eat my arm," she declared.

He was so woozy in the head that he actually tried to take her observation seriously. He wondered if those air crash victims in the Andes could have eaten their own nonessential body parts for strength, a finger or a whole hand to get started on their trek, the forearm the next day, then up to the shoulder. Where would the critical point come? A leg—as long as the other was left to hop onward to safety?

"There are a lot of your body parts I could snack on," he said, and she took his arm with small warm hands and squeezed.

He thought he heard a skittering in the brush as they came down toward the shed, probably another coyote or some jackrabbit tucking back into its hole.

And then Billy Gudger was standing right there in the sun, clasping at his pistol with both hands as if a breeze might come up and pluck it away from him.

"*Shit!*" Jack Liffey yelled, and it seemed to startle the young man.

"Don't move don't move don't move!" Billy Gudger acted bewildered.

"What you going to want . . . ?" Tien started in with a menacing throb in her voice.

"Hush," Jack Liffey said. His mind was back into high gear, pushing the weariness and the cruel disappointment away. "Billy, you don't want to hurt anybody. We can all work together to find a solution for this."

The young man seemed frozen, immobilized by some struggle inside himself.

"Please don't let yourself believe that because you did something once, you have to go on doing it," Jack Liffey said. "Every one of us is better than the worst things we do." He rememberered someone saying that, perhaps Father Greg Boyle.

The young man gagged a couple of times and then a word emerged. It sounded like "Agape."

Could it possible have been *agape*? Jack Liffey knew it was Greek, but he couldn't for the life of him remember what it meant.

"It's okay, Billy. Just be calm."

The young man was crying, trembling with it, tears gushing down his cheeks. "I want. Help."

"Sure, of course you do. I'll help you. I'll stay with you and make sure things work out. I'm a little cold and sore right now. Could we go somewhere more comfortable and talk?"

Billy Gudger nodded crazily, almost as if his head had taken off on its own and he couldn't stop it. The young man kept his distance, but motioned them along a spur road. Jack Liffey relaxed a notch inside. If the young man had meant to kill them, the time to do it was passing. As long as they didn't antagonize him, they had a chance to get back to civilization where a gunshot would be impossible. Tien came along quietly, holding Jack Liffey's arm like a C-clamp and apparently trusting him to handle things. The black VW was parked just out of sight where the side road stopped dead in a box canyon.

They were made to swear not to cause trouble and then put into the folded-down backseat again. Billy Gudger was still having trouble talking, and his eyes were red-rimmed and a little crazy.

The car roared to life and then slowly joggled down out of the hills, and Jack Liffey decided a soothing voice was a good idea so he went on at random about redemption and the transforming power of kindness.

"When I was a child, Billy, I was very lonely like you and I walked along a path that I thought was the path of honor, but all of a sudden one day I came to a fork and I didn't know what to do. I didn't even know the path of life had forks back then. I thought the path I was on was perfectly simple. There was a kind of fierce personal honor that I followed like a pole star, and the only alternative was these fantasies I had of incredible violence. If my honor was violated, I had to obliterate whatever caused it. But then I stumbled on a fork that I didn't know was there. I started to see another world along this other road where I might be able to love things that weren't perfect as well as hate the bad. It was a world where things were a lot less simple, but I realized that I shared coming to that place with thinkers all through history and they all found ways to say good-bye to their violent dreams. It's the fork to growing up, Billy. And I took it."

"I'm so tired," the young man said.

"That's because you've been holding onto everything by yourself. I'll take some of your burden now."

The young man nodded. "Please. I can't think any more now. We can talk soon."

"That's fine," Jack Liffey said. "Remember, I'm with you, whatever you need."

Tien rested her head against his chest, and he realized none of them had slept very much that long, long night.

twenty

Waking from Sleep

He kept getting the impression that Billy Gudger wanted to apologize for something as he drove, but the apologies aborted themselves, one after another, in chagrined head bobs until Jack Liffey
and Tien Joubert found themselves back in the dismal house and
ankle-cuffed to the old sleeper sofa again and the TV was on loud to
a soap opera, and it was as if the intervening night and morning had
never existed, except that all three of them had somehow got muddy
and wounded and exhausted. In some curious prudery, Billy draped
a knitted afghan over Tien's shoulders so he wouldn't have to look
at her fluorescent blue brassiere.

Billy sat down in the overstuffed chair under the flying ducks, and
he played with the pistol idly as if it were something else. Jack Liffey
knew he had to stay focused and keep his spirits well up to deal with
Billy on some very intense level now. If he was going to get a break
this time it wouldn't be a physical opening, but some manner of
worming his way through a chink in the young man's psyche. After
all the failing relationships that he had navigated through, Jack
Liffey felt he had developed a pretty good ear for the moment-to-
moment—the shadings that were revealed as hearts shifted imperceptibly toward danger or away. And he knew that trying too hard,

or seeming to, could drag you right back to the thing you feared the most, so he needed as delicate a touch as he could possibly devise, but he was so weary it was hard even to stay awake.

Billy Gudger stared intently at the floor. Without warning he looked up and spoke with a fierce petulance.

"You betrayed me and ran away. I don't know how I could ever trust you again."

Jack Liffey was taken aback. Having recently been driven far into the night in order to be murdered, it was hard to readjust to seeing his attempted escape as a kind of betrayal. "Billy, I'm sorry you feel that I failed you. I can understand how that makes you feel. Sometimes it's best after a bad experience not to try to rebuild things on the same ground, but to start all over again. We need to find a ground to build our friendship on that we both trust."

"I just don't know." The young man crossed his arms, and from somewhere deep inside himself, Jack Liffey was surprised to find he could muster a sense of empathy for all that deranged loneliness.

"I know next to nothing about toadstones," he said. "That's certainly something you have on me. Could you tell me about them?"

"I hope you had fun in Santa Royale with your obliging little slut!" a stringy blond woman on the TV proclaimed.

"It's a bufonite," Billy Gudger blurted, as if correcting the diction of the woman on the screen. He halted and glared at Jack Liffey, considering whether he was going to explain the term, but finally gave in and his tone softened. "That's a kind of bony fossil. I told you. Many of them were just the teeth and palate bones of a fish that stuck together and fossilized that way, but people believed they formed in the heads of toads, I don't know why. They wore them for good luck and to ward off evil spells. My mom is three parts gypsy and she always had lots of seeing powers, and she told me that most of the toadstones in museums and private collections were just what the scientists thought, fossilized teeth and palate bones, but every once in a while there was a real one that actually had formed in the head of a toad. And not just toads, either. There was a time when I was little when I started slurring words and they thought I had a brain tumor and they did an X-ray. Mom says she saw the X-ray and though there was no tumor, there was very clearly a toadstone, like a calcified kidney stone or something down by the medulla. Maybe it should be called a Billystone." He chuckled, but the humor collapsed instantly. "Mom said it would protect me always, but it hasn't done a very good job."

"Did you look at the X-ray?"

He shook his head. "I was afraid to."

"Afraid you'd see it or afraid you wouldn't?"

"Either way, it would be out of my control. Who wants to know something you can't control?"

"Can you always control things? Isn't it better sometimes to sit back and let things take their own course?"

"Oh, no. What if things went the wrong way and they didn't work out at all? What if something made you look stupid or people laughed at you?"

That's the human condition in a nutshell, Jack Liffey thought.

"You were sleeping with our own *therapist*!" a man on TV brayed.

"Didn't anybody every tell you about the little bird?"

"What bird?"

Tien Joubert stirred, watching his performance intently.

"If you catch a little bird in your hands, you can feel its heart beating against your palms, but you can never make it do what you want it to do. It's too delicate and frightened and too willful, and if you try to make it do something, you'll end up breaking its tiny bones and killing it. All you can do is let it fly in the room and patiently wait until it lands on your shoulder. You give it what it needs and slowly you become its friend."

Billy Gudger's eyes had got their nervous look again, flitting to strange corners of the room, as if looking for the little bird on the wing.

"But sometimes the bird chooses to land somewhere else again and again, and you have to accept that, too. You just have to wait."

"That sounds like the lie people always tell you to get their own way. I'm so tired of talking."

"Giving people the freedom to be themselves is what friendship is about. It opens your heart and makes you bigger inside. I want us both to be able to be who we are."

"I don't *know*." His eyes finally came to rest on the smashed-open cellular phone in the middle of the floor. "Too-Tired Billy," he said, as if selecting his own Homeric epithet.

The night of sleeplessness and emotional pandemonium was getting to them all.

"Don't go off half-cocked," a voice blurted from the television. "At least wait until you're full-cocked."

"I can't think right now."

"I'll be your friend, Billy. You don't have to try to force me."

The young man's head rolled to one side and the pistol fell between his thighs and he was fast asleep. Jack Liffey gauged the distance across the room and knew it was hopeless to get that far with his leg manacled to the heavy sofa. And even with the two of them on the floor, straining together, they would never be able to budge the heavy sleeper-sofa.

While he was still inspecting alternatives in his head, the sofa heaved and Tien Joubert was abruptly on her knees on the hooked rug, then stretching out full length until her fingertips reached the smashed cell phone and dragged it toward her. The broken dial pad trailed jerkily on the rug, drawn on by a skein of fine wires. She punched at the dial pad after she gathered it in, but couldn't get a light to come on. Then she hit what he thought was probably redial on the body of the phone itself and though he could hear nothing, he saw her attention rivet to the telephone. She pressed it to her ear, waited a half minute and began speaking rapidly in Vietnamese. She rattled on for a couple of minutes and then hit another button and pushed the phone back where it had been.

She clung to the afghan and slithered back onto the sofa to nestle against him.

"Did you get through?"

"Only place I could call. Last number I call yesterday was Thang Le and the *Quan Sats*. Part of peace treaty I not tell you about, secret stuff just like Paris, I offer them work in import business."

"You got them on the line just now?"

"I get their machine."

"What did you tell their machine?"

"I say this crazy roundeye guy, he keep big bars of gold bullion in his freezer. They can come and get it like picking daisy from baby."

Jack Liffey let his head loll back against the sofa. "Oh, Lord. Did you have some reason for picking the freezer?"

He could feel her shrug. "I see it when he drag me through room there. I just think of it."

He laughed ruefully to himself for a moment. It was too ghastly and farcical a picture, a half dozen *Quan Sats* invading the house in their black jumpsuits and balaclavas, waving little spray guns as they hurled up the lid of the freezer chest to see the rump of Billy Gudger's very dead mother.

He watched Billy Gudger slumped in the chair opposite, his mouth open and drooling a little, the pistol fallen between his legs and pointing straight back at his own private parts, really nothing more than a vulnerable and broken child who had never had much of a chance in the world. He wondered if he had an obligation to wake the young man and warn him about the danger heading his way. He had offered to be his friend, and this would certainly be the final betrayal. Some friend, he thought. On the other hand, it would end their ordeal in an instant if the *Quan Sats* came in quickly and quietly. After all, he had a peace treaty with them.

"We're going to have to send her to a convalescent home, you know that," a man on television ranted.

"You think it will work?" Jack Liffey asked.

"Gold bars? Oh, yeah, sure. Those guys big on gold bars—like chocolate chip cookie for starve little boy." She seemed to notice his torn Penney's shirt. "You know, this shirt you got here really sucks.

I mean even before it get torn and all. I get you really good shirt like from Rodeo Drive for thirty bucks."

He smiled and she sighed and lost interest in the shirt. Her head sagged against him and she dozed off.

He lay back feeling her regular tiny breathing against his shoulder, like some delicate forest creature. The contact and his own weariness led him to picture other women who had slept against him and how it had made him feel. One night, not long after Maeve was born, Kathy had fallen asleep in exhaustion right in the middle of intercourse and he had stayed inside her for the longest time, noticing her milk-engorged breasts and her new stretch marks, a little chagrined by the nod-off *in flagrante delicto* but full of tenderness for her bone-weariness and then finally chuckling at the absurdity of it all and losing his erection all at once. He didn't let himself think about Kathy much, not in tender moments like that, because she'd been so important to him once, and his jobless rages and drinking and his failure as a father had been so painful.

And he recalled Lori Bright—a fading movie star, older than he was, who had crossed his path once like an express train out of hell—and he remembered the time she had fallen off into a little sniff sleep, toking some downer, after working overtime to prove her sexual prowess with a number of little steel studs and a wicker box, and then all at once she had started snoring away like a buzz saw on the silk sheets. In the abstract that raucous snore should have broken all the glamour illusions, but he'd found that nothing at all could do that. Once you'd grown up watching a face on a fifty-foot screen, it rooted itself so firmly in your daydreams that reality never had a prayer.

Marlena, too, had once dropped off to sleep in his lap after drinking too much rough red wine. Then she had gone to great lengths to make it up to him. Remembering that long exhausting inexpressibly tender morning, Jack Liffey fell asleep, too.

* * *

It was an unearthly screeching, like an owl caught in a trap, that awoke Jack Liffey and the first thing he saw was a big plastic bottle of dish detergent on the TV and he didn't see how dish detergent could have made that noise. Then he saw a Vietnamese man in a black jumpsuit hovering over Billy Gudger who had been thoroughly taped to his own chair with his own duct tape, like a fly in a spider web, his arms completely hidden under a skein of gray tape.

Billy's cheek seemed to be bleeding down his chin and beads of slow blood dribbled onto his shirt. The Vietnamese brandished a supermarket box cutter in front of Billy, like a treat he was withholding from a pet.

"Where gold at, fucker?"

Tien Joubert was sitting bolt awake, too, and for the longest time Jack Liffey felt quite detached from the scene, as if watching it through a pane of armored glass.

Another black-clad Vietnamese hove into the room and though he had a ski mask on, it was unmistakably Thang Le. Thang Le took in the scene and spoke quickly to Tien.

"He say they open freezer and find only fat frozen woman."

"That's Billy's mom."

Tien looked startled. "He kill his own mother?"

"It looks like it. I think it was probably half an accident, and half a kind of reflex that takes him over when people laugh at him. He's a pretty troubled kid."

"Well, fuck him." She spoke fast to Thang Le.

"What did you say?"

"I tell him he must have move gold last night when we asleep."

"Tien, don't do this!"

"I say, fuck this bad boy. He was going kill us. He kill Phuong, he kill his own *mother*. Let him feel scare a little."

"It's not right. Stop them."

There was another hopeless screech of pain and terror and Jack Liffey was glad the other Vietnamese had moved in front so he couldn't see what was going on.

"There's no gold!" Jack Liffey shouted. "Tien said that to get you here. There's *no* gold. I swear it!" He wasn't sure how much English they knew.

They turned the TV up a notch as a hopeless wail banged around the small room.

> *It was distinguished by the name of the reptile, and called the Toad-Stone, Bufonites, Capaudine, Krottenstien; but all its fancied power vanished on the discovery of its being nothing but the fossil tooth of the Sea-Wolf.*
> —Thomas Pennant, *British Zoology* (1776)

The darkness was so close now, billowing around his shoulders. The sudden pain. Those voices gabbling and crying out. Was one of them Mr. Liffey? The horrible razor thing came closer again and he felt a searing burn in his forehead. He yelled and tugged at his arms but they were held fast. Gold gold, somebody kept asking about gold. Was it an Asian voice? It came from a thickening in the darkness that had finally come very close indeed.

"Mr. Liffey, help me!"

The fire reached his shoulder, coming into him suddenly out of the murk. He could barely see. It wasn't fair. No one would come to his side. Abandoned just as he was going to reach out. But he knew he had done something terrible and now he had to be punished. Another gathering of the darkness swept around him like dark wings, blotting out the room. Fire entered his knee, his chest.

"Ma!" he keened. "*Ma!*"

"Tien, stop them. I'll never sleep with you again if you let them do this. I mean it!"

Tien Joubert turned and hissed once at Jack Liffey, like an enraged cat, and then she spoke rapidly in Vietnamese and the two home invaders looked at her. "Guys, no gold here. Big trick. Sorry. I make it up to you later. You only place I could call on broke phone."

Thang Le glared at her for a while. Then he picked up Billy's own pistol and in perfectly clear English asked, "Did this piece of garbage kill Phuong?"

"Yes," Tien said.

Thang Le pressed the pistol against Billy Gudger's forehead.

"Mr. Liffey," Billy Gudger cried out. "I want you to have my toad-stone!"

The pistol went off with a sickening wet burst in the room, and the Vietnamese raiders were gone in a blink.

Jack Liffey glanced only once and knew it was not a sight that would ever leave him.

"What's toadstone?" Tien asked.

"Just a superstition." It would have transgressed some scruple to explain it to her now.

The cops were slow in getting there, even after the gunshot and the screams, and over the rest of the day Jack Liffey felt as if he was writing the same story over and over from scratch, writing it and then having it ripped away from him. There were the Tustin Cops, then a man and woman from the Orange County Sheriff's, luckily not Margin, and then two hard-bitten men in dark suits and permanent scowls from the F.B.I. The one fact they both withheld was the identity of the *Quan Sats*. They had no idea how the housebreakers had got there, perhaps they had followed Tien's fancy Porsche, or they suspected there were valuables in the house for some other reason. Nobody believed them but everybody knew about Vietnamese home invasions and the reluctance to name names. It wasn't until six in the evening that they got out of the Tustin Police Station on Camino.

"Come home with me," Tien said. "I sorry they killed the guy. I make it all up to you like the bee's knees."

He'd been dreading this, but her indifference in the face of Billy's pain did make it a bit easier. "I live with someone, Tien. I can't get around that."

"I make you happy in bed. You know it."

"There are things that don't work between Marlena and me and things that do, and I owe it to her to give it an extra shot to try to make it work."

"I got stuff I ain't even show you yet in bed. I even arrange you have some young stuff on the side if you want. I make you rich, get you good shirt and pants, not this junk."

"Marlena's a good woman with a heart as big as little Saigon. You'd like her. I can't just tip her out with the old newspapers."

"I say I give Rolex and Jag, but I know that make you mad." She took a deep breath. This was not the first disappointment in her life and it certainly wasn't even a very big one compared to some of the others. "If bad stuff with this Marleta get bigger than good stuff, you come back to me any time, Mr. Jack."

"Thanks for the offer," he said. "You're worth a lot, too."

King Canute

*The vast beds of toad-stone or lava in many parts of this
country.* —Charles Darwin, *Philosophical Transactions* (1784)

"This feels kind of dumb," Rogelio said. "You wanna go some
place?"

"Let's stay a bit and see who comes out alive," Maeve said. She
had just bicycled all they way up PCH to Mar Vista to see her father
and tell him she'd got an A on her physics test, the one subject that
was her brick wall, and she had been informed in an urgent whisper
that her dad had just come home a half hour before her. Rogelio had
had a big grimace on his kindly face and he had hustled her out the
side door without much explanation while a lot of yelling was going
on inside in two voices.

They were sitting on the front bench seat of Rogelio's chopped
and lowered 1950 Mercury, with the grill changed to a set of
chromed vertical bars like shark's teeth. It was just about the coolest
car she'd ever seen.

"What color you going to make it?" she asked. It was all gray
primer now.

"I thought candy-apple maroon. You know, that lacquer paint
that makes it look about a foot deep."

"Yeah, way cool. And tuck and roll seats?"

"I can get that cheap in TJ, though everybody says they put rotting cabbage inside the tuck and rolls. But that's lies. TJ does good work if you know where to go."

"Of course it does. Do you know what the fight in there is about?"

"Oh, yeah. Your dad's gonna really be in the doghouse awhile I think. He came back looking even more beat up than last time, but he told Mar some Viet Nam woman he met on the job down there and he had a thing for a while. He came back to say he was sorry and he wants to work on staying with her, if she'll let him. Mar's a bit put out, you can bet."

"I can guess. My dad does have a little trouble sometimes keeping his pants zipped."

They both fell silent during a particularly loud bit of yelling from Marlena and something that sounded like glass breaking.

"I guess affairs like that only really happen when other stuff in the relationship is going wrong," Maeve said. "But I don't remember him doing it to mom. He just got drunk and introverted when he lost his job. Then she started seeing some guy at work who was nice to her and that flipped dad out."

"Yeah, it's worse when women do it."

"It is *not!*"

"Well, you know, you can get pregnant with somebody else's baby."

"That's not what you meant, though. You think women have to be faithful while men get to go gallivanting around all they want."

He thought about it a moment. "Yeah, I guess that's not fair, is it?"

"No way."

"Wanna make out a bit?" He looked away shyly and fondled the chrome slam-shifter set in the floor.

"Rocky, I'm only thirteen and three-quarters."

"No kidding. *Wow*, I'm sorry, Maeve. Honest, I didn't know. You seem so old and smart and stuff. And you're, you know, like, growing pretty *big*."

"Thanks for the offer. You're a really sweet guy."

Something else in the house broke and they both winced.

"What do you think of my aunt?" he asked.

"I think she's really really super. Her heart is right up there in front for everybody who needs it."

Rogelio nodded. "Yeah. She had a bad time, too. You got to ask her about it sometime. One of these days I'm gonna get some *carnales* together and go down and pound on some biker trash who really dissed her bad when she was young."

"Is violence the answer to everything?"

"No, but sometimes you just gotta stand up to be a man."

"So that's what being a man is."

He ran his hands around the tiny steering wheel which was made of welded, chromed chain links. "Yeah, I think so. So what do you think of your dad?"

"What do you think of him?" she countered.

"He's a good guy to me, really listens to me. To tell the truth, Aunt Mar is hard to handle sometimes and he's pretty good with her. What do you think?"

She leaned back in the seat and rolled her head a bit. "Well, outside of this zipper problem that he seems to have when some woman makes herself available, I'm pretty crazy about him. Do you know who King Canute was?"

"Huh-uh."

"It's an old legend. This old English king loved giving orders and he went down to the ocean one day and told the tide to stop coming in. I always picture Canute in a big gold throne out in the breakers, screaming at the waves to stay back."

"That's your dad?"

"Sort of. It's like this bad tide is coming in and hurting people, including Dad. And he's like a rock standing up out there in the ocean where the tide is going past and kind of yelling at it to stop. He's not stopping much of it, but he's not giving up either."

Rogelio chuckled. "Yeah, I can see that. Your old man tried so hard to get me a computer operator job and I just couldn't do it."

"I'll bet you can do it."

He grimaced. "I tried but it scared me."

"Could I help you study up for it?"

He glanced over at her, surprised.

"We can make out a bit, if you want," she added. "But you can only touch my breast through my bra."